BEVE

H

D

BOOKS BY STUART WOODS

FICTION

Shoot Him If He Runs[†]

Fresh Disasters[†]

Short Straw

Dark Harbor[†]

Iron Orchid[*]

Two-Dollar Bill[†]

The Prince of Beverly Hills

Reckless Abandon[†]

Capital Crimes[‡]

Dirty Work[†]

Blood Orchid[*]

The Short Forever[†]

Orchid Blues[*]

Cold Paradise[†]

L.A. Dead[†]

The Run[‡]

Worst Fears Realized[†]

Orchid Beach[*]

Swimming to Catalina[†]

Dead in the Water[†]

Dirt[†]

Choke

Imperfect Strangers

Heat

Dead Eyes

L.A. Times

Santa Fe Rules

New York Dead[†]

Palindrome

Grass Roots[‡]

White Cargo

Deep Lie[‡]

Under the Lake

Run Before the Wind[‡]

Chiefs[‡]

TRAVEL

A Romantic's Guide to the Country Inns of Britain and Ireland (*1979*)

MEMOIR

Blue Water, Green Skipper (*1977*)

[*]A Holly Barker Novel [†]A Stone Barrington Novel [‡]A Will Lee Novel

BEVERLY HILLS DEAD

STUART WOODS

G. P. PUTNAM'S SONS | NEW YORK

G. P. PUTNAM'S SONS
Publishers Since 1838
Published by the Penguin Group
Penguin Group (USA) Inc., 375 Hudson Street, New York, New York 10014, USA •
Penguin Group (Canada), 90 Eglinton Avenue East, Suite 700, Toronto, Ontario M4P 2Y3,
Canada (a division of Pearson Penguin Canada Inc.) • Penguin Books Ltd,
80 Strand, London WC2R 0RL, England • Penguin Ireland, 25 St Stephen's Green,
Dublin 2, Ireland (a division of Penguin Books Ltd) • Penguin Group (Australia),
250 Camberwell Road, Camberwell, Victoria 3124, Australia (a division of
Pearson Australia Group Pty Ltd) • Penguin Books India Pvt Ltd,
11 Community Centre, Panchsheel Park, New Delhi–110 017, India •
Penguin Group (NZ), 67 Apollo Drive, Rosedale, North Shore 0632,
New Zealand (a division of Pearson New Zealand Ltd) • Penguin Books (South Africa)
(Pty) Ltd, 24 Sturdee Avenue, Rosebank, Johannesburg 2196, South Africa

Penguin Books Ltd, Registered Offices:
80 Strand, London WC2R 0RL, England

Library of Congress Cataloging-in-Publication Data

Woods, Stuart.
Beverly Hills dead / Stuart Woods.
p.   cm.
ISBN 978-0-399-15469-0
1. Beverly Hills (Calif.)—Fiction.   I. Title.
PS3573.O642B48   2007   2007028158
813'.54—dc22

Printed in the United States of America
1   3   5   7   9   10   8   6   4   2

Book design by Susan Walsh

This is a work of fiction. Names, characters, places, and incidents either are the product
of the author's imagination or are used fictitiously, and any resemblance to actual persons, living or dead, businesses, companies, events, or locales is entirely coincidental.

While the author has made every effort to provide accurate telephone numbers and
Internet addresses at the time of publication, neither the publisher nor the author
assumes any responsibility for errors, or for changes that occur after publication.
Further, the publisher does not have any control over and does not assume any
responsibility for author or third-party websites or their content.

This book is for
David and Susan Lederman.

BEVERLY
HILLS
DEAD

Rick Barron took one last look through the viewfinder, then he turned to the assistant director. "Conversation," he said.

The AD held up a megaphone and shouted, "Conversation!"

At once, a hundred and fifty extras, packed into a set that was a replica of Sardi's, the famous theater-district restaurant in New York, began to talk.

"Action," Rick said quietly.

"Speed," the camera operator replied.

Waiters began to move among the tables.

"Cue the entrance," Rick said.

"Entrance," the AD said into a microphone hanging around his neck. He signaled the dolly man, and the camera began to roll smoothly down the restaurant's main aisle toward the entrance of the restaurant.

The front door opened, and his leading lady, Glenna Gleason, wearing a gorgeous evening gown and followed by another actress and two actors, all in evening dress, walked in and were greeted by a Vincent Sardi look-alike. As they walked past the small bar and entered the dining room, the camera backtracked, and, on cue, all the diners stood and applauded.

Glenna managed to look shocked, then delighted as she followed "Sardi" to their table along the wall. The camera stopped and moved in closer as a microphone boom was lowered over the false wall to pick up their dialogue.

"My God," Glenna said. "I didn't know it could be like this."

The actor on her left turned to her. "Katherine," he said, "it's going to be like this from now on."

On Rick's signal, the camera began to dolly slowly away from the table and, keeping Glenna's party in the center of the frame, rose to a height of twelve feet and stopped.

"Keep the conversation going," Rick said from his chair on the boom next to the camera. He sat and watched the stopwatch in his hand for ninety seconds, which was what they needed to roll under the closing titles. "Cut!" he yelled, finally. "Print it! That's a wrap!" It was the fourth take, and it was perfect. They had shot the three scenes set at Sardi's all on the same day, and now it was done: Rick had made his first feature film as a director. He sagged with relief as the camera operator pounded him on the back.

Then, to his astonishment, every actor on the set rose from his seat and gave the director a standing ovation. Rick stood up, holding on to the camera for support, then turned and faced the bulk of the crowd. "Cut!" he yelled again. "Start the party!"

A part of the rear wall of the set was rolled away, revealing a huge buffet table and a bar serving real booze instead of the tea in the prop glasses on the table. The crowd of extras surged toward the food and drink, and Rick signaled the boom operator to lower the camera to the floor. He hopped off and slid into a banquette beside his wife, giving her a big kiss. "Glenna, my darling, that was great. It's going to be wonderful, the whole thing."

Two of the actors got up from the table and made way for Eddie Harris, the chairman of Centurion Studios, and Sidney Brooks, the famous New York playwright, who had written the script for *Times Square Dance*.

"Rick," Eddie said, "congratulations."

Champagne appeared and was poured.

"I thought that last scene went beautifully," Brooks said to everybody.

"Sid, we're going to do your script proud," Rick said. "Just give me a couple of days, and I'll show you a rough cut."

"I can't wait," Brooks replied.

"I have to go pee," Glenna said, and Rick let her out of the banquette. The actor playing her husband got up, too, leaving Rick, Eddie Harris and Sidney Brooks at the table.

"Fellas," Brooks said, "I have to tell you something."

Rick looked at the man across the table. For the first time since he had met the playwright, the man looked less than happy.

"What's up, Sid?" Eddie asked.

"I wanted to tell you before it hits the papers tomorrow," Brooks said.

"Tell us what?" Rick asked.

"I've been subpoenaed by the House Un-American Activities Committee, along with eighteen other people, mostly writers but a few actors and one director."

"Oh, shit," Eddie said. "Well, don't worry about it; get a good lawyer."

"I'm sorry, Sid," Rick said, "but Eddie is right about the lawyer."

"There's a meeting tomorrow," Brooks replied. "I want to tell you fellows . . ."

"You don't need to tell us anything," Eddie said.

"You mean, you'd rather not know, don't you, Eddie?"

"The first thing your lawyer is going to tell you is to shut up," Eddie said. "I'm just giving you a head start; don't say anything to anybody, unless your lawyer approves it first."

"I'm not looking to drag anybody into this," Brooks said. "I just want to be honest with you. This picture has been the best experience I've had since I came out here four years ago; it's the first picture that's given me the same sort of satisfaction that writing a play used to."

"Look, Sid," Rick said, "these people are going to hold their hearings, grill some movie stars, and then it'll be over. Six months from now you'll have put it behind you."

Brooks set a briefcase on the table, opened it and pulled out a thick manila envelope. "I've been working on this for two years," he said. "I've never told anybody about it, but it's the best thing I've ever written for either the stage or film, and after the wonderful experience I've had with the production of *Times Square Dance*, I want you fellows to produce it, and, Rick, I'd be delighted if you'd direct again."

"Thank you, Sid," Rick said, and he meant it. "I'll read it tonight."

"Tell your agent to call Rick in the morning," Eddie said. "We'll have a deal before lunchtime."

"But you haven't even read it, Eddie," Brooks said, laughing.

"I don't need to. I'll buy it sight unseen."

Rick knew that wasn't quite true, but he knew that Eddie expected to like the script; he would want Rick's opinion first, though.

"It's a western," Brooks said.

"*What*?" Rick exclaimed. "The theater's urban genius has written a western?"

"The grittiest, down-and-dirtiest western you ever saw," Brooks said. "I love westerns, and I've always wanted to write one; to tell you the truth, it's the principal reason I came out here, just to get the opportunity. I've had the idea for a long time, but it wouldn't work on the stage, and I didn't want it produced without the level of participation you fellows have given me."

"Thank you, Sid," Rick said.

Glenna returned from the ladies' room and sat down. "I called home," she said. "The girls are fine, and I told Rosie to give them dinner and put them to bed. I take it we'll be here for a while."

"I think we will," Rick said. "I think I'd better circulate and thank everybody." He handed Brooks's script to her. "Guard this with your life," he said. "It's the next Sidney Brooks film."

"Oh, is there a part for me?" she asked excitedly.

"I haven't read it yet, sweetheart; I'll let you know tomorrow." Rick got up and began making his way around the Sardi's set, shaking hands, hugging and kissing and enduring many claps on the back.

A moment later, Eddie Harris caught up with him. "Listen, kid," he said, leaning into Rick's ear. "If that script is any good we need to get it into production fast."

"I'm supposed to personally produce the new war film," Rick said. "We could do it right after that."

"I got a bad feeling about these HUAC hearings," Eddie said. "I'd rather have Sid's film in the can, even if we have to postpone production on the war movie."

"Okay. I'll call you when I've read it," Rick said. Eddie fell away, and Rick continued his rounds, but his euphoria at finishing shooting had been pricked by Eddie Harris, and air was leaking out.

2

The wrap party was over by eight. Rick drove Glenna to her cottage/dressing room to change out of her gown, then home. They looked in on their daughters, Louise, two, and Glenn, three months, and found them happily asleep. Glenna went to bed with a novel, and Rick settled into his study to read Sidney Brooks's new script.

It was just as down-and-dirty as Sid had said it was, probably the most realistic depiction of the Old West that Rick had come across, and he loved it. He knew Eddie Harris would still be up, and he called him.

"Eddie Harris."

"It's me; the script is terrific. We may take some heat for the realism, but it's worth fighting for."

"Then buy it. Pay him more than he expects; he may need the money soon."

"You're really worried about the committee hearings?"

"Never underestimate how far politicians will go to get their names in the papers."

"You know what's-his-name, don't you? The California congressman who's on the committee?"

"Dick Nixon? Yeah, I know him, and as far as I'm concerned he's a real shit. He beat Helen Gahagan Douglas by telling people she was a Communist, which she in no way, shape or form was, and I won't ask him for a favor."

"You know anybody else on the committee?"

"Nah, they're all from New Jersey or the South or someplace."

"Is there anything we can do to help Sid?"

"It's too soon to tell. All we can do right now is to pay him well and up front for his script."

"Up front?"

"It's the least we can do after the job he did on *Times Square Dance*. What's the new script called?"

"*Bitter Creek*. It's about a fight over water rights."

"Tried-and-true western theme."

"Believe me, nothing about this is tried-and-true. There are no heroes, just people who are less bad than other people."

"Will it sell tickets?"

"Yes. There are at least three roles that leading actors would kill for and one really good female role, a woman who runs a ranch after her husband is murdered."

"Glenna?"

"Only if she really wants to do it. I wouldn't try to persuade her; it's so different from everything else she's done. Think of a younger Marjorie Main."

"That sure doesn't sound like Glenna."

"I think that's what she'll say, too."

"Okay, kid, I'll see you tomorrow." Eddie hung up.

Rick poured himself half a drink and reflected on what his life might be like now were it not for Eddie Harris's friendship. Rick had still been a cop when he had witnessed a horrible traffic accident involving Centurion's biggest star at the time, Clete Barrow. A woman had run a stop sign and had been killed as a result. Rick had been quick-witted enough to get the actor out of there and, at Barrow's urging, called Eddie Harris. Before he knew what had hit him,

Rick had become Centurion's head of security, and since that date, Eddie had given him more and more responsibility.

When Rick had had to get out of L.A. because of a shooting and had joined the navy, Eddie had continued to pay his salary, and when he returned, his knee shot up, Eddie had found the best knee surgeon west of the Mississippi to fix it. Now, with studio founder Sol Weinman dead, Eddie was chairman and CEO, and Rick had his old job as head of production.

Rick's career as a cop was already on the rocks when he met Eddie, and if not for Eddie, he'd probably be a down-at-the-heels private eye, doing divorce work.

Rick emptied his glass and went up to bed. Glenna was still awake.

"So, is there a part for me?"

"There's only one decent female role," Rick replied, "a sort of younger Marjorie Main character."

Glenna made a face. "Not for me. I'm not ready for character roles."

"That's what I thought you'd say." He tossed the script on the bed and began to undress. "Read it, though; I don't want you to come back after you've seen the picture and yell at me for not giving you the role."

"I don't yell."

"Yes you do when you don't get the roles you want." Rick got into bed.

"*Mmm,* no pajamas, huh?" she asked. "What could that mean?"

"Just that I'm available."

Glenna took a deep breath. "Before I make that decision, I want to ask you something."

"Shoot."

"An unintentionally ironic reply," she said. "Did you shoot Chick Stampano?"

Rick drew in a quick breath. That was completely unexpected. Stampano had been a slick Mafia thug and blackmailer who had preyed on rising actresses, Glenna among them. He had also given her a horrible beating that had put her in the hospital for weeks. "Why are you asking me that after what, four years?"

"I have an opinion; I just want a fact. I want to know if my husband would kill for me."

"Yes," Rick said.

"Yes he would, or yes he did?"

Rick turned and looked her in the eye. "Both," he said.

"And that's why you joined the navy, instead of coming to look for me?"

"Yes."

Glenna shucked off her silk nightgown and wrapped herself around him. "I'm so glad," she said.

"Glad I joined the navy?"

"Glad it was you who dealt with Stampano." She kissed him on the neck. "Did it make you feel guilty?"

"No," Rick replied, "not for a moment. It made me feel sick for a moment, but I knew I had done the right thing. I had already talked with the navy recruiter and had taken my physical. They were able to get me into training almost immediately. I'm surprised Eddie didn't tell you all of this."

"He came to see me at the hospital and told me some things but not everything. As soon as I could, I got out and went to New York. Eddie didn't have a chance to explain further, and I wasn't sure I wanted to know. Did you have problems with the police?"

"My friend Ben Morrison was the investigating officer. He bought me enough time to get out of town, then he spread a rumor that I'd gone to Canada to enlist in the Royal Canadian Air Force. When I came back to L.A., after I was wounded, the whole thing had blown over. Nobody seemed to want to know anything, except Bugsy Siegel, who still wanted my head on a platter."

"Eddie took care of that, didn't he? I mean, I know the conventional wisdom was that the mob murdered him, but I never believed that."

"Neither did I, but Eddie never said another word about it after he brought me the newspaper with Ben Siegel's picture on the front page, missing part of his head."

She snuggled closer. "Was there something you wanted to do to me?"

"I want to do everything to you."

She kissed him again. "Then do it."

And he did.

3

Rick got up early, careful not to wake Glenna, dressed and left the house without breakfast. He got into Eddie Harris's old 1940 Continental convertible, drove out to Clover Field in Santa Monica, then to his father's hangar at Barron Flying Service. He parked out back and walked into the hangar. His father was standing before Centurion Studios' Douglas DC–3, which, after being confiscated for military use and used as a general's personal transport during the war, had finally been released to its owner. Jack Barron and his people were renovating the airplane thoroughly.

"Morning, Dad," Rick said.

"How you doing, Son?" Jack said, offering his hand.

"How's she coming?"

"Couple more weeks, I guess. The interior is mostly done, and I'll have the overhauled engines back next week. We're repolishing the aluminum, starting today, and we'll put the Centurion name back on her when we're done."

"I'll tell Eddie Harris," Rick said. "He's tired of driving to Palm Springs on the weekend, and he'll be glad to fly again."

"How's work?"

"Just great. We wrapped on a new picture yesterday, the one that I directed, and we'll start the editing and other postproduction work today." Jack had heard enough conversations about Rick's work that he knew the jargon by now.

"You're moving up in the world, boy. You know, when you quit the Beverly Hills police force and took that job as the studio cop, I thought you were headed downhill. In fact, I was kinda hoping it wouldn't work out, so I could have you back out here as my partner, doing the flying."

"Sorry to disappoint you," Rick said, laughing.

"How are my granddaughters?"

"Thriving. Louise is talking a blue streak, and Glenn is a sweetheart, so far."

"Wait till she's two; you were a hellion at two."

"You're coming to lunch on Sunday, right?"

"Wouldn't miss it."

"I'll let you get back to work, then." Rick left him, went back to his car and drove to the studio. The guard at the gate gave him a smart salute, and he drove to the administration building and parked in his reserved spot. He went upstairs to his office, which had belonged to Eddie before studio founder Sol Weinman had died. Eddie now worked in Sol's palatial office next door. Rick passed through the outer reception room and the inner secretaries' office, where two women kept things running.

One of them handed him an envelope. "This just came. It's the final budget for the war movie."

"Thanks," Rick said, "but it looks like we're going to be postponing that."

"You want to send out a memo?"

"Later this morning; I'll let you know." Rick went into his mahogany-paneled office and sat down at his desk. Immediately, his phone buzzed.

"Hyman Greenbaum for you," the secretary said. Sidney Brooks's agent wasn't wasting any time.

Rick picked up the phone. "Morning, Hyman, here's the deal: I'll pay fifty percent more for *Bitter Creek* than I did for *Times Square Dance*, all the money on signing, the usual revisions and polishing, all other stipulations as per the last contract."

There was a brief silence before Greenbaum could speak. "This is a negotiation?" he asked, finally. "With negotiations like this, what will I do for a living from now on?"

"Don't worry; you can tell Sid you fought like a tiger for the deal, and I'll back you up. Get me a contract over here this morning; we want to start preproduction immediately."

"Anything you say, Rick," Greenbaum said.

Rick hung up, and his phone buzzed again. "Just a reminder," the secretary said. "You have an appointment with your architect in ten minutes."

"Oh, right," Rick said. "And take a memo to the preproduction staff: Eddie Harris and I are postponing production of *Pacific Invasion* in order to begin preproduction immediately on a new Sidney Brooks script, *Bitter Creek*, a western. Meeting in my office at nine A.M. tomorrow morning. Hold that until the contract arrives from Hyman Greenbaum, then send it out. Also, come in and get the script, get it retyped and run off a hundred copies as soon as possible, and send each member of the preproduction team a copy with the memo."

"Will do," she said. She came in and got the script. "What's going with this? No revisions? How come I never heard of this?"

"Because I read it only last night."

"It must really be something," she said.

"It really is, but don't take time to read it until the copies come in."

"Peter James, the architect, is outside."

"Send him in." Rick walked over to the conference table and met the young man there. "Good morning, Peter."

"Good morning, Rick." He spread out the plans on the table. "Your revisions are done; you want to go over them?"

"Tell you what, take them to the house and go over them with Glenna, then let's meet out at the site at twelve-thirty. I'll call her and tell her you're coming."

"That's great. The pilings are going in this morning."

"Make them deep; I don't want the place swept out to sea."

"Don't worry."

The architect left, and Rick called home and woke up Glenna. "You'd better roll your ass out of bed; Peter James is on his way over there with the revisions on the beach house."

"How long have I got?"

"Fifteen minutes, tops. We're going to meet at the site at twelve-thirty; I'll bring sandwiches."

"I don't know how you can do all this at the crack of dawn," she said.

"It's ten-fifteen."

"Okay, okay." She hung up.

Rick went through some papers on his desk and found the *Los Angeles Times* staring up at him:

HUAC SUBPOENAS FORTY-ONE

He read the lead paragraph, then set the paper aside for later. Among the papers on his desk was a manila envelope, the kind for interoffice communications, with two rows of lines for names of addressees. It was a new, previously unused envelope, and his was the only name written on it, so he couldn't tell who the sender was. Also, it was sealed with red sealing wax, which was very unusual. Ordinarily, such an envelope was secured only with a piece of string wound around a paper disk. He broke the seal, unwound the string and shook the contents of the envelope out on his desk.

There was only one sheet of paper. He picked it up and looked at it. It was a photostatic copy of a membership card of the Communist Party, made out in the name of Sidney Mark Brooks, dated 1935 and showing a New York City address.

Rick was startled. He had never seen one of these before, nor had he, to the best of his knowledge, known anyone who was a Communist. There were rumors around town, of course, but he had never paid much attention to them. He had trouble imagining Sid Brooks as a bomb thrower, or even a subversive.

He put the photostat back in the envelope, walked over to the coffee table in front of the sofa, picked up the Ronson table lighter, took it to the fireplace and set fire to the envelope and its contents, watching until it had completely burned, then stirred the ashes.

He didn't know who had sent it, and he didn't care. He didn't care about Sid Brooks's politics, either. He went back to his desk and tried to put it out of his mind.

4

A t noon Rick left his office with a picnic lunch prepared by the studio commissary and drove down to Santa Monica, then out the Pacific Highway to Malibu.

At the insistence of Eddie Harris, Rick had started investing in real estate not long after getting his medical discharge from the navy in early '44, at first borrowing money to do it. As his income rose, he bought more, among the properties three beach lots in the village of Malibu. After the war he began thinking about building on the beach, and, as materials became more available in the postwar environment, he and Glenna had hired Peter James to design a house for them.

The lots were half a mile south of the Malibu colony, an enclave of movie stars and the very rich, which together fronted four hundred feet on a gorgeous stretch of beach and stretched for more than three hundred feet from the highway to the beach.

A pile driver had been set up, making tremendous noise every time the weight was hoisted and fell. Half a dozen piles were already in place. He found Peter James in conversation with a man who appeared to be the foreman and greeted both men. Glenna was nowhere in sight, though it was twelve-thirty.

"They're making really good progress," Peter said, "and we're going very deep, as you asked. A couple more days of this, and we can start framing."

Glenna drove up in Rick's old 1938 Ford convertible and got out. "Piles!" she yelled over the noise. "How exciting!"

Peter took them over to where a tabletop had been set on a pair of sawhorses and spread out the plans. He pointed out the changes that Glenna had asked for, and Rick agreed with everything.

"One more thing, Peter," Rick said. "The room on either end that we were going to build later? Build them now."

"Oh, Honey!" Glenna shrieked. "You've made my day!"

"What the hell," Rick said, "we'll go the whole hog."

They talked for a few more minutes about the way the house would sit on the land, then Glenna said, "I'm hungry; did you bring lunch?"

Rick went to the car and got the picnic basket and a blanket, and Peter walked over to the foreman and told him to break for lunch. The noise abruptly ceased.

"Let's go down to the beach and eat there," Rick said, and he led the way. As he reached the edge of the sand he looked back to see Glenna in conversation with one of the workmen. Wearing a baseball cap and naked above the waist, he was tall and well-muscled. He was also deeply tanned and bathed in sweat from his work. To Rick's surprise, she indicated that he should follow her, and they began walking toward the beach.

"Rick," she said as they approached, "I want you to meet somebody; this is Vance. Vance, this is my husband, Rick, and our architect, Peter. I've asked Vance to join us for lunch."

"Sure," Rick said. He was mystified about this, but Glenna had her reasons, he supposed. The young man was very handsome; maybe that had something to do with it. He felt a little jealous.

Rick spread the blanket, and Glenna distributed the food and drink from the basket, then they settled down to eat.

"Vance is an actor," Glenna said, and then Rick understood.

"Where are you from, Vance?" Rick asked.

"England, a small village in Kent."

"I don't hear an accent."

"It's better with the crew if they think I'm American."

Rick laughed. "I understand. How long have you been in L.A.?"

"About four months."

"Looking for work?"

"Mostly, I work at this," Vance said, waving a hand toward the pile driver. "I only get weekends off, and to tell you the truth I don't have much of an idea about how to look for acting work."

"Have you had any experience?"

"I ran away from home when I was fifteen and joined a touring repertory company. Mostly, I moved scenery around, but now and then I got a small part with a few lines. After a year or so, I got bigger parts and stopped moving scenery."

"Did you ever make it to the West End?"

"I got a second lead in a comedy that ran for a year; then, when they brought the production to New York, I came with it. It ran for five weeks, then closed. The troup went home, and I stayed to look for work on Broadway. I found nothing, and it was bloody cold in New York, so I came out here. At least, I'm not freezing to death."

They talked for a bit longer, then finished their lunch, and Glenna began putting the dishes back into the basket, while Peter dealt with the trash.

"Do you know who I am?" Rick asked Vance.

"You're her husband," Vance said. "I certainly know who *she* is."

Rick laughed and handed him his business card. "Tell you what, Vance," he said, "you tell your boss that your career in the construction business is at an end, then be in my office at eleven tomorrow morning. Do you own a suit?"

"I do."

"Wear it, and bring your English accent, too. I'll leave a pass for you at the front gate. Do you have an agent?"

"No."

"I'll recommend a couple of people."

"Thank you very much, Mr. . . . " he looked at the card, "Barron."

"What's your last name, Vance?"

"Calder."

"Vance Calder. That sounds pretty good. What's your real name?"

"Vance Calder."

"How old are you?"

Vance looked around to see if anyone could hear him. "Nineteen."

"Jesus," Rick said, "I thought you were twenty-five."

"I've always looked older. When I was fourteen, people thought I was eighteen, and so on."

"That's an advantage at your age. From now on, don't tell anybody how old you are; they'll just think you're lying about your age, the way everybody out here does."

"All right."

"See you tomorrow." Rick joined Glenna and walked her back to her car. "Thanks," he said.

"You didn't notice him, did you?"

"No, I didn't."

"I think he's stunning, Rick; very sexy, too."

"He's probably queer, like half the boy actors in L.A."

"Don't you believe it for a moment," she said.

5

B efore Rick left the house the following morning he called his assistant director on *Times Square Dance*. "Hi, Billy, I'd like you to set up a screen test this morning, and I want you to direct it. I'm sorry it's such a rush, but it's important."

"Sure, Rick. Who's the girl?"

"Guy. His name is Vance Calder, and he's coming to my office at eleven. I'll talk to him for a few minutes and then send him over to the little stage."

"What sort of stuff do you want?"

"I want a dramatic scene and a comedy scene, then I want you to dress him in cowboy gear—nothing Roy Rogers, just plain stuff—then take him out to the back lot and shoot him handling a gun, throwing a rope and riding a horse."

"Does he know how to ride?"

"I have no idea. Tell you what, for the interior stuff, use the comedy scene on about page thirty of *Times Square Dance* and the dramatic scene toward the end, when he tells Katherine how good she is. In the dramatic scene, have him use an English accent."

"Okay. I can even put the real set back together."

"If it's no trouble. Take the time to light this guy well; he's very tan, so he won't need a lot of makeup. You can pick him up at my office at eleven-fifteen."

"Okay."

"And get the film to the lab tonight; I want to see it before noon tomorrow."

"Will do."

Rick hung up and left for the studio.

When he walked into his office there were half a dozen people seated around his conference table, drinking coffee and eating pastries. "Morning, all," Rick said. "Sorry I'm late, but I have a good excuse."

"What's that, Rick?" somebody asked.

"I'm not going to tell you." Rick pulled up a chair, poured himself some coffee and chose a Danish from what remained. "Okay," he said, "let's get started."

Everybody pulled out legal pads and pencils and settled down.

"As you've already heard, we've postponed *Pacific Invasion* in favor of Sidney Brooks's new original script, *Bitter Creek.*"

"It's a great script, Rick," somebody said.

"I think so, too. Unless somebody at this table comes up with some necessary changes because of logistics, I'm not even going to give Sid notes. Anybody got anything like that? Speak now, or . . ."

Nobody said anything.

"Okay. Let's start with locations."

"There's nothing in the script that can't be shot on the back lot, Rick," somebody said.

"We're not going to shoot a foot of film on the back lot."

"Where do you want to shoot it?" the man who was in charge of location scouting said.

"I want you to tell me," Rick said. "I'd prefer a place where nobody has ever shot anything before."

Everybody was very quiet.

"Manny," Rick said to the location man, "I want you to leave tomorrow on a scouting trip. Call my father at Barron Flying Service at Clover Field and charter an airplane. Look at the Sierras, look at Colorado, look at . . . I don't know, Montana, some place like that."

"How about Monument Valley?" Manny asked.

"That's John Ford's backyard," Rick said. "He owns it, and he can keep it. This is a cattle and water western, so I want enough grass to support cattle and a river worth fighting over, and Monument Valley doesn't have either of those. I wouldn't mind some snow-capped mountains in the background, either. We're probably going to have to build some early ranch houses, so if you can find some that will do, that'll be a plus. They'll need to be simple, though, maybe even raw. I want you back here in ten days, a week, if you can manage it."

"Anything else?" Manny asked.

"Nope."

"Then I'd better go home and pack and get out my atlas." Manny gathered his things and left the room.

"Costumes," Rick said, turning to Elsa Cameron, the studio's chief staff designer.

"We've got it all in my warehouse," Elsa replied.

Rick shook his head. "I don't want to see so much as a hat or a dress in this picture that has ever been used in a picture before. I want you to research the era, which is the 1870s, get photographs and work from the clothes real people wore."

"This is going to be fun," Elsa said.

"Then go get started," Rick said. He turned to Ruth Gannon, the casting director. "Ruth, I expect you've already got a list of actors for every part."

Ruth slid a memo across the table, and Rick caught it and slid it back. She looked surprised.

"I want this film cast with a lot of actors who've never been seen before in a feature film; look for stage actors and people new in town, maybe some old-timers who haven't worked for a long time. Look at acting teachers at the schools around town for middle-aged types; look at kids in their classes. I want fresh faces."

"Okay," Ruth said. "Who do you have in mind for the leads?"

"For the girl, the young widow, I want a young character actress, not gorgeous but not unattractive, one who's willing to bring her looks down a peg for the part. As for the male leads, I'm testing an actor today who may be right for the second lead; I'll know more tomorrow. Again, I want fresh faces, even for the star's role."

"I'll go call some agents," Ruth said.

"Call the acting teachers first. See who among their students they recommend."

She gave him a wave and left.

His associate producer, Howard Cross, spoke up. "Who do you want to shoot it?"

"I hear Basil Weathers is shooting something at RKO."

"He's a Brit and a first-timer here. You want a Brit to shoot a western?"

"I want a fresh eye; a Brit would kill to shoot a western. Find out when Weathers wraps on the RKO film, and if it's soon, get him over here to see me."

"I'll call his agent. What about lighting?"

"We'll let our cameraman pick him."

"Right. Anything else?"

"I'm going to produce and direct. I'll give you single-card coproducer, though."

"Okay."

"I want you to handpick the stunt guys on this one. There are going to be some rough scenes, and I want them to look really rough."

"I'll take care of it."

"That's it, then. Keep me posted." With everybody gone, Rick started on the paperwork on his desk. Vance Calder wasn't due for an hour.

Calder was announced and brought into Rick's office at eleven sharp. He was wearing a Savile Row suit and expensive linen and shoes. His hair was beautifully cut. The two men shook hands, and Rick sat him down on the sofa and took a chair.

"I hope you haven't made any plans for the rest of the day," Rick said.

"No, I'm out of work now."

"Not for long. An assistant director I like is going to come and get you in a few minutes, and you're going to shoot a screen test, two scenes from a film we've just finished shooting, one with an American accent, one English. The clothes you're wearing will be fine, and that will save time."

"All right," Calder said.

"Then he's going to take you out to the back lot for some outdoor stuff, and we'll provide you with the proper clothes. Have you ever ridden a horse?"

"I had a pony as a child, spent a lot of time pretending to be Tom Mix. I rode to the hounds a couple of times in my teens and didn't die." His accent was stage English now.

"That's a start," Rick said. "Tell me, how does an out-of-work actor with a construction job come up with that suit?"

"It was made when I was a working actor, in London. I think I may still owe the tailor for it."

The door opened, and Rick stood up. "Hi, Billy. Vance, this is Bill Thomas. He's going to direct you today. Billy, this is Vance Calder." The two young men shook hands and started to leave the office, but Calder returned.

"Rick, there's something I have to tell you. I lied to you yesterday, and I don't think that's a good way for us to start out."

"What did you lie about?"

"My real name is Herbert Willis. Calder is my mother's maiden name, and she had an uncle named Vance. It was legally changed in London a couple of years ago."

"Herbert Willis, huh? Glenna's real name is Louise Brecht. Keep both of them to yourself," Rick said.

6

The following midmorning, Rick got a call from Billy Thomas. "The stuff I shot yesterday is back. You want to me to clean it up or you want to see it raw?"

"Raw, as soon as possible."

"I'll have it put up in your screening room in half an hour."

"See you then."

In half an hour Rick walked into the screening room between his and Eddie Harris's office. Eddie was already there.

"What, you weren't going to invite me?"

"I figured you'd already know," Rick replied. "You know everything that's happening around here."

"I hear you offered Sid Brooks's agent a hundred and fifty grand for his screenplay. That's a big raise over the last picture."

"The last one was an adaptation; this is an original. Besides, you said to be generous, and I didn't want to get into a negotiation."

Bill Thomas came in and sat behind them. "We're ready," he said.

The lights went down, and the film popped onto the screen. The scene hadn't started yet, and Vance Calder was pacing nervously up and down.

"Uh, oh," Eddie said. "He's green."

"Oh, shut up, Eddie."

Bill Thomas's voice came from offscreen. "All right, places."

An actress walked into the frame, and Calder turned to face her. He took a deep breath and let it out slowly. Quickly, he was very still.

"Action," Thomas said.

The scene began, and Rick was struck by how suddenly calm the actor was. The two traded lines, and the girl turned her back. Vance took her shoulders, turned her back and delivered the funniest line in the movie.

Eddie Harris laughed out loud, and so did Rick.

The scene continued for two minutes, then Thomas yelled, "Cut. Print."

"How was it?" Vance asked.

"We won't need another one," Thomas replied. "Next scene, places." Calder, who had begun pacing again, took a breath. "Action."

This scene, the dramatic one, played more slowly, and Calder used his own accent.

"Is he a Brit or an American?" Eddie asked, surprised.

"What, you didn't know?" Rick replied.

The scene ran a little over three minutes, then Thomas cut but left the camera turning. "Face the camera, Vance," he said.

Vance faced the camera.

"Smile."

Vance smiled.

"He's going to need some dental work," Eddie said.

Thomas asked for left and right profiles and a rear shot, then asked Vance to face the camera again. "What's your name?"

"Vance Calder."

"How old are you?"

"None of your business."

"Cut. That's a wrap. Let's go out to the back lot." The projector stopped, and the lights went up. "He's putting up the outdoor stuff," Thomas said.

"I'll send him to the dentist today," Rick said. "After he meets Hyman Greenbaum."

Eddie said nothing.

The lights went down again, and the film began with the camera pointing down a western street set. A man on a running horse appeared, headed straight for the camera. As he approached, he brought the horse up short, simultaneously dismounting, drawing a six-gun and fanning six shots directly at the camera.

The scene changed abruptly to a shot from a car with the horse running alongside. To Rick's astonishment, Calder leapt from the running horse, hit the ground, vaulted over his mount, then back again, then into the saddle. He whipped a Winchester out of a saddle holster and began firing it at a full run, then he brought the horse up short and reared him, his hat raised in one hand. The shot was pure Tom Mix. The film stopped, and the lights came up.

"That's it," Thomas said.

"I asked you to shoot him roping," Rick said.

"He refused to do it. Said he knows nothing about roping and he wasn't going to make an ass of himself on film."

Eddie burst out laughing. "Where the hell did you find this guy?"

"Glenna spotted him the day before yesterday on the construction crew out at our new beach house."

"Is he American or English?"

"English."

"You know what I'm thinking," Eddie said.

"You're thinking of Clete Barrow." Barrow had been Centurion's biggest star and Rick's closest friend until he was killed in the war, at Dunkirk. "He's nothing like Clete, except that he's English, a terrific actor and a terrific athlete, but I know what you mean."

"I hope you didn't let him off the lot without signing him."

"Later today. He's having lunch with Hyman Greenbaum. Don't worry; I'll have him signed before the day is out."

"Be careful of Hyman; he's the best."

"That's why I sent Vance to him."

Vance Calder entered the Brown Derby and was shown imme-diately to a table where a man in his fifties stood up and offered his hand. "Hello, I'm Hyman Greenbaum," he said. He was a big man who looked like he had played football in college.

"How do you do, Mr. Greenbaum. I'm Vance Calder."

"Call me Hy, Vance, and have a seat."

Vance sat down and declined a drink.

"This is interesting," Hy said. "The only other time Rick Barron ever sent anybody to me was the girl he married, Glenna Gleason."

"Then I'm flattered," Vance said.

They looked at a menu and ordered.

"Rick and Eddie Harris had a look at your test this morning," Hy said. "I have an appointment out there at two o'clock. That means they liked it."

"Who's Eddie Harris?"

"He's the chairman of Centurion Pictures, Rick's boss."

"I thought Rick was the boss."

"No. He's the head of production, which means he's the boss of moviemaking, except he reports to Eddie."

"I see."

"Centurion is a good place for you to be," Hy said. "They're the newest of the major studios . . . well, nearly major."

"Do you think they'll offer me a contract?" Vance asked.

"Yes, but we won't take it. We'll take a three picture deal, with options. That means they can fire you whenever they like."

"Wouldn't a long-term contract be safer?"

"I'm glad you're concerned about safety; I'm a cautious man, myself. But you don't want to be a salaried employee of a studio; you want to stay independent, so you can work wherever you like. That's what the smart stars are doing."

Vance nodded. Lunch came, and they ate.

"Let me give you a little sermon," Hy said.

Vance smiled. "I'm accustomed to sermons; my father is an Anglican priest."

Hy nodded. "Then you know to sit quietly and not ask questions."

Vance looked sober. "Yes."

"Here we go. I've seen a lot of young people come out here since the advent of talkies—even before—and it goes something like this: most of them end up pumping gas and waiting tables. If they're beautiful and talented, they get a studio contract, starting at two hundred a week, more, if the studio wants them badly enough.

"The studio puts them in whatever movies they need them for, never mind quality. If they think they're going to be hot, they give them better pictures, and their salary goes up to five or eight hundred a week. If they're star material, pretty soon they're making two thousand.

"At first, they buy a new car, a convertible, usually, and get a better apartment. Then, after a raise, they get a mortgage and buy a little house. As the money continues to go up, they buy a more expensive car and a bigger house. Then, if they're lucky, they go independent.

"One day, when they've been out of work for a couple of months, a script arrives. It isn't a good script, but it's being shot in a nice place, say the South of France, and the costar is somebody they want to fuck. Oh, and the mortage and car payments are overdue. The movie doesn't do well, and the next script isn't quite as good. Then they're offered second leads in even worse pictures, and in a couple of years they're pretty much done, and they haven't turned thirty-five yet."

"I understand," Vance said.

"I'll get you decent money for the first picture, and we'll hold out for the lead. Here's what you do: don't buy a car until you can pay cash for it, and it should be used; you live modestly and don't go to expensive restaurants, unless the studio or somebody else is paying. You keep putting money in the bank. You don't marry a costar."

Vance laughed.

"You don't buy a house until you can pay cash. You don't ever take a job because of the location or the costar or even the director. You take jobs for good scripts, that's all. If you can stick to that program, you'll become very rich, and I'll help you invest your money. You'll form your own production company and become a partner of the studio, instead of just working for a fee. And you can marry anyone you like.

"My agency gets ten percent of every dollar you earn, whether it's from salary, profits, investments or partnership. That will get to be a big number, but we'll earn it."

"Of course," Vance said.

"They're going to want you to see a dentist," Hy said. "I'll make them pay for it."

"Thank you for your advice, Hy," Vance said. "I assure you, I'll take it. Now let me tell you a little about me: I drive a Whizzer."

"A *what*?"

"A Whizzer. It's a little engine bolted onto a bicycle, and it goes about thirty miles an hour downhill with a tailwind. I live in a rooming house in Santa Monica, where I'm very comfortable, and I saved money when I was running a pile-driving machine. I promise you I will change my circumstances carefully.

"I'm very impressed with both Rick Barron and you, but there's something you must understand: there is no one's judgment that I trust more than my own, and, while I will always be grateful for your counsel on every aspect of my career, I will always reserve the right to overrule it. If we can proceed on that basis, I would be very pleased to have you represent me."

Hyman Greenbaum reached across the table, and Vance Calder took his hand.

"Check," Hy said to a passing waiter. "Let's take a drive out to Centurion. Did you ride the Whizzer here?"

"No, I phoned for a taxi."

"You'll ride home in a studio car," Hy said. "One thing: they're going to offer you a part in a western, an original script by one of the best writers out here, Sidney Brooks. You'll take the part immediately, without reading the script, but that will never happen again."

"All right."

"One other thing, Vance: are you, by any chance, a member of the Communist Party, or have you ever been to one of their meetings?"

"I am not, and I have not."

"Have you ever signed a petition for aid to the Russians or the Republican side of the Spanish Civil War or war orphans or *anything*?"

"I have not."

They stood up, and Hy Greenbaum showed him to the door, where his car was waiting. "You're going to have a long and very successful career," he said.

7

Hyman Greenbaum took a chair across from Rick's desk, while Vance Calder cooled his heels in Rick's reception room.

"I want to see his test," Hy said immediately.

"The screening room is tied up right now," Rick said. "I'll run it for you later."

Hy smiled a little smile. "It was that good, huh?"

"It was all right."

"No seven-year contract," Hy said.

"What do you want, Hy?"

"A two-picture deal with an option; fifty grand for the first one, a hundred for the second."

"Not a chance," Rick said.

"What are you offering?"

"A five-picture deal, starting at ten grand, adding another ten grand every time we pick up his option. And I'll give him a nice dressing room."

"Three pictures; twenty-five, fifty and a hundred. And he gets a cottage. And he gets the lead in the Sid Brooks picture."

"All right," Rick said. "Three pictures; fifteen, twenty-five and fifty. He gets the lead, and he'll share a cottage. That's it, Hy."

"The kid needs a car," Hy said. "He's riding around on a bicycle with a motor, something called a Whizzer. He'll get killed."

"I'll loan him one until he gets on his feet."

"Oh, and he gets script approval."

"Not for the first three pictures, Hy. We want him to do as well as you do, and I promise you I'll handle him carefully. It's not in our interests for him to appear in a mediocre movie."

"No more than two pictures a year," Hy said. "Let's not wear him out."

Rick shook his head. "It's important for him to be seen a lot early in his career. Later, we'll see."

"You'll pick up his dental bill."

Rick nodded. "We've got a good man right down the street; he gets all our business."

"This kid is going to be very big, Rick."

"I hope so."

"All right, you've got a deal."

The two men stood and shook hands. "I'll send you a contract tomorrow morning and a check for five grand," Rick said.

"Done."

"Let's get him in here," Rick said, pressing a button on his intercom. "Show Mr. Calder in, please."

Vance walked into the room, and Rick shook his hand. "Welcome to Centurion, Vance," he said. "I think you're going to do very well here."

"Thank you, Rick," Vance said.

"Sit down, I want to tell you about the next few weeks."

Everybody sat down.

"We're in preproduction for a new script by Sidney Brooks, called *Bitter Creek*. It's going to be a tough, gritty western with a lot of fresh faces, yours among them. You're going to play the lead, and you'll have a script when you leave here. We'll start shooting the exteriors in about four or five weeks—sooner if we find an amenable location in a hurry. You'll probably be living in a tent for a month. In the meantime, you have a lot of work to do. I want you to ride as much as you can out on the back lot. You looked good in the test, but I want you perfectly at home in the saddle, and I don't want you saddle sore on location. Our head wrangler will teach you a lot of stuff you don't know yet, including roping cattle, and you'll spend some time on the firing range, working with guns.

"You'll need some dental work to make you look good in the closeups, and we'll send you to the studio's dentist for that. You'll be rehearsing with other members of the cast, with an acting coach, learning your lines, and you'll spend a couple of hours every day in the gym; we want to strengthen your upper body a bit and put a little more muscle on you for the part. After this film, you can decide how much working out you want to do, but it's important to your career that you be fit. Any questions?"

"When do I start all this?"

"Be in the gym at nine tomorrow morning. My secretary will give you a map of our lot, so you can find your way around." Rick reached into a pocket and tossed him a set of keys. "There's the key to your dressing room and a '38 Ford convertible outside in my parking spot; you can use it until the film is over, and after that I'll sell it to you if you like it."

"Thank you, Rick."

"Your dressing room will be half a duplex cottage at number 4A G Street. You'll see it on the map. You can sleep there, if you like, and save some money on rent. You'll have a pass for your car that will get you through the gate, but the guards will know you almost immediately. If you need clothes for a special occasion, see Marge in wardrobe, and she'll loan you what you need. Get fitted for a tuxedo today; you're invited to dinner at Eddie Harris's house tomorrow evening at seven. Don't bring a girl; Eddie's wife, Suzanne, will pair you with somebody. Is there anything else you need?"

"I'm probably going to need a lawyer," Vance said.

"Hy will recommend somebody, I'm sure. Anything else?"

"I can't think of anything."

"Don't hesitate to call me if you do. In the meantime, don't get into any traffic accidents, don't get anybody pregnant and, generally speaking, keep your nose clean. You'll get into the columns soon, but we want it to be at a time of our choosing. One of the publicity people will interview you for a studio bio, and we'll have a lot of still pictures taken. If you need a date for an event, publicity will fix you up with a contract player. Be nice to her."

"Of course."

"Your screen test is put up in my screening room next door." Rick handed him an envelope. "Here's your script. Good luck." He stood up, shook the actor's hand and showed him and his agent to the screening room, leaving them there.

Rick called Eddie Harris and sketched out the deal for him.

"Fine with me," Eddie said. "Good job, and you keep that kid happy."

"Don't worry; he's happy, and he's going to stay that way."

"He's going to be our Clark Gable and our Clete Barrow, all wrapped up in one."

"He just might be. He'll be at your house for dinner tomorrow night."

"Good. Did you give him Glenna's car?"

"Yes."

"Don't bother to pick out a new one; it's already in the parking lot next to your spot, by way of thanks for her spotting Calder."

"Thanks Eddie."

"You heard from Manny, the location maven, yet?"

"He's probably still in the air. Don't worry; he'll come up with something."

"I expect so. See you later, kid."

Rick hung up and turned his attention to the pile of mail on his desk. He went through a few things, then he came to an internal mail envelope, sealed with wax.

"Now what?" Rick said aloud. He broke the seal and shook out the single sheet of paper onto his desk. It was another photostat of a Communist Party of America card.

The name on it was that of one Louise Brecht, of a Milwaukee address. Rick sat, frozen, staring at the card. He didn't burn this one.

8

Rick left his office a little after six and found a brand-new, cream-colored, 1947 Cadillac convertible, waiting for him, or rather for Glenna. That was very generous of Eddie, he thought as he walked around it, admiring its lines. It was a lot bigger than the old '38 Ford, but Glenna would get used to it.

Rick had been driving the Ford since the day he had joined Centurion as its security chief in 1939. It had been garaged at the motor pool while he was in the navy and used in an occasional film, and when he got home, it was returned to him. No civilian cars had been built during the war years, and he went back to driving it as soon as his knee wound had healed enough to allow him to bend his leg. When Eddie Harris had tired of his 1940 Continental convertible, Rick had taken it and passed on the Ford to Glenna. Now new cars were coming out of Detroit again, and the Cadillac seemed the best of the lot.

He got into the car, fiddled with knobs to see what they were for, tried raising and lowering the top, then snapped down the tonneau cover. He drove out of the studio and headed for Beverly Hills, driving slowly. His enjoyment was tempered by his bafflement over the receipt of a Communist Party card with Glenna's original name on it. Not that he cared whether Glenna was a Communist or not, but he had thought she was a Roosevelt Democrat, as he was, and there was a nagging worry attached to Eddie's view of the upcoming HUAC hearings.

He parked the new convertible in the circular driveway and went inside, finding Glenna on the back terrace feeding the baby Glenn her bottle while little Louise, or Lou, as they called her, watched.

"Hi, there," she said, offering her lips for a kiss.

He accepted the offer, then sat down next to her. "Good news and bad news," he said.

"Good news first," she said.

"Vance Calder's screen test was outstanding; I signed him to a three-picture deal this afternoon. He's going to play the lead in *Bitter Creek*."

"Wow! That's moving fast."

"I'm just glad you spotted him before another studio did."

"What's the bad news?"

"I gave him your car."

"What?"

"It's your own fault; you discovered him."

"But I love that car."

"The poor guy was riding around town on a motorbike. We couldn't have that, could we?"

"But *my* car?"

"Don't worry; Eddie found you something to drive. It's sitting outside." He gave her the keys.

Glenna got up, handed him the baby and the bottle and left. A moment later Rick heard a shriek from the front of the house, then the sound of running feet in the hallway.

"A Cadillac!" she screamed, as she made it back to the rear terrace.

"I believe that's what it is. And it's yours, not the studio's. The registration is on the steering column, and it's in your name, a gift from Eddie for discovering Vance Calder."

"Can we go for a drive after the baby's fed?"

"We can after *I'm* fed."

The children's nurse, an Irish girl named Rosie, joined them. "All done?" she asked.

"Yes, Rosie, you can tuck them in, if you will, and will you let Hannah know we'll dine as soon as she's ready?"

"Yes, ma'am." Rosie left with the two girls.

Glenna took Rick's hand. "Why is it that life just gets better and better? What have we done to deserve all this?"

"Hard work and clean living, I guess."

"Do you know how many people in this country have nothing?" she asked.

"A lot fewer than had nothing ten years ago," Rick replied. "We're in a postwar boom, and things are looking pretty rosy."

"Well, we've defeated facism," she said, "and that's something, too. Now we can look forward to a better world."

"What's your idea of a better world?"

"When everybody has as much as we do."

"In order for that to happen, we'd have to have a lot less."

"Wouldn't you settle for a lot less, if everybody could have a lot more?"

"You mean like in Russia?"

"Well, not as long as Stalin is in charge, but when he's gone things will improve."

"Glenna, my darling, the rewards of our work are not preventing anyone else from getting ahead, except the people who would like to have our jobs. What the Communists do is drag everybody down without elevating anybody, except their party elite." He thought now would be a good time to ask her about the party card, but then they were called to dinner, and later, when they were driving around Beverly Hills in her new convertible, it would have spoiled her euphoria. There was no reason to mention it to her, really. He put it out of his mind.

———

T hree days later Rick was at his desk when a phone call came from Manny, the location director.

"Manny? Where are you?"

"I'm in a place called Jackson Hole, Wyoming," he said. "I spent a day in Colorado, then I heard about this place."

"What's in Jackson Hole?"

"Absolutely nothing; it's perfect!"

"Tell me about it."

"It's ranch land, with the Grand Teton Mountains in the background. I found a sixteen-thousand-acre ranch owned by an elderly couple who lost two boys in the war. It has every location we need, except the town; we'll have to build that. Lots of cattle on the ranch."

"What about housing for the cast and crew?"

"I found a war-surplus dealer in Denver who has a whole bunch of prefab barracks buildings sitting in his storage yard."

"You think the unions would sit still for their people living in open barracks, on cots?"

"There's a version that has one-man rooms and another that has two-man rooms. They were used as bachelor officers' quarters on military bases, and we can buy them for five hundred bucks apiece."

"Who assembles them?"

"The war-surplus guy. He trucks them up here and puts them up for fifteen hundred apiece, including running hot and cold water and toilets. We'll have to put in a septic field for a couple of grand."

"Are they heated?"

"A couple of pot-bellied stoves in each, plus we can wire each room for an electric heater."

"How many will we need?"

"We can get away with six," Manny said. "There's room in the main ranch house for you and the two stars. We can assign first-level people to the two-man rooms, which are fairly roomy: a single bed, a comfortable chair and a radio. We'll need another, open building for a mess hall and bar; there's no entertainment around here. I figure we can run a picture every night."

"What else do we need?"

"The dealer has half a dozen surplus trucks we could use and a whole bunch of Jeeps. There's a good five-thousand-foot dirt landing strip; we could fly the first-level people up here and bus everybody else. We'll need a bunch of phone lines, but those are available. It's really beautiful up here, Rick. You're going to love it."

"All right, Manny, draw up a list of everything and a budget and special-delivery it to me tomorrow. Then you go ahead and start putting everything together. How much is the use of the ranch and ranch house going to cost us?"

"Five grand, and they're tickled to get it."

"How long do you need to put the whole thing together and be ready for us?"

"Two, maybe three weeks."

"I'll give you a month, but you have to think of everything."

"Leave it to me."

"Thanks, Manny. I look forward to your budget." He hung up, feeling a surge of enthusiasm for his new project. He walked to Eddie's office and filled him in.

"Okay, you start exteriors in a month. What's your shooting schedule up there?"

"Five weeks, and they'll be building sets for the interiors while we're up there. We'll be back here before the snow flies up there, then we'll need another three weeks for interiors, and we'll be in postproduction."

"So, even if you have to deal with bad weather, we could handle a spring release?"

"That should be fine."

"How's casting coming?"

"It's going quickly. Because we're using so many new faces, most of the cast is working for scale."

"You got a budget yet?"

"No. In a couple of days, though, and it will be very complete."

"Can you bring this in for a million dollars?"

"Less, I expect."

"Looks like you've got yourself a western, kid."

"Looks like I have."

9

L ater that afternoon a call came from Rick's father.
"Hey, Dad."

"Hey, Boy. Your airplane's finished."

"Good news!"

"Yeah, I flight-tested her yesterday, and the overhauled engines are right on the money. We're painting that Centurion thing on her right now."

"So she's ready to fly?"

"She is."

"I might want her tomorrow; I'll call you about that."

Jack hung up, and Rick pressed the intercom button. "Please get me a flying weather forecast for tomorrow and as far into the future as possible from L.A. to Jackson Hole, Wyoming. I'll want it in writing."

His secretary came back a few minutes later. "They say it's ideal from tomorrow through the weekend and maybe beyond. I'm sending a messenger over there to pick up the written copy."

"Great." Rick buzzed Eddie Harris.

"Yeah?"

"Your airplane is ready to fly, Eddie; what say we take the girls and Sid Brooks and his wife up to Jackson Hole for the weekend, take a look at our locations?"

"That sounds great, kiddo."

"We'll meet out at Clover Field at nine A.M., then?"

"Good."

"Tell Suzanne the nights will be chilly."

"Okay. And remember, you, Glenna and Vance are expected here for dinner tonight."

"Right." Rick hung up and called Glenna and put the trip to her. She was enthusiastic.

"Can I bring the girls?" she asked.

"Too much for them and for us," Rick said. "Rosie and Hannah can handle them."

"Okay. What time?"

"We're meeting at Dad's place at nine tomorrow morning, and don't forget dinner tonight at the Harrises'."

"You're on."

Rick hung up and called Sidney Brooks.

"Hi, Rick, your production people have been keeping me abreast of work on *Bitter Creek*. I hear it's going well."

"It certainly is, and we've found a location for the exteriors at a place called Jackson Hole, Wyoming. Eddie and I are going to take our wives and fly up there tomorrow morning for the weekend. Would you and your wife like to join us?"

"Would I! Absolutely!"

"We're meeting tomorrow morning at nine at Clover Field at a big hangar called Barron Flying Service. It's my dad's place."

"I'll find it."

"Bring outdoor clothes and something warm for the evenings. Nothing fancy for the ladies."

"We'll be there."

"See you then." Rick hung up and buzzed his secretary. "Track down Manny White up in Jackson Hole and tell him six of us . . . No, wait a minute. Get me Vance Calder first. He's probably on the back lot."

Fifteen minutes later, Vance was on the phone. "Hello, Rick."

"Vance we've found a location up in Wyoming, and we're going up there tomorrow morning for the weekend. I'd like you to come."

"Love to."

"Bring a girl, if you like."

"There's nobody to bring, at the moment."

"Meet us at Clover Field tomorrow morning at nine at Barron Flying Service. It's a big hangar. Bring outdoor gear, and tell your girl to bring a jacket for the evenings, and don't forget dinner tonight."

"I'll be there."

Rick buzzed his secretary again. "Okay, now find Manny White and tell him eight of us are coming up there tomorrow morning for the weekend. Tell him to find us the best accommodations he can for three nights and to scout around for someplace to eat. Oh, and tell him to find us some horses, too."

"There's a bar up there he's been using for an office; I'll try him there."

"Tell him to hire us some decent transportation, too."

"Will do."

Rick hung up and called his father. "Okay, Dad, we're on for nine A.M. tomorrow."

"She'll be ready. You'll need full fuel?"

"Right. We'll probably need some internal fuel, too; as I remember, there's a bar in the cabin."

"I'll stop at the liquor store on the way home tonight."

"Thanks, Dad. What sort of heating does the airplane have?"

"It's got two good heaters, so you should be comfortable, but if you want me to, I'll buy some blankets, just in case."

"Good. Get expensive ones; these passengers are used to that. I'll reimburse you, of course. And please be sure the oxygen bottles are charged."

"Wilco."

He hung up and called the studio commissary. "Hi, this is Rick Barron. I'm going to need a picnic lunch for eight people—the works—plus paper plates and utensils, delivered to Barron Flying Service at eight A.M. tomorrow morning. Can you handle that?"

"Yes, sir. Hot food or cold?"

"Cold is just fine. Put in some beer, wine and Cokes, too."

"It'll be there, Mr. Barron."

Rick got out his charts of the west and plotted a course that would take them over Death Valley, then Nevada and cut the northwest corner of Utah and the southeast corner of Idaho. The field at Jackson was just over the Idaho-Wyoming border.

He calculated the distance at 680 miles, which was good, since he'd have a maximum range of about 1,300 miles, no refueling, coming or going. There were mountains all along the route, many of them nearly 10,000 feet; he'd go at 13,000 so his passengers wouldn't need oxygen, though he would, to be safe.

His secretary buzzed him. "Manny White's on the phone."

Rick picked it up. "Hey, Manny."

"Hi, there. I hear you're coming to see me."

"That's right, and I'm bringing Eddie Harris, Sidney Brooks and Vance Calder and their women."

"I spoke to the people who own the ranch, Mac and Ellie Cooper, and they're happy to have you all stay at the main house. It's big and comfortable, and they have a full-time cook, so all your needs will be taken care of. I've rented their big '41 Ford station wagon, and I've already got two Jeeps here, too. And they've got a barn full of horses, so you can ride all you like. There's good fly fishing in the Snake River, if you want that."

"What, no tennis and golf? No beach club?"

"We'll save that for when we're on location in Palm Beach."

"All right, look for us around two P.M. at the Jackson airfield. We'll have lunch on the airplane."

"We'll be ready for you. And Rick, bring me some cash, will you?"

"Okay."

Rick scribbled out a chit and called his secretary in. "Get me this in cash, today, please; I won't be in tomorrow."

"How do you want it?"

"Six thousand in hundreds, the rest in fifties and twenties."

When she came back with the money, Rick stuffed the fat envelope into his briefcase and rechecked his planning, excited about the flight.

10

Rick and Glenna arrived a little late for dinner at the Harris home to find everyone else already there. The Sam Goldwyns, old friends of Eddie's and Susan's, were there, along with Rick's friend, David Niven, who was with a girl they didn't know. Niven's wife had died the year before, when she had fallen down the cellar stairs at the home of Tyrone Power while playing a party game, and Rick was glad to see David out and around again.

Vance Calder, who looked perfectly at home in his borrowed tuxedo, was paired with Adele Mannheim, the widowed sister of the late Sol Weinman, Centurion's founder, who had been Rick's dinner partner on his first visit to this house. She was a charming woman, now in her sixties, and Vance, Rick was pleased to see, was paying a lot of attention to her.

Everyone waited for Rick and Glenna to finish a drink, and then Suzanne had them called to dinner.

After dinner, the ladies left the gentlemen to their brandy and cigars, both of which, Rick noticed, Vance declined, as did he.

"Sam," Eddie said to Goldwyn, "what do you think of all this business with the House Un-American Activities Committee?"

Goldwyn shrugged. "I think if they look hard enough they'll find a few Communists under a few rocks, maybe even some people we know. I don't know what will come of it, but I don't think it's a good thing."

"Neither do I," Eddie said.

"You know," Goldwyn said, "when I read the Constitution it makes me think that these people shouldn't be asking the questions they're asking. It's nobody's business what a fellow's politics are in this country. Or am I right?"

"You're right, Sam," Eddie said.

"Young man," Goldwyn said to Vance, "are you an American citizen yet?"

"No, Mr. Goldwyn," Vance replied. "I haven't been here long enough to qualify; I hope to become a citizen as soon as I'm elegible."

"Well, if that's what you want, let me give you some advice: don't talk politics with anybody, and don't sign anything."

"Sam," Eddie said, "Vance has just signed a contract with us. I'm glad we got to him before he heard your advice."

"Yes, well, that's your misfortune, young man; you should have signed with me."

Niven spoke up. "You did very well, Vance."

Everybody laughed.

"There's a lot of self-appointed policemen of other people's politics in this town," Goldwyn said, "and some of them think that people who come from where I do aren't real Americans. Some of them don't like my religion, either. I won't be working with these people no more."

"That's sad," Eddie said.

"I'm not sad!" Goldwyn said. "I'm the happiest fellow, and I'm not going to let these people tell me how to run my business."

"Good for you, Sam," Eddie said. "Let's go join the ladies." They got up and moved back into the living room.

Rick and Vance were seated next to each other.

"How did you like Adele?" Rick asked.

"She's lovely. I enjoyed her company."

"Good. I didn't want to mention it before, but she's a large stock-holder in Centurion. You know, the first time I came to this house I wore a tuxedo borrowed from wardrobe, and I was seated next to Adele. The other guests were the Goldwyns and the Clark Gables."

"How did you happen to join Centurion, Rick?" Vance asked.

"It's too long a story for tonight. Maybe I'll get a chance to tell you this weekend."

"I'm looking forward to the weekend."

"Good. Bring some riding clothes, and I don't mean tweeds."

"Wardrobe has already fixed me up," Vance said.

Rick turned to Niven. "David, we're flying up to a beautiful place in Wyoming tomorrow. There's some trout fishing up there. Would you like to come with us? There's room on the airplane."

"That sounds wonderful, Rick," Niven replied, "but I have two invitations this weekend that I can't get out of. Word has got 'round that I'm socializing again, I guess. I'd love to another time."

"David and I once went trout fishing in Oregon with Clark Gable and Clete Barrow," Rick said to Vance.

"And England declared war that weekend," Niven remembered. "Clete and I were on our way to England in a matter of days." He leaned a little closer. "And I don't think Sam has ever forgiven me for walking out on my contract."

By ten, the party was over, and the guests went their separate ways.

Driving home, with Glenna at the wheel of her new convertible, she said, "I thought Vance did awfully well, don't you?"

"Yes, I do. He paid the proper amount of attention to Adele."

"What did you gentlemen talk about over dinner?" she asked.

"Politics."

"Ugh," she said.

11

The Centurion Douglas DC–3 was sitting out in front of the Barron Flying Service hangar, her newly polished aluminum skin gleaming, when Rick and Glenna arrived.

"She's beautiful," Glenna said. "Eddie is going to be pleased."

Rick opened the trunk of the car so a lineman could get their luggage out of the car and aboard the airplane. "Wait until you see the interior," he said, leading her around to the door.

They stepped aboard. There were a pair of facing sofas up front and a beautifully crafted refreshment area; to the rear were a dozen large and comfortable seats, only one on each side of the aisle. "This is very nice."

"The airplane will seat as many as thirty-two," Rick said, "but it's configured for a maximum of eighteen, with three on each sofa, and today, we're only eight, so we'll get excellent range and good speed."

Other cars began to arrive, and Vance had come alone, so they were only seven. Soon everybody was aboard, waiting for Rick and his dad to finish the preflight inspection.

"She's gorgeous," Eddie Harris said, surveying his newly renovated airplane.

"She's as perfect as I know how to make her," Jack Barron said.

"She's better than new," Rick said. "Thanks, Dad, and now we'd better get going." He passed out earplugs, made sure everyone was comfortably seated and belted in, then he went forward to the cockpit.

Vance tugged at his sleeve as he passed. "Rick, do you mind if I sit up front?"

"No, come ahead," Rick said. "There's a headset hanging on your yoke, there," he said, pointing. "Fasten your seat belt, and we're off." Rick began working through his checklist, then started each engine. The big 1,200-horsepower radials rumbled smoothly, and Rick nudged the throttles forward and began taxiing to the runway. He stopped at the end and went through the run-up checklist.

"Clover tower," Rick said on the radio. "Douglas 123 Tango Foxtrot ready for takeoff on two one."

"Tango Foxtrot cleared for takeoff," the tower operator replied.

Rick taxied onto the runway, turned the airplane and moved the throttles forward. Shortly, the tailwheel was off the ground, and a moment after that they were airborne and crossing Santa Monica Beach, then out over the Pacific. Rick began climbing and turning parallel to the beach, then he called Los Angleles Control, reported his position and was cleared en route. He tuned in the Palmdale radio beacon and turned northeast toward it. By Palmdale he was at his cruising altitude of 13,000 feet in smooth air, with a nice tailwind. He calculated his groundspeed at just over 200 knots, or about 230 statute miles per hour.

He punched the button for the intercom and switched on the cabin speaker. "All right, everybody," he said, "we're at our cruising altitude of thirteen thousand feet, making good time. Our flight should be about four and a half hours, so that should put us in at the Jackson Airport in a little over four hours from now. If we encounter turbulence and have to climb higher, you may need to put on your oxygen mask, which is near your seat, but please don't do that until I ask you to.

"Our route is across Nevada, then over the northwest corner of Utah, then over the southeast corner of Idaho, then Jackson. There should be some spectacular mountain scenery below us along the way, and don't worry; we won't bump into anything. Glenna and Suzanne will serve lunch around noon."

Rick leaned the engines for maximum cruise speed and switched on the autopilot. "There," he said to Vance over the intercom, "we're on our way."

"I didn't realize you were going to be our pilot," Vance said. "Have you been flying long?"

"All my life. First, in my Dad's lap. I was flying left seat with him when I was twelve, and I got my license at sixteen. Have you ever flown before?"

"Once: a five-pound, half-hour ride in an old Jenny at Biggin Hill, in Kent. I threw up, and then I was fine."

"If you have any problems with airsickness, there's a bag in the pocket by your knee."

"Nope, that was first-time nervousness," Vance said.

"I was five minutes into my first combat mission when I threw up into my lap. After that, I was fine."

"What were you flying, the Thunderbolt?"

"No, those didn't come along until '43. We flew the Grumman Wildcat. We were at Guadalcanal in August of '42, supporting the landings, when a big Japanese transport force turned up to reinforce the island. My squadron led the attack that sank the aircraft carrier *Ryujo,* but I took some anti-aircraft fire that punched a hole in my airplane and messed up my right knee. After that, it was hospital ships, then San Diego, then back to L.A., where Eddie Harris got me to the best knee man on the West Coast. I got a medical discharge in early '44."

"I guess I was lucky; I was too young for conscription," Vance said. "I tried to enlist when I was fifteen, but my mother heard about it and turned up at the recruiting office with my birth certificate and practically led me out by the ear. I've always felt guilty about not serving."

"Don't. Your conscience should be clear."

"I suppose so."

Vance began asking questions about the airplane, and they passed most of the trip talking about flying. Rick turned off the autopilot and let Vance fly the airplane for a few minutes, but then lunch was served, and he turned it back on.

Rick picked up the radio beacon at Jackson half an hour out and homed in on it. The weather was clear, and the windsock showed him the active runway. He made a smooth landing and taxied up to the terminal.

Manny White was waiting for them with a big Ford station wagon and a pickup truck for the luggage, driven by a Cooper Ranch cowboy. Rick made arrangements for hangaring and refueling, and twenty minutes later they were at the Cooper Ranch.

The Coopers—MacKenzie, known as Mac, and his wife, Eleanor, called Ellie—a weathered-looking pair of sixty or so, were warm and welcoming and showed them to their rooms. When everyone had had a chance to freshen up, Manny loaded them all into the station wagon and gave them a tour of the huge spread, pointing out locations as they went.

"You did good, Manny," Rick said halfway through. "It's perfect."

Eddie Harris, uncharacteristically, seemed speechless, awed by the towering Tetons and the gorgeous landscape.

They dined on home-grown roast beef at the ranch house that night, supplemented by bottles from a case of wine Eddie had brought. He was deep in conversation with the Coopers at his end of the table, while the other end carried on its own conversation.

After dinner, Mac Cooper led them into the rustic living room and showed Eddie and Rick a map of the area with the ranch boundaries marked. Manny had told them that the Coopers had lost two sons in the war, but except to express the visitors' condolences, nothing more was said about it. Cooper told them that during the war he had had something over 7,000 head of cattle on the place, selling exclusively to the military. He was down to something over 4,000 head now and was selling briskly to the civilian market.

They were at an elevation of around 6,500 feet, and the thin air made everyone tired. They were all in bed by nine o'clock.

Rick settled into a comfortable bed with Glenna.

"Sid Brooks's wife is worried," she said sleepily to Rick.

"What's Alice worried about?"

"The committee business," she said, then she turned over and fell asleep.

Rick was not far behind her.

12

Rick slept like a stone until after ten o'clock. To his surprise, Glenna was already out of bed. He showered and shaved, went downstairs for coffee and found everyone but Eddie on the front porch with their cups.

"Morning, all," he said, and everyone returned his greeting. "Is Eddie still in bed?" he asked Suzanne.

"No. He's deep in conversation with Mac Cooper, in his study," she replied.

Manny appeared and walked everyone around the immediate environs of the ranch house, showing them the bunkhouse, the mess hall, the barns and corrals and the place that was being prepared for the war-surplus barracks buildings.

"They're arriving on Tuesday," Manny said, "and they'll all be up by the end of next week."

After their tour they went to a corral and met the ranch foreman, Dick Torrey, who had a wrangler choose horses for them. The animals were saddled, then Torrey led them away from the ranch house for an hour's ride. They arrived at a low bluff on the Snake River, where the ranch's chuck wagon awaited them and served lunch while a wrangler picketed their horses.

They sat around a rough-hewn portable table on sawhorses and ate the good food.

"I think I'm going to enjoy shooting up here," Rick said, "and I'll be sorry to leave."

"You can visit as often as you like," Eddie said. "I bought the place this morning."

His wife's mouth dropped open. "You *what*?"

"Mac and Ellie Cooper expected their sons to carry on here, but that is not to be, so they've decided to retire and build a new, smaller house for themselves a couple of miles up the river on fifty acres they've kept."

Suzanne was having difficulty with this. "You bought a *ranch*?"

Eddie nodded. "This ranch, nearly sixteen thousand acres of it. It's a going concern, you know, and Dick Torrey is going to run it for me."

"But you are the most urban person I know," Suzanne said.

"I could get used to this," Eddie said, waving an arm. "In fact, I'm already used to it. I even like being on a horse."

"How much do you expect we'll use the place?"

"As often as we like," Eddie replied. "After all, we have an airplane; let's use it."

"Congratulations, Eddie," Rick said.

"You'll all be welcome any time."

"When do you close on the place?"

"Well, I've got to find legal and accounting representation in the state, then incorporate. I expect it will be about three months. The Coopers will stay on in the big house until their new one is finished. Suzanne and I probably won't see the place again until next summer."

"It ought to be a great investment," Vance said.

Eddie grinned, "I think so, too. Not to mention the fun Suzanne will have decorating it."

"I've got to start making lists," Suzanne said.

That night after dinner the four men made themselves comfortable in Mac Cooper's study.

"Eddie, Rick," Sid Brooks said, "we had a meeting a couple of nights ago."

"What sort of meeting?" Eddie asked.

"A strategy meeting. There were two lawyers from New York there, and we hired two West Coast attorneys. We're going to make this a First Amendment issue. The idea is, if we have freedom of speech, we have the right not to speak, and if we have the right to choose our politics, we have the right not to talk about it."

"I'm a lawyer," Eddie said, "and I think that's a novel approach."

"You sound disapproving," Sid said.

"If I were your lawyer, I'd advise you to take the Fifth, rather than depend on an untested legal strategy."

"When you take the Fifth, everybody thinks you're guilty of something, and we're not guilty of anything. Anyway, we have a liberal Supreme Court right now, and if we lose in the hearings, we can appeal with the hope of success."

"There are what, nineteen of you?"

"Forty-one were subpoenaed; nineteen of us are going to be un-friendly witnesses, as they've begun to call us. There's also a group being formed called the Committee for the First Amendment, people who aren't politically suspect, who are going to send a dele-gation to the hearings to morally support us."

"I know," Eddie said. "I'm a member, and I'll be there."

"I'd like to go, too," Rick said.

"You're going to be shooting a movie right here," Eddie pointed out, "and anyway, I'm the public face of the studio, since Sol Wein-man died. You leave this to me."

"As you wish," Rick said, but he was disappointed.

"Eddie's right, Rick," Sid said. "You're better off keeping your head down; this could get messy. And I want to thank both of you for paying for my script up front. That gives me a financial cushion, and I may need it."

"The least we could do," Eddie said.

"I'm grateful for the trip up here," Sid said. "Alice has been worried sick about all this, and, I have to admit, I have been, too. It's good to get away from L.A. for a few days and breathe some fresh air without the press all over us. I haven't been this relaxed for weeks."

"Our pleasure," Eddie replied.

Vance, who had said nothing until now, spoke up. "I guess I'm going to have to read the U.S. Constitution," he said, "if I'm going to understand any of this."

13

They landed at Santa Monica on Monday evening, their return flight longer than the trip out, because of the westerly winds. Everybody piled out of the airplane, and the linemen got their luggage unloaded and into the trunks of their respective cars.

On the way home, Rick felt very satisfied with their weekend. "We got a lot done," he said to Glenna.

"You sure did, but nothing compared to Eddie."

Rick laughed. "That was a surprise; I didn't have a clue. I just knew he and Mac Cooper were spending a lot of time together."

"When will you go back to start shooting?"

"A couple of weeks. Everything will be in place by then, and we'll be trucking up equipment and crew in advance of that."

"What do you want me to do while you're gone?"

Rick looked at her, surprised. "Why, I want you and the girls to come with me. Didn't you know?"

"Well, you didn't mention it until now."

"I'm sorry. I just assumed you'd think the same way. I think we'd enjoy the time together up there."

"You're going to be busy as hell, and I'm going to be spending a lot of time with Ellie Cooper, quilting or something."

"Would you rather not go?"

"No, I want to go, but I want to be able to bail out if I get . . . whatever the reverse of cabin fever is."

"Sure, you can go home any time you like." He had a thought. "Listen, all your experience is in front of the camera; how'd you like to spend some time behind it?"

"What do you mean?"

"How would you like to be an associate producer?"

She thought about that. "You mean, order people around?"

"No, I mean we'd carve out some responsibility for you, and you'd be in charge, reporting to the producer."

"And that would be you?"

"No, that would be Leo Goldman. He's a bright new guy who's seriously on the make, and I think you'll like him."

"And if I don't like his decisions, can I appeal to you?"

"No. Leo would probably fire you."

"I'll have to think about that," she said.

V ance Calder went back to his rooming house, cleaned out the last of his belongings and put them into the '38 Ford convertible; he had already sold the Whizzer to the guy across the hall for sixty dollars. He gave his landlady a check, then drove to Centurion Studios, to his cottage/dressing room.

The place had a living room with a foldout sofa, dressing room, bath and kitchenette. It was snug, but it was a lot more room than he was accustomed to.

He put away the last of his things: three pairs of Levis, some work shirts, boots and underwear, and his one suit, two good shirts and one pair of good shoes. It wasn't much of a wardrobe, but when he left New York he was so broke he couldn't even afford a bus ticket. He took a commuter bus to a New Jersey station, then hitchhiked all the way across the country, carrying one suitcase and a backpack, along with a rolled-up sleeping bag. It took him twelve days, and he slept in barns, the backs of rolling trucks and in the woods. Along the way he gained a real appreciation of the size, diversity and wealth of this amazing country.

A short time ago he had been making two dollars an hour as an equipment operator. Now, all of a sudden, he had a place of his own, a car and a little over four thousand dollars; also an agent, a lawyer, a three-picture contract and, if he worked hard and played his cards right, a career. He sat down and wrote his parents a long letter, detailing everything that had happened to him over the past weeks and giving them the studio as a mailing address.

He unpacked half a bottle of good Scotch, poured himself a drink and got back into the Ford, taking the bottle with him. Slowly, he drove around the studio, taking it all in. He drove down the set streets: the New York brownstones, the downtown business street, the small-town set, with its village square and pond and, on the back lot, the western street. The studio police never stopped him because they knew the car.

On his way back to his cottage he noticed lights on in the motor pool, and he turned in and stopped. Hiram, who ran the place, slid out from under an elderly Rolls Royce and looked at him.

"Hey, Vance, what brings you around, car trouble?"

"No, Hiram. The car is just great. I was just driving around, looking at the place. You want a drink?" He held up the bottle.

"Don't mind if I do," Hiram said. He stood up, walked to his desk and found a coffee cup, watching as Vance half-filled it. "Down the hatch," he said and took a swig. "Good stuff."

"Black Label. I splurged."

"How's it going for you?"

"It's a dream, Hiram; don't pinch me."

Hiram laughed.

"That's quite an old crate," Vance said, nodding at the Rolls.

"Yes, it is, and it's in perfect shape, or it will be when I finish this little job. You want to see something really special?"

"Sure."

Beckoning for Vance to follow, Hiram walked over to a rear corner of the big garage, switched on the overhead lights and pulled a sheet of canvas off a car. "What do you think of that?" he asked.

Vance stared at the sleek black roadster. "My God," he said, "is that a Mercedes SSK?"

"You bet it is."

"I thought they were all destroyed in the war."

"Not this one, though Clete Barrow tried hard enough."

"This was Clete Barrow's car?"

"Hasn't Rick told you the story?"

"No, he hasn't."

Hiram climbed into the passenger seat and motioned for Vance to sit behind the wheel. "Well," he said when they were settled, "this goes back to '39. Rick Barron was a cop on the Beverly Hills police force at the time, and he had just been busted from detective to patrolman. He and his captain didn't get along."

"Why not?"

"I'll let Rick tell you that part, but don't ask him right out."

"All right."

"Anyway, late one night, he's sitting at the corner of Sunset and Camden in his patrol car, and Clete Barrow, driving this car, came barreling down Sunset and made scrap metal out of an old Ford driven by a woman who had run the stop sign.

"The Mercedes spins across Sunset into a hedge, throwing Clete out. Rick runs over there, recognizes Clete, finds out he isn't hurt much, checks on the woman, who, he says, was hamburger. Then he did something really smart: Clete gave him Eddie Harris's home number, so instead of taking Clete to a hospital, where the cops and the press would have been all over him, he calls in another car to deal with the wreck and, after taking the plates and the registration off the Mercedes, calls Eddie and takes Clete to the studio.

"They get the famous Dr. Judson over here to check out Clete, and Eddie and Rick fall into conversation. Eddie likes him, and within seventy-two hours, Rick has a new job as head of security for the studio. The rest, as they say, is history."

"And you fixed the car?"

"We had to order the parts from Germany, and they came in on the last German merchant ship before the war started. I worked on it in my spare time for two years, until I had it back in mint condition, as you see it. It hasn't been driven since."

"Why not?"

"Rick inherited the car when Clete was killed in the war, and I guess he's never had the heart to use it."

"Seems like a waste," Vance said.

"Yeah, well. Maybe they'll use it in a picture, or something."

"What do you suppose it's worth, Hiram?"

"Christ only knows. More than anything else in this barn, that's for sure. More than a new Cadillac."

Vance tried to imagine himself driving it.

"Well, I gotta get back to work, get this job done and get home. The little woman is saving supper for me."

"Thanks for the look at the SSK," Vance said.

"Thanks for the drink."

Vance got back into the car, drove back to his cottage and heated up a can of chili con carne for dinner.

14

At breakfast the following morning, Glenna said, "Okay, I'll do it."

"Do what?"

"Don't mess with me this early in the morning," she said. "How much do I get paid?"

"Five hundred a week."

"How much does Leo Goldman get paid?"

"None of your business. Glenna, I wasn't kidding when I said that Leo can fire you, if you don't do a good job."

"I know you weren't; you're a hard man, mister."

"Oh, and I guess so that the kids won't die, you'd better bring Rosie along. And I won't take her pay out of yours."

"That's mighty white of you."

"I know it is; I wouldn't do that for a producer who wasn't my wife."

Rick arrived at his office to find Leo Goldman, a large, bearlike, bullet-headed man in his late twenties, waiting for him. He had joined Centurion after slugging his boss at Metro. Eddie had thought his action was "admirable." "Morning, Leo," Rick said. "I'm glad you're here; we've got things to talk about."

"We sure have," Leo said, following him into his office and taking a chair.

"Something on your mind?"

"I hear you went up to Jackson Hole this weekend to work on the picture."

Rick immediately realized that he should have invited Leo, but it had never crossed his mind. "I'm sorry, Leo. I didn't intend to leave you out of anything important. It was a weekend off, that's all. We took the wives, but we did get a look at the locations Manny had picked out."

"*Manny* decides on locations?"

"Manny finds them; the director decides."

"Look, if you don't want me on this picture, just say so. In fact, if you don't want me at the studio, say so, and I'll tear up my contract."

"Listen to me, Leo," Rick said. "If I didn't want you on the picture or at the studio, you wouldn't be here. Anyway, you were still cleaning up your last production over the weekend, weren't you?"

"I could have shook loose."

"Leo, I promise you that no decision was made over the weekend that is in any way going to impact on your job."

"You'd better not ever do that."

"Leo, I've apologized, and I'm not going to do it again, but don't *ever* tell me I'd *better not* do something. I suggest you get a grip on yourself and start addressing what we're going to do with this script."

Leo took a deep breath and let it out. "All right, I had my say. Let's go to work."

"Good. Manny is still up there dealing with getting some war-surplus barracks put together. Call my father, Jack Barron, at Barron Flying Service, at Clover Field, and he'll get you flown up there."

"When do you want me to leave?"

"As soon as you can get a list of equipment and crew that will have to be trucked and bussed up there, and get them rolling. You'll be there two or three days before they arrive, and Manny will work out some office space and transportation for you." He gave Leo Manny's phone number at the local saloon. "He'll have some phone lines in for us in a few days. Also, set up a meeting here to finalize casting."

"I hear we've already got a leading man."

"That's right. His name is Vance Calder, and he's going to be very good. He has a three-picture deal with us."

"I saw him out on the back lot doing stuff on horses. The guys out there are impressed; one of them told me Calder could win money at the rodeo."

"He'd better not, or our insurance is blown. I'll make sure he understands."

"I'd like a trailer to work in, so I won't be tied to a desk."

"Good idea; get me one, too. Have you met my wife?"

"No, but of course, I've seen her pictures."

"She's coming up to Wyoming for the shoot, and I've hired her as an associate producer at five hundred a week; get that in the budget."

"You told me I'd be single-card credited as associate producer."

"You've been promoted. Now you're executive in charge of production."

"Well, I can't argue with that, as long as the title describes what I do."

"Leo, don't push your luck. I'm still producer and director, and, in case you've forgotten, I'm head of all production for the studio, so you work for me."

"Yeah, okay."

"Don't worry, I'll share the best-picture Oscar with you."

Leo laughed out loud. "From your lips to God's ear."

"Carve out some stuff for Glenna to be in charge of; costumes would be good. A couple of other things: she's smart, and she's a good organizer. I've told her that if she does a lousy job you can fire her, so don't take any crap from her. Also, don't ride her because she's my wife."

"You give me a thin line to walk."

"I want you to treat all the people who report to you decently, and that includes Glenna. You've been here for one picture, so by now you should know that's studio policy."

"Sure, I do; don't worry. I'll get along with Glenna, but what happens if she comes to you, complaining about me?"

"I'll send her right back to you."

"How about our star? Is he going to be a handful?"

"Vance is too smart for that. Go out to the back lot and introduce yourself. Get to know him and help him in any way you can. If he works out he's going to make a lot of money for the studio over the next few years, maybe even longer."

"I'll do that. By the way, for what it's worth, I hear the locations are good."

"We've got sixteen thousand acres to choose from. The owners of the place, Mac and Ellie Cooper, are sweet people, and you treat them with kid gloves. Between you and me, Eddie Harris bought the place from them this weekend, but they'll still be living in the ranch house."

"Where will I be living?"

"Work that out to your satisfaction with Manny; there won't be room in the main house." There would be room, Rick knew, but he didn't want to live with Leo.

"Speaking of casting, what are we doing for extras?"

"When you get up there go into town and take a look at the locals, especially the men, the guys who hang out in the saloon. They're a salty-looking bunch, and, sober, they'd look great on camera. Don't mess with the ranch hands; they've got four thousand head of cattle to deal with. If you need anybody from L.A., call casting, and they'll scare them up for you."

"Okay, anything else?"

Rick stood up and held out his hand. "This will be the first time we've worked together, Leo; let's do it right."

Leo grinned, shook his hand and left.

Watching him go, Rick hoped he had been firm enough with him. Leo reminded him of a touchy bull he had seen at the ranch, all muscle and no finesse.

15

Rick was near the end of his day. Casting had nearly been completed and the various contracts issued. Just before five, his secretary buzzed.

"Jed Crawford from the extras union is on the phone."

"Okay," Rick said, pushing the button. "Jed, how are you?"

"Not so good, Rick; I hear you're about to start shooting a western, and I haven't heard anything about how many extras you want to use."

"We're shooting out of state, Jed; we probably won't need any L.A. people."

"That's unfriendly, Rick."

"I'm sorry you think that, Jed; I certainly don't intend for it to be. In fact I don't anticipate using more than half a dozen extras, and we'll hire them locally, as much for their cattle-handling skills as for anything else."

"We've got plenty of guys who can ride horses and handle cattle."

"So, you want me to hire here, then transport them to the location, then feed and house them for a month, so that we can use them in two or three scenes, is that it?"

"That's about the size of it."

"Jed, have you read the contract lately? I mean, we signed it only a couple of months ago, both of us, and it excludes out-of-state extras."

"It would be nice if you used a few of our people, and it won't be nice if you don't."

"Do I hear just the hint of a threat in that sentence, Jed? Because if that's what it is, then this conversation is going to take a different turn."

"Take it easy, Rick; you'll have a heart attack."

"Not over this, I won't."

"Be seeing you." Crawford hung up, and Rick went back to work.

Five minutes later his secretary buzzed again. "A Mickey Cohen is on the phone."

"Put him on hold." Rick thought about this for a minute. Mickey Cohen had stepped in and taken over many of Ben "Bugsy" Siegel's responsibilities after Bugsy had had an eye blown out of his skull while sitting in his girlfriend's living room, and those responsibilities, apparently, included using the extras union for the purpose of extortion. Rick picked up the phone.

"Rick Barron."

"Hi, Rick. This is Mickey Cohen."

Rick waited a couple of beats before replying. "Who?"

"Come on, Rick. You wouldn't have taken the call if you didn't know who I am."

"I've heard of you."

"What have you heard?"

"I've heard you're the new Bugsy Siegel."

"Ben wouldn't like to hear you call him that name, Rick."

"Okay, I'll wait for *his* call."

"Consider this his call."

"What do you want, Mr. Cohen?"

"I understand you just had what could be interpreted as an unfriendly conversation with Mr. Crawford of the extras union."

"I had a business discussion with Mr. Crawford; he was what I interpreted as unfriendly. Are you an official of the extras union?"

"Not in a formal way; I'm sort of a counselor to them."

"Well, you can counsel them all you like, but this studio is a signator of a contract with the extras union that doesn't say anything about my having to deal with counselors. Crawford knows that; if you have any questions about it, get him to explain it to you."

"I'm sorry you're taking that attitude, Rick; it would be so much simpler just to have a nice chat about this and come to an arrangement that benefits everybody."

"Listen, Mickey," Rick said, forcing himself to sound more conciliatory, "let me be frank with you: I didn't deal with Bugsy Siegel or Chick Stampano, and I'm not going to deal with you."

"Yeah, I heard about how you dealt with Stampano."

Rick had blown off the top of Stampano's head, after he had beaten up Glenna. "Don't believe everything you hear."

"Oh, I believe that story, all right. You're a tough guy who takes the law into his own hands."

"Only when dealing with people who take the law into their own hands."

"You're an ex-cop, aren't you?"

"I still carry an LAPD badge," Rick said. And he did. Eddie Harris had paid a hundred and fifty bucks for it to a corrupt former chief of police, and Rick was actually listed on the rolls of the department as a detective lieutenant.

"That doesn't concern me, since I never do anything illegal."

Rick couldn't suppress a short laugh. "That doesn't really concern me, Mickey, because you and I are never going to do anything together that doesn't involve a lot of cops and lawyers."

"Listen, you want to place a bet, call me."

"Not even that."

"Well, I'm sorry you can't take a more flexible view of our contract terms," Cohen said. "But pretty soon, you're going to need extras for something shot in California, and that could get rocky."

"Mickey, if you and Jed Crawford want your names and the union spread all over the front pages of the trade papers, then do your worst. I can promise you this: I will never lose so much as a day's shooting because my extras don't show, and if you ever interfere with our business I'll see you in federal court. You do know that interference with a trade union is a federal offense these days, don't you?"

"Bye-bye, Rick."

Rick hung up and walked over to Eddie Harris's office.

"Got a minute?"

"Sure. You want a drink?" Eddie got up and went to his bar.

"Yeah, some of that bourbon of yours."

Eddie poured two drinks, handed Rick one and sat down.

"I just had a phone call from Jed Crawford at the extras union, followed closely by a call from Mickey Cohen."

Eddie's eyebrows went up. "Yeah?"

Rick gave him the substance and detail of each conversation.

"That's exactly what I would have said, Rick," Eddie said, "except maybe more profanely."

"You think we're going to have trouble?"

"Yeah, I do. Cohen made his demands and was rebuffed; he's not the kind of guy who will take that lying down."

"Should I start going around armed?"

"I don't think you'll get shot at, but I think it's a good time to go on location in Wyoming. Cohen will wait until we need forty extras for an expensive scene, then he'll make his move."

"What will we do then?"

"I'll brief the lawyers tomorrow and have them draw up a lawsuit. I won't even make a phone call; the minute they're in breach of contract I'll have them served, and Cohen, too, and I'll call the trades and the columnists personally. I think I can arrange for the FBI to have a chat with Cohen, too. We'll have our extras the next day. Until then I think it would be a good idea to have a backup scene ready to shoot, if we should have extras problems."

"Okay, Eddie."

"You make movies, kiddo; I'll do what I do."

For a moment, Rick thought this might be a good time to mention the Communist Party card with Glenna's name on it, but he didn't.

16

After a day's delay for weather, Rick loaded Glenna and the girls, their nurse, Rosie, and Sidney and Alice Brooks and Vance Calder onto the DC–3, along with another pilot, who would return the airplane to Santa Monica. Their flight was a little bumpier than the last one, but they landed midafternoon in Jackson, where Manny White and a small army bus were waiting for them.

"What's with the bus?" Rick asked, while their considerable luggage was being unloaded.

"I bought it," Manny said. "It cost nine hundred bucks. I bought six Jeeps, too, for two hundred apiece. And something else I'll show you when we get to the ranch. I'm telling you, this war surplus thing is a location manager's dream."

When they arrived at the ranch, the place had been transformed; it looked more like a small army base than a working ranch, with neat rows of barracks and former military vehicles scattered about. Parked next to one of the barracks was a Caterpillar bulldozer, painted olive drab.

"What the hell is that for?" Rick asked, pointing at the machine.

"For keeping the ranch roads in good shape," Manny explained. "We had some rain last week, and they needed work, if we're going to truck equipment and cast around. It was twelve hundred dollars, and it had six hours of use on the meter. The bus has thirteen hundred miles on it."

"What are we going to do with all this stuff when we're done?"

"Sell it or move it back to L.A., if there's something we can use there."

"Okay, Manny, whatever you say, as long as we're on budget."

"We're under budget."

"Now tell me what the problems are."

"Well, we've had an unavoidable delay on the phone lines, but the good news is we have our own Western Union service. Our cable address is BCREEK."

"When do we get the phones?"

"At least a week, maybe ten days. I've been over and over this with them, and it really is the best they can do. They're in the middle of installing new equipment at the central office. Our lines have all been run out here, and the phones installed; they just don't work yet."

"Send an explanatory wire to Eddie Harris," Rick said.

Rick greeted Mac and Ellie Cooper, then moved his family into the ranch house. He gave Vance the same room he had used before, and soon they were comfortably settled.

At dinner, Mac, the normally terse rancher, was particularly ebullient. "Rick, this movie business is a hoot; it's like hosting an invading army."

"That's a good description, Mac," Rick replied. "I'll ask our people to hold down the looting and pillaging."

Mac laughed uproariously. "When you get a minute, I want to show you the house Ellie and I have designed for ourselves. We poured the footings the last couple of days."

"It's a pity you don't need any piles driven," Rick said. "Vance would be your man for that. His former career."

"I can pour footings, too," Vance said, "but I warn you, I get two bucks an hour."

"Is that what Rick's paying you?" Mac asked.

"I wish," Rick said.

Sid Brooks stayed for three days, doing some polishing on the script, then returned to L.A. with the airplane, while his wife, Alice, stayed on.

"I'm grateful to you for letting Alice stay, Rick," he said. "She's extremely nervous about the HUAC hearings, and it's better to have her up here and out of it. I'll be back, if you want me, when I return from Washington."

"I'd love to have you back, Sid," Rick said.

"That's good to know; the writer isn't usually welcome on the set."

"That's because you're all such royal pains in the ass," Rick explained. "Where's Basil?" he asked. The director of photography was not at dinner.

"He lit out of here late this afternoon," Mac said. "Something about taking pictures of the thunderstorms over the mountains."

They were having drinks after dinner when Basil turned up, dirty but happy. "I got some gorgeous stuff," he said to Rick. "We had a sunset with thunder and lightning, and I got a lovely shot of Vance's double riding in from the direction of the mountains and watering his horse in the river."

"I have a double?" Vance asked.

"Of course," Basil replied. "He'll stand in for you when we're lighting; we don't want you sweating through your makeup under those hot lights. You've got a stunt double, too."

"I don't wear makeup, and I don't think there are any stunts in the script I can't handle myself," Vance said.

"Vance," Rick said, "we can't afford to have you hurt while we're making this picture. Also, our insurers don't like it when you start falling off horses and jumping off cliffs."

Vance shrugged.

After dinner, Manny White showed up with a telegram for Rick.

GOOD LUCK ON YOUR SHOOT. PHONE ME WHEN
YOU CAN. WE NEED TO TALK. EDDIE.

17

L eo Goldman hit the ground running. Before sunset on his first
day in Jackson Hole he had selected the smaller of two
Airstream trailers, earmarking the larger one for Rick Barron. He had
unpacked his clothes and his briefcase and moved into the trailer,
which had a water and septic hookup and a gas bottle outside to run
the stove. He had wandered the barracks, introducing himself to
and ingratiating himself with everybody he ran into, cast and crew.
By the time Rick arrived on location, everybody was accustomed to
reporting to Leo.

Leo had anticipated every problem and had his fingers on every
button. He had mapped the way to every location, and, if necessary,
he could unhook his trailer from the utilities, hitch it to his Jeep and
tow it anywhere the cameras went. Leo had learned the ropes, beginning in the mail room, during six years at Metro Goldwyn
Mayer, the grandest of the studios, and he had absorbed both its or-
ganizational brilliance and its many excesses. He knew how to get a
movie made, as long as he didn't have to write, photograph or direct it, and he knew how to use the machinery of a studio to his own
advantage.

Something else he had absorbed from his betters at Metro was an
abiding hatred of Communists and anybody who sympathized
with them, and he had been royally pissed off to see Sidney Brooks

getting off the war-surplus bus at the Cooper ranch. Leo had joined a nascent organization that styled itself, rather grandly, the Motion Picture Alliance for the Preservation of American Ideals, known as MPA, an outfit that included Walt Disney, John Wayne, Cecil B. DeMille and a lot of other well-placed producers and actors in town whom Leo wanted to get to know under favorable circumstances.

Sidney Brooks, he knew, was going to be an early target of HUAC, and he, for one, hoped the bastard got gutted, along with all his fellow travelers. Leo had gone over the casting lists for *Bitter Creek* with a fine-toothed comb, looking for Reds, but, since so many of the cast were new to pictures, he had only found two suspects, and he had managed to squelch the employment of both of them without calling undue attention to himself.

He had also gone over Brooks's script, searching for any trace of Communist propaganda that he could root out. Somewhat disappointingly, he had found nothing he could legitimately complain about, and he was smart enough to know that it was a damned fine script that would reflect well upon him as its executive in charge of production. He had learned, too, that Brooks had already been paid, so there was no way he could interfere with that.

Leo liked Eddie Harris, whom he considered to be almost as smart as he was, and he thought Rick Barron was okay, too, though he had not yet tested the political views of either man. He had heard that Eddie was going to Washington in support of those who had been subpoenaed, and he didn't like that much, but there was no percentage in his challenging Eddie on that, or on much of anything else, either. After all, he worked for these two guys, even if he did have plans to change that some time in the future.

Leo was a Jew, and this was the first time he had worked for somebody who wasn't Jewish, and at first that circumstance had made him uncertain of his judgment of Eddie and Rick. Soon, though, he discovered that, WASPy as they were, they were little different from their Jewish counterparts at other studios, and it impressed him that the brilliant Sol Weinman, who had founded Centurion, had hired them both. Also, he had never heard an anti-. Semitic remark by anybody at Centurion, which was more than he could say for some other places around L.A.

Now, as he sat in his Airstream, surrounded by the paperwork that validated his talents as an organizer, he was nonplussed by only one thing: Glenna Gleason. What the hell was a movie star doing working as an associate producer, even if her husband was the director?

Leo's experience of female movie stars was broad and deep; he had worked with Claudette Colbert, Norma Shearer, Rita Hayworth, Bette Davis and, God help him, Joan Crawford, and not one of them would have ever allowed herself to be anybody's associate anything, let alone producer.

A t eight o'clock on the first full day of work, Glenna knocked on the door of Leo's trailer.

"Yeah?" Leo shouted through the door.

"It's Glenna Gleason," she called back.

He opened the door and showed her in. "Hi, Glenna. Good to meet you. You ready to go to work?"

"I am," she said. She was wearing jeans and a work shirt and sturdy boots.

"Siddown," Leo said, pushing a chair toward her. "Here's what I'm gonna do," he said. "I'm putting you in charge of wardrobe and the secretarial pool, both of them important things on this picture. The secretaries may be more important than wardrobe, since that's pretty much settled."

"All right," Glenna replied.

Leo noticed that without a star's makeup and wardrobe she was suprisingly wholesome looking, in a shiksa sort of way. There was something a little odd about her face, as if she had been slugged a few times and had needed repairs, but, still, it was a good face. She was, what, twenty-five, twenty-six? Still had a career ahead of her, especially with her husband so well plugged into the studio. "Is there anything else that particularly interests you?"

"The animals," she said. "I wouldn't mind dealing with the wranglers and cowboys."

Leo grinned. Fine with him, since he didn't know shit about either horses or cowboys and was glad to have them off his back. "They're all yours," he said. "You go through the script and see when and where we're going to need the livestock and the guys."

"I've already done that," Glenna said, holding up a copy of the script.

"Good girl!" She wasn't stupid; that was the sort of thing he himself would have done in her position. "Anything else?"

"Can't think of anything right now, but as we move along I might see someplace else where I think I can help."

"Sing out," Leo said, "and let me know if you need my help on anything." He looked at his watch. "We're on the first setup, out by the corral. Go on out there and tell the wardrobe lady she's reporting to you, and the head wrangler, too." He'd see how she could handle that.

"Thanks, Leo," Glenna said, then left.

Leo had already planned how he was going to handle this: he was going to give her her head, and if she got into too much trouble, he'd *hand* her her head. He wouldn't have to complain to Rick; he'd see it happen sooner than Leo would.

Leo went back to his papers.

18

Sidney Brooks had been back at his house in Beverly Hills for less than an hour when the phone rang. "Hello?"

"Sid, it's Al James." Alan James, formerly Alvin Jankowski, was a rising movie actor; they had been friends back in New York, when they were both members of the Group Theater and looked down on anybody who went to Hollywood. James had been subpoenaed, too.

"Hi, Al."

"I've been trying to reach you. Where've you been?"

"I spent a few days up in Wyoming, where they're shooting my script."

"How is it up there?"

"Gorgeous. What's up, Al?"

"We need to talk. Can you have dinner?"

"Okay."

"Seven o'clock at Benny's?"

"Okay, see you there."

Al had been at the big meeting where Sid and the others discussed their trategy for the HUAC hearings, and he had been uncharacteristically quiet. Sid wondered why he wanted to talk now.

Benny's was sort of a bush-league Musso & Frank, a hangout of writers and actors, mostly at a time in their careers when they hadn't made it and were looking for the commiseration of their peers. Sid hadn't been there for a long time, and he doubted if Al had, either. He found the actor in a dimly lit booth in the back of the restaurant, looking glum, no more than a sip of whiskey left in his glass. "How goes it, boychick?" he said jocularly. He couldn't get a grin out of his old friend.

"What are you drinking?" James asked.

"Whatever you just had."

James held up two fingers, and a waiter brought them over, along with menus. "Are you ever sorry you came out here?" Al asked.

Sid took a deep breath and thought about that. "I was, at first, when they were fucking with my scripts. I've gotten to a point, though, when they're doing that less and less. The people at Centurion haven't asked me for a single, substantive change on *Bitter Creek*, just a little polishing. Now I think I'm happy to be out here."

"I'm not."

"What, you miss the snows of New York?"

"I miss the theater."

Sid laughed. "You miss eight shows a week, rain or shine?" Al had a reputation for being lazy.

"Sometimes, I actually do," James replied.

"Come on, Al, I remember when you hated going to rehearsals, and we practically had to root you out of Sardi's to get you to matinees on time. You were made for the movies."

The actor lifted his handsome head a little and smiled, revealing his beautiful Hollywood dental work. "You have a point. We wrapped on *Dark Promise* earlier this week. I saw a rough cut this morning, and it's going to be really, really good. The studio says I'll get nominated."

"Please accept my premature congratulations," Sid said.

"My agent, Max Wyler, says I'm up for something even better: a Faulkner script. There's a chance of back-to-back nominations."

"Faulkner and who else?" Sid asked, laughing. "I don't think Bill has ever written a whole draft that anybody could shoot."

"There'll be some good lines of his in it, though; I haven't seen the script yet. The rumor is Kazan is going to direct."

"Sounds like a nice package, so why are you so depressed?"

"Let's order," James said. They both opted for the steak, which was Benny's claim to fame. James didn't answer the question.

"How did Alice like Jackson Hole?"

"She loves it. In fact, she's going to stay up there and keep an eye on how they handle the dialogue for me while I go to Washington."

"Alice in Wyoming for a month? I don't believe it. There can't be any shopping up there."

"She doesn't want to be here," Sid said.

James nodded. "I'm glad I'm not married," he said.

"I thought you and that actress were headed that way."

"Not any more; she ran for the hills."

"The hearings?"

"Oh, it's not her; it's her agent. He's warned her off me, told her she could become tainted by the association, ruin her promising career."

"Oh."

"Have you noticed that some people don't want to be seen with you any more? Don't even want to talk to you?"

"No, I can't say that I have."

"People at the studio?"

"Eddie Harris and, especially, Rick Barron have been just great. They paid me up front for the script, so I've got a cushion now."

"I wish I could say that."

"Didn't you get the rest of your money when you wrapped your picture?"

"Yeah, but there's the mortage and the cars." Al lived very well but paycheck to paycheck.

"Well, I'm a little flush; if you need a loan I can come up with a few grand."

"Thanks, Sid, but I don't think you're going to want to loan me money."

Sid wanted to ask what he meant by that, but their steaks arrived, and they began eating. He remained silent. He would let Al spit out whatever it was in his own time.

"What are you writing next?" Al asked.

"I'm going to option an old novel that I think would make a great romantic comedy."

"What's it called?"

"I'll tell you when I've got the option in my pocket."

Al grinned. "Smart."

Finally, Sid couldn't take it any more. "Come on, Al, what's eating you?"

Al put down his knife and fork and signaled for another Scotch. "I met with the HUAC investigator this week, my lawyer and I."

Sid looked at him askance. "Al, is that a good idea? We all agreed not to talk to them until we're in Washington."

"He wasn't a bad guy, really. He's kind of in the same bind we are, getting a lot of pressure from the committee."

"Go on."

"He wants me to name names."

Sid stopped eating and swallowed hard. "Whose names?"

"He started with everybody I ever saw at a meeting."

"And you agreed to that?" Sid was becoming alarmed.

Al shook his head. "No, I held my ground."

Sid relaxed a little. "That's good. You shouldn't even have met with him."

"Sort of, I mean."

"Sort of?"

"After a lot of talking he finally said I didn't have to name anybody the committee doesn't already know about."

"Why would they want you to name names they already know? That doesn't make any sense."

"It makes sense to them. They don't think the way you and I think. They want witnesses to name names in the hearings."

"Al, you didn't agree to this, surely."

"Sid, my career is taking off. I have the prospect of two nominations in successive years, maybe even two Oscars. I'd be made for life. I could write my own ticket. Should I give up all that for a bunch of people, most of whom I never even liked? I haven't paid any dues or been to a party meeting in four years, not until I got subpoenaed. I thought they'd forgotten about me, that I was out."

"The party tends to have a long memory," Sid agreed.

"So do the studios," Al said. "If I make the wrong move here, I'm done in pictures; I'll never work again."

"There's always New York and the theater. You said you miss it." Sid said.

"Sid, you have a bigger reputation there than I do. What reputation I have is out here. And I can't live on the few hundred a week I'd get for a play."

"Al, what are you going to do?" There, he had asked the question, and he tensed for the answer.

"They've asked me to name six people, all of them known to the committee."

Sid didn't speak; he just stared at his friend, whose jaw was working, but nothing was coming out.

Finally Alan James spoke. "You're one of them," he said.

19

S id Brooks got Alan James into his car and drove him home. Al, he knew, would never have made it without crashing his car; he had probably consumed half a bottle of Scotch at Benny's.

Al mumbled unintelligibly during the ten-minute drive. At his place in the Hollywood Hills, Sid got him out of the car and over his shoulder in a fireman's carry he had learned in the Boy Scouts. The front door was unlocked, and Sid struggled up the stairs with the nearly unconscious actor and dumped him on his bed. He sat him up, stripped off his coat, loosened his tie and belt and let him fall back on the bed. He pulled off his shoes, spread a blanket over him and positioned a wastebasket where he could vomit into it. "Good-bye, Al," he said. "I don't think we'll be seeing each other any more." He walked out of the house, putting the door on the latch, and drove home to Beverly Hills.

Sid let himself into the house and turned on some lights. He walked around the place, inspecting it as if he had never seen it. They had bought the house two years before, but they had only just finished the renovations and decorations. He walked into his beautifully paneled study, poured himself a Scotch and sank into his comfortable leather chair, the one where he did most of his thinking. His typewriter sat, waiting, on his desk, a stack of foolscap next to it, a coffee mug of sharpened pencils nearby.

A place to work and everything he needed to do it—that had been his dream when he was younger. If this were New York, he and Alice would be crammed into a three-room apartment, bursting at the seams with their stuff. He had told himself that he was coming out here for the weather and the paycheck, but this house was what he had come for. This was the first time in their lives that he and Alice had been ahead of the game: money in the bank, the cars paid for, an investment in a small, six-unit apartment building in Santa Monica. They had made it. He dozed.

The doorbell woke him. Sunlight was streaming through the study windows, reflecting off the walnut paneling. He looked at the clock on his desk: just after ten o'clock. His Scotch glass was on the floor next to the chair in the middle of a wet spot. He struggled to his feet, slapped himself to wake up. The doorbell rang again, more insistently.

Sid opened the door to find two men in suits. They flashed badges. "Mr. Brooks?"

"Yes?"

"I'm Sergeant Flynn, LAPD. This is my partner, Detective Schmidt. May we come in?"

What was this? Sid thought. Some new kind of harassment? "Sure," he said, opening the door. He showed them into the living room and pointed at a sofa. "Have a seat."

The two men sat down, and the sergeant opened a notebook. Sid took a wingchair.

"Were you at a restaurant called Benny's in Hollywood last night?"

"Yes. I had dinner with a friend."

"What was your friend's name?"

"Alan James."

"Did the two of you leave together?"

"Yes, we did."

"Was Mr. James drunk?"

"I don't think that's too strong a word to use."

"What happened then?"

"Well, he was in no condition to drive, so I took him home, carried him bodily up the stairs, put him to bed, then came home."

"What time did you leave him?"

"Couldn't have been later than ten o'clock." Sid began to feel uneasy; this wasn't the kind of questioning he had expected. When would they get around to party membership?

"How would you describe Mr. James's condition when you left him?"

"I think he had fallen asleep or passed out by the time I left."

"Did you and Mr. James argue about anything last night, either at the restaurant or after you left?"

Sid shook his head. "Not really."

"What does that mean?"

"It means we had a discussion, but not what I'd call an argument, nothing heated."

"Were you close friends?"

"We've known each other for a good ten, eleven years starting in New York." Then he caught the past tense of the policeman's question. "Has something happened to Al James?"

"His housekeeper found him dead in his bathroom this morning. His throat had been cut with a straight razor."

Sid sucked in a breath and held it for a moment. "He was on the bed when I left; I spread a blanket over him."

"Did anyone see you leave Mr. James's house last night?"

"I've no idea. I didn't see anyone."

"What kind of car do you drive?"

Sid was almost grateful for these questions, to keep talking. "A 1941 Buick convertible."

"What color?"

"Kind of a medium green. It's in the garage."

"Was the top up or down last night?"

"Down; still is."

"Good; that squares with what a witness told us; a neighbor, walking her dog."

"I didn't see her."

"She saw you, and the coroner says Mr. James died around three A.M., so you're not a suspect."

"You think he was murdered?" This had not occurred to him.

"Looks like a suicide," the sergeant said. "Do you know if Mr. James had any family in the Los Angeles area?"

"No, he didn't. He had parents in New York. Their name is Jankowski. I think his father's name is Myron. He had a brother, too, but I don't remember his name."

"Would you have a phone number for Mr. and Mrs. Jankowski?"

"No, but they live on the Lower East Side; I expect they're in the phone book."

"Do you know them at all?"

"I was introduced to them once at the opening of a play I wrote that Al appeared in. That was the only time I ever saw them: two minutes, maybe. The brother was there, too, but as I said, I can't remember his name."

"And there's no one in L.A. we can contact?"

Sid shook his head. "Al was unmarried, and he told me last night that he and his girlfriend had broken up. His agent's name is Max Wyler. I think he's at the William Morris Agency. You should call him; he can contact Al's family. He'll know who Al's lawyer is. Was."

"Thank you, that's a good idea. Do you have any idea why Mr. James would take his own life? Did he say anything last night that would have made you think he might do that?"

Sid stared at the coffee table. "He seemed depressed." He looked up at the detective. "He had made a decision, and it's possible he may have regretted it."

The two detectives stood up, and Sid walked them to the door.

"How did you learn that we had dinner last night?" he asked.

"When you drove him home, Mr. James's car remained parked in front of the restaurant. Someone there called him at home this morning to ask him to move it, because it was blocking their deliveries. A police officer answered the phone at Mr. James's house."

Sid nodded. "Thank you for letting me know."

"Thank you for your help, Mr. Brooks. Good morning."

Sid watched them walk to their car, then he closed the door, leaned against it and began to cry.

20

Rick sat under a huge umbrella he shared with the camera and watched his actors slog through the scene. It had rained a lot since they had started shooting, but they were on schedule. It was going to be a wetter picture than he had planned, but the weather added character to their footage: the peaks of the Tetons obscured by cloud, an occasional flash of lightning behind the actors, their wet clothing, the mud.

"Cut. Print that," he said.

"Cut. Print it!" the assistant director shouted for the benefit of those who could not hear Rick, who tended to speak softly.

"We'll break for lunch. Next setup by two o'clock, please."

The AD repeated his instructions.

Rick went over to Susan Stafford, their leading lady. "Susie, I think you've got this character exactly right, and it's good to see that this early in our schedule."

Susie glowed. "Thank you, Rick. I've worked hard on her."

"Vance is a lucky actor."

"Listen," she said, "where did this guy come from? He seems to have been hatched as a working actor, and I've never heard of him, not in New York or L.A."

"He's English, and . . ."

"*English?*"

"Yes, and he toured in rep over there, then did a second lead in the West End and came to New York with the play, which ran for only a few weeks, then he came west."

"I'm flabbergasted," she said. "He's so real I thought you'd found him around here somewhere."

"I guess that's what talent is. We've got him for a three-picture deal."

"What are the other two?"

"Sid Brooks is working on adapting a novel for a romantic comedy, and I want to take a look at it. Beyond that, I don't know, yet."

"Whatever he does, I hope you'll consider me; I love working with him."

"Sure, I will."

Manny White, the location director approached. "Rick, I'm told we'll have phones before the day is out."

"That's a relief," Rick said, though they had gotten along perfectly well with only the telegraph connection.

"Alice Brooks got a telegram from Sid this morning," Manny said. "Alan James killed himself last night."

Rick was stunned. "He was what, thirty-five?"

"About that."

"Does anybody know why?"

"The telegram asked Alice to call Sid as soon as possible; maybe we'll know more after she speaks to him."

Rick got onto the bus with the others, and they were driven back to the ranch house. He went upstairs to change his clothes and boots, and found Glenna there, doing the same, while keeping up a running conversation with their little girls.

"We need to hire a laundress, maybe two, and buy some washing machines," she said. "Though I don't know where we're going to dry things in this weather."

"Indoors, I should think."

She laughed. "Well, yes."

"Talk to Manny about it. By the way, we just heard that Alan James killed himself last night. Sid telegraphed the news to Alice."

"Good God, why?"

Rick shrugged. "The phones are going in today; maybe we'll know more later. But James was one of those who were subpoenaed, and the hearings are soon. That could have had something to do with it."

"You should call Sid when you can and see how he is."

"I'll do that."

They went downstairs for lunch, and Rick shared the news with those at the table. Only Leo Goldman seemed not to react.

"Rick, did you know James?" Vance asked.

"A little. We were at a dinner party with him once. Nice guy, I thought."

"Does this have something to do with the hearings?" Vance asked.

"I wouldn't be surprised. I hope we'll know more later today, when we have telephones that work."

Ellie Cooper spoke up. "Now you see why we've never had a phone," she said. "We would have had to pay for the poles and the stringing of the wire for about five miles."

"I never missed it much," Mac said. "I've lived on ranches all my life and never in a house with a telephone."

"It's a great convenience, as long as you don't give anybody your number," Rick said and got a laugh.

When the day's shooting was over, Rick arrived back at the ranch house to hear a phone ringing in the living room. He picked it up. "Hello?"

"Rick? It's Eddie."

"Hi, Eddie."

"You've got a phone!"

"We have, for better or worse; you're our first call."

"Manny sent me a telegram. How's it going?"

"It's been raining like hell, but it's going to look good on the screen."

"If you say so."

"You heard about Alan James, I guess."

"Yeah, I did. It's got to be because of the hearings; he was going to testify."

"I should think so. Anything else back there I should know about?"

"I had a call from Mickey Cohen."

"Oh, yeah?"

"Yeah. I told him to go fuck himself."

"In those words?"

"I told him to go fuck himself politely. You sound tired."

"Yeah, I am. I think I'll have a nap before dinner."

"Go ahead, kiddo. I'm glad you're in touch now, and I'll try not to bug you too much. Oh, by the way, the first footage came back from the lab today, and it's gorgeous. Basil was a good choice."

"Thanks, Eddie." They had flown the first few days' shooting back to L.A. Rick intended to do that once a week. The editor was working at the studio, so by the time they got home he would have assembled a rough cut.

Rick started up the stairs, then he remembered. He went back to the phone, called the operator and placed a call to Sid Brooks's home.

"Hello."

"Hi, Sid, it's Rick."

"You've got a phone!"

"Yes, we do. I heard about your telegram to Alice, and I'm sorry. You were friends, weren't you, going back to New York?"

"That's right, though I hadn't seen as much of him since we both came out here. I had dinner with Al the night before, and he was morose, got very drunk. I took him home, and, apparently, he got up during the night and cut his throat."

"God, that's awful. Did this have something to do with the hearings?"

"Yes, it did. Can I tell you something in confidence?"

"Sure, Sid."

"Al had decided to be a friendly witness before the committee; he was going to name names but ones that the committee already knew about."

Rick wanted to ask if Sid was one of them, but he didn't. "That's terrible, and I have the feeling that Alan is only the first casualty."

"My phone's been ringing all day," Sid said. "We're getting together a memorial service at Temple Emanuel in Beverly Hills."

"May the studio send flowers?"

"Some of us have spread the word to make donations to our defense committee instead, but I don't expect Centurion to do that, Rick; it's just for individuals."

"Was Alan a member of Temple Emanuel?"

"Yes, though not a very observant one."

"We'll make a quiet donation to the synagogue in his memory, then."

"That's very thoughtful of you, Rick."

"Sid, are you all right? That's a serious question. I want to know."

"I'm shaken up some, but I'm all right. Don't worry, Rick; I'm not going to do anything stupid."

"If Alice wants to go home now, I'll get her on an airplane. We're sending the exposed stock back once a week; there's one going in the morning."

"Thanks. I'll let you know."

Rick gave him the new phone number. "Call me, if there's anything you need."

"Thank you, Rick."

They said good-bye and hung up. Rick trudged up the stairs, tired and a little depressed.

21

V ance Calder had just gotten out of a bath and was standing at the bathroom sink, naked, shaving. The bathroom door opened, and Vance turned to see Susan Stafford standing in the doorway.

"Hi, Susie," he said.

Her eyes were not on his. "Sorry, Vance. Didn't know you were in there." She started to close the door.

"Come on in and run yourself a bath," he said, then went back to shaving. She closed the door behind her and turned on the taps. He glanced in the mirror and saw her take off her robe. "You were great in that scene this afternoon," he said.

"Thanks, Vance. So were you. Rick told me you're English; I was astonished."

Vance grinned. "I've been staying in character since I got here, working on the accent. I've hung around some with the cowboys and wranglers on the place, had supper at their bunkhouse a couple of times. That helped."

"How old are you?" she asked.

He glanced in the mirror, but he couldn't see her. He thought she must be sitting on the edge of the tub. "None of your fucking business," he said, laughing. He splashed water on his face, pulled the plug and reached for a towel. Susie was tall and slender, with not very large breasts. He'd heard a rumor that she had a girlfriend back in L.A. and that she wasn't interested in men. He didn't believe it. When she spoke again, her voice was closer.

"What about the business of fucking?" she asked from somewhere around the nape of his neck.

He felt her press against his back, and her arms went around him, one hand on his belly. She reached down and let the hand brush across his crotch. He turned around, and she climbed him like a tree, until her knees were resting on the edge of the sink.

"Seeing as it's you," he said, "we're open for business."

She reached down and took him in her hand, then slid him inside her. "Yes, we are," she said.

Vance took hold of her slim buttocks and helped her move. She was making sweet little noises that he loved, and they remained in that position until she came, but he held back.

"Your tub is going to run over," he said.

"Then we'd better get into it," she replied.

The two of them nearly made the tub overflow.

"Archimedes would be proud," he said.

She laughed and snuggled into his shoulder, holding his balls in her hand. "I think I'm older than you," she said.

"How old are you?"

"None of your fucking business."

Vance had learned nearly everything he knew about sex from a leading lady with whom he had lived for three months on a tour of the English midlands with a play. He had seen her passport, so he had known that she was forty but never let her know he knew, since he had been sixteen at the time. "That's okay with me," he said. "I tend to think of people I like as being about my age, no matter how old they are."

"A good practice," she said. "Do you like me?"

"I admired you from the moment we rehearsed our first scene," he said. "Now, I like you, too."

"Can you tap-dance?" she asked.

"Is that a euphemism?"

She laughed. "I tend to call things what they are and not employ euphemisms. I mean, can you tap-dance?"

"As it happens, yes. I learned from an old music hall performer—that's the English version of vaudeville—during a tour of a play we did together."

"Do you sing?"

"I'm untrained, but I do."

"Some of the cast are talking about doing a show for everybody on our last night on location. Why don't you and I work up a number together?"

"I think we've already worked up a number together," he replied, cupping a breast in his hand and pinching her nipple.

"Well, yes, but I don't think we'd better do this for an audience. People might talk."

He laughed loudly. "Yeah, I guess they would, wouldn't they? What sort of number did you have in mind?"

"Well, being a Brit, you must know 'Burlington Bertie.' That's music hall, isn't it?"

"It is, and it's one of the numbers my friend taught me. I can choreograph it for us."

"Like Fred Astaire and Judy Garland?"

"Better."

"I expect wardrobe could come up with some costumes."

"I expect so," he agreed.

"Let's keep it a secret, though; we'll surprise everybody."

"Where will we rehearse?"

"Late at night, in my room," she said.

"Sounds perfect."

"No, this is perfect," she said, climbing on top of him and guiding him inside her again.

"I can't argue with that," Vance said.

This time they both climaxed.

That night before dinner, when they had kissed the girls good night, Rick told Glenna about his conversation with Susan Stafford about Vance. "It's nice that she likes him," he said.

"Yes, it is, and he likes her, too."

"He told you so?"

"He didn't have to; they were fucking in the bathroom an hour ago."

"You're kidding!"

"Nope. I caught a glimpse of her walking in on him while he was shaving, and he was stark naked. And then the door closed."

"Wow."

"They were in the tub together, too; I could hear the sloshing. They must have got a lot of water on the floor."

"I guess it's the old fuck-your-costar-on-location tradition."

"Could be. I'll bet they'll sit next to each other at dinner tonight."

"Well, it's nice that they have a diversion while we're here; makes for a happier shoot, I think."

"It does, if they continue to get along," Glenna said. "If they don't, then your job could get a lot tougher."

"Ow," Rick said. "I hadn't thought of that."

"Better watch for signs," Glenna said. "You don't want one or both of them stalking off the set if there's a tiff."

"Thanks for the tip," Rick said.

"You know, it's a while since you and I have had a bath together," Glenna said.

"Let's remedy that after dinner."

"It's a date."

V ance and Susie sat next to each other at dinner.

22

S id Brooks was packing for the trip to Washington when the phone rang. "Hello?"

"It's Alice."

"Finally."

"There's been a line for the use of the phones."

"How's the shoot going?"

"Fine. You'll be pleased with how your lines sound. How was Alan's memorial service?"

"It was about what you'd expect: the nineteen unfriendly witnesses were all there but not more than a couple of dozen other people, none of them well-known to the public. No actors, no writers, no producers or directors; no representatives of the studios."

"I'm not surprised. When are you off to Washington?"

"I'm being picked up in an hour."

"Are you still determined to be an unfriendly witness, Sid?"

"Yes, I am."

"Isn't that what caused Alan to kill himself?"

"No, I think it was his decision to be a *friendly* witness that made him do that. He was going to name me, among others. He said he had made a deal to name only people the committee already knew about."

"So the committee knows about you?"

"Apparently so."

"Sid, if you refuse to talk they're going to destroy you."

"No, they won't; they'll just convict us of contempt of Congress, then we'll appeal and the Supreme Court will overturn the convictions. Then it will be over."

"Over? Do you seriously believe that?"

"What else can the committee do to us?"

"Not the committee; the industry. Nobody's going to give you work, if you do this. You'll be branded forever as a Communist."

"A lot of people will still give me work; there are sympathetic employers in town, you know."

"You're deluding yourself, Sid. You'll be destroyed, and that will destroy us."

"How will that destroy us?"

"I'm not a Communist, Sid, and I don't want to be thought of as one. If you're shunned in the community, I'll be shunned, too, don't you see?"

"Alice, I have some more packing to do, so let's talk about this when I'm back from Washington. It shouldn't be more than a week."

"Good-bye, Sid, and good luck; you're going to need it from now on." She hung up.

Sid hung up, too, then the phone rang again. "Hello?"

"Sid, it's Hy Greenbaum." Hy was his agent and a powerful one.

"Good morning, Hy."

"You're off to Washington this morning?"

"In less than an hour."

"We have to talk, Sid."

"Okay, let's talk."

"I had a meeting early this morning with the chief investigator of HUAC."

"I'll bet that was a nice chat."

"Did you know that Alan James was going to testify as a friendly witness?"

"Yes, he told me at dinner the night before he killed himself."

"Did he mention that he was going to name half a dozen people?"

"Yes."

"Did he mention that you were one of them?"

"Yes."

"And you understand that means the committee already knows about you from some other source?"

"I understand that; all the people Alan was going to name are known to the committee to be party members."

"Sid, if you walk into that hearing you're going to be walking into a buzz saw."

"I don't think so, Hy; we've talked this through with our lawyers, and we think the Supreme Court will back us in this."

"And what about when you get back out here? Do you think the studios are going to back you?"

"I think they'll remain neutral."

"Sid, I talked to two studio heads this morning. They're leaving tomorrow for New York. There's going to be a meeting of all the studio heads at the Waldorf in a few days, and the consensus is, they're going to institute a blacklist."

"But Hy, Eric Johnston, the head of their group, the Motion Picture Association, has already said publicly there will never be a blacklist."

"Johnston doesn't have a vote. I'm telling you what's going to happen."

"I can't believe they'll do that to us; we make them too much money, and that's all they care about."

"Sid there are other interests working hard to convince them that employing you or any of the unfriendly witnesses will *cost* them money. If they believe that, how do you think they will act?"

"Hy, I'm already committed to this."

"Sid, there's a way out for you. You can come out of this untainted if you'll just listen to me."

"I'm listening, Hy."

"The investigator told me less than fifteen minutes ago that you can testify as a friendly witness in Alan's stead, that you can make a statement for the record that you are or were a Party member, and you can state your reasons for staying in or getting out, whatever they are. Then, in the questioning that follows, you'll name the five other people Alan was going to name. You'll be on the stand for less than half an hour, and you'll spout a few platitudes about what a great country this is and how you would never do anything to harm it. At the end, you'll be dismissed with the committee's thanks. That will be a kind of coded message to others involved in this, and you will not be blacklisted."

"Hy, if I do that, no one I know will ever speak to me again."

"Wrong. No *Communist* you know will ever speak to you again. How many people is that? And all of them will be disgraced; they won't be in any position to harm you."

"Hy, it all boils down to this: the committee has no right to demand of an American citizen that he explain his political views; they don't have a constitutional leg to stand on."

"Sid, the party has advocated the violent overthrow of the United States government. If you're a member, then you're tarred with that brush; that's the leg they have to stand on."

"Well, *I* don't advocate the violent overthrow of the government, and I'll be glad to tell them that."

"If you cooperate with them they'll believe you; if you don't, they'll just . . ."

"Hy, I'm not going to become a friendly witness; if I did, I might have to do what Al James did."

"You'll lose everything, Sid: your career, your home, your wife."

"My wife? Nonsense, I just talked to her."

"Did she offer her undying support?"

"Not exactly. In fact, she said pretty much what you're saying."

"Well, there you are."

"Hy, if I begin losing things, am I going to lose my agent?"

"I hope not, Sid. You and Dalton Trumbo are the highest paid writers in Hollywood, and I want to see you both survive this. I think of you as my friend, and I'll do everything I can to help you, regardless of what you say before the committee. Just don't tie my hands."

"Thank you, Hy. I appreciate that. When I get back from Washington, let's have lunch and talk about where to go from here, okay?"

"Okay, Sid. I guess all I can do is wish you luck."

"Thanks, Hy."

Sid hung up and went back to his packing.

23

S aturday nights during the location shoot, Manny White staged a square dance for the cast and crew. He hired a western band and a caller, and everybody caught on to the moves quickly. Rick was amazed at how everybody had somehow acquired western outfits—fancy shirts, fringed skirts and cowboy boots—and he and Glenna enjoyed the dancing as much as everybody else.

On Friday, he had sent Alice Brooks back to L.A. on the airplane with the film stock. All the participants in the hearings—friendly and unfriendly witnesses, the members of the Committee for the First Amendment, who had chartered an airplane, the lawyers and investigators—were in Washington now. Eddie Harris was there, too, on his way to New York for the studio heads' meeting at the Waldorf. Rick hadn't spoken to him since his first call after the phones had begun working, their only communication having been telegrams about the donation to Temple Emanuel in Alan James's memory.

On Sunday, their only day off, Rick and Glenna put the girls and their nurse, Rosie, in a Jeep and drove out to the riverbank with a picnic lunch. Rosie took the girls down to a sandy bank to wade, and Rick and Glenna had a moment alone.

"Did you speak to Alice before she left?" Rick asked.

"Yes, and she was very upset."

"She seemed very quiet and uncommunicative."

"That's how I knew she was upset. I tried to get her to open up, but she wouldn't. She's very angry with Sid, I think, about his choice not to cooperate with the committee."

"I think that's a mistake, too, at least as far as his career is concerned, but he feels it's some sort of moral imperative to oppose the committee, that he's acting to protect the constitutional rights of all Americans."

"Do you think Sid is really a Communist?"

"Glenna, I haven't told you this—in fact, I haven't told anybody, not even Eddie—but a few weeks ago I got an internal mail envelope at the studio that contained a photostat of Sid's party card."

"Who the hell would send you that?"

"I don't know. Just somebody at the studio; could be anybody."

"That's a shitty thing to do to Sid."

"Yes, it is. And I have to tell you, the next day I got another envelope that had another photostat of a party card, this one with your name on it."

Glenna's mouth dropped open. "With *my* name on it?"

"Louise Brecht, with a Milwaukee address."

"That's impossible; I never joined the party."

"I'm glad to hear that. Did you know any people who did?"

"There was a little group, half a dozen people I socialized with. I don't know if they were actual members, but they tossed around a lot of party-style rhetoric."

"Were you close to any of them?"

"I went out with one of the guys for a while; I guess you could call him my boyfriend. He's how I met the others."

"Did you ever go to a meeting or sign any petitions or anything?"

"No, but I went to a couple of cocktail parties with him, and he tried to get me to go to some sort of rally once, something about supporting aid to the Soviet Union. Why didn't you tell me about this before?"

"I didn't know what to think; I didn't know you when you lived in Milwaukee, and I don't know any of your friends from that time, except Barbara Kane, your old roommate." Barbara Kane had been Martha Werner, and she and Glenna had gone to high school together. Rick had gotten her a contract at Centurion, and she was doing well in supporting roles, mostly in comedies.

"Martha/Barbara ran with a different, wilder kind of crowd," Glenna said. "Lots of drinking and sex. The men she liked didn't go to political meetings; they hung out in pool halls."

"Did any of the people in your group come out to L.A.?"

"I don't know; after I broke up with Hal—Harold Schmidt—I didn't see any of them anymore. We had different interests. Why do you think somebody would fake a party card like that?"

"My first thought was blackmail, but I haven't heard anything more about it."

"Do you think the card with Sid's name on it was a fake, too?"

"I don't doubt that Sid was or maybe still is a party member, but I have no way of knowing whether the card I was sent was real or fake."

"Now that I think about it, I'm glad you didn't tell me about this before; in fact, I'm sorry you told me about it now."

"I think it's better that you know. If anything else comes up about this, then you might see a connection you might not have otherwise."

"This is going to get ugly, isn't it?"

"It already has, considering what happened with Alan James. The hearings start tomorrow morning."

"I have this really ominous feeling," Glenna said. "Is that why you offered me the associate producer's job? To give me something to do If I got caught up in a political scandal?"

"Of course not; there's no reason to think that will happen."

"There's got to be a reason for somebody sending you that card."

"If it comes up again, I'll deal with it, don't worry."

She put her hand on his cheek and kissed him. "I know you'll protect me, but I'm going to worry anyway."

When they were back at the ranch house, Rick walked over to Leo Goldman's trailer and found him, as usual, working.

"Hi, Rick. Come in," Leo said.

"You ought to take a day off now and then," Rick said, settling into a chair.

"I'm happier working," Leo said. "I don't ride horses or square dance."

"Well, I won't argue with you. There's something I want to ask you about, though."

"Shoot."

"A few weeks ago, right after I bought the *Bitter Creek* script, I got two pieces of internal studio mail, on successive days: each of them was an envelope containing a photostat of a Communist Party card, one in the name of someone I've dealt with who might very well be a party member; the other, in the name of someone I know for sure is not a member."

"Who were they?"

"I'd rather not say. Since I know one of them was a fake, the other may be, too. I just wondered if you had received anything like that in the interoffice mail."

Leo shook his head. "No. If I had I would have come to you about it. God knows, I don't want any Reds on the productions I work on."

"You're anti-Communist, then?"

"Damn right. Aren't you?"

"I don't really care much about the politics of the people I work with, Leo; all I expect from them is talent, ability and hard work."

"You don't care if they're trying to get propaganda into our scripts?"

"I think I'd spot it if they did, and I'd take it out."

"So would I. I went over the *Bitter Creek* script very carefully," Leo said.

"Did you find anything suspect?"

"Not a word."

"Well, then, we know that Sid Brooks is not trying to use our productions for propaganda."

"I guess not. Is Sid a Communist?"

"I don't know; I've never asked him, and he's never volunteered that information. You know that he's been subpoenaed by HUAC and that he's testifying this week in Washington."

"Sure, I read the papers and the trades."

"Leo, when Sid gets back, are you going to have any problem working with him?"

"I guess that depends on his testimony before the committee."

Rick nodded. "Thanks for being frank with me, Leo, and if you come across anything like the internal mail I received, please bring it to my attention."

"Sure, I will, Rick."

Rick walked back to the ranch house for dinner, wondering what he would do if two people who worked for him wouldn't work with each other because of their political views.

24

Sid Brooks had stewed in Washington for a week. He had attended some of the committee hearings, but he had stopped
going after hearing the testimony of screenwriter John Howard
Lawson, who, he thought, had made such an ass of himself by
upbraiding the committee that he had been an embarrassment to
the cause of the others. By the time Sid was called to testify, he was
convinced that, under the influence of two Party lawyers sent to
advise them, the unfriendly witnesses had taken the wrong tack. Sid
resolved to change that, if he could.

Finally, he was called before the committee and was sworn. The
committee's chairman, J. Parnell Thomas of New Jersey, began the
questioning.

THOMAS: Mr. Brooks, are you a screenwriter?

BROOKS: Yes, Mr. Chairman, but I hope I may read a short
statement before being questioned.

THOMAS: You may not. You may answer our questions.

BROOKS: It won't take more than five minutes, sir.

THOMAS: I asked you if you are a screenwriter.

BROOKS: Yes, sir.

THOMAS: How many motion pictures have you written?

BROOKS: Fourteen that have been produced, sir. May I say that I have never inserted in any of them any propaganda of any sort? I am only concerned with the drama or comedy in the work when I write, not politics.

THOMAS: Are you saying that you are not now nor have you ever been a member of the Communist Party?

BROOKS: Mr. Chairman, I believe it has already been pointed out to you at length that this committee has no right to question an American citizen about his political beliefs. The First Amendment . . .

THOMAS: That's it; this witness is dismissed.

BROOKS: Mr. Chairman . . .

THOMAS: I'll have the sergeant-at-arms remove the witness, if he doesn't go quietly.

Sid stood up, humiliated, folded his written statement and stuffed it into a pocket. A uniformed man appeared at his side and showed him the door. For this, he had flown across the country and spent ten days in a hotel?

In the hallway outside there was a barrage of questions from the gathered press. "Here's my statement," he yelled, shoving the typed pages into the hands of the nearest reporter. "That's what this committee wouldn't allow me to say." He elbowed his way through the crowd and somehow got out of the Capitol, into a taxi and back to his hotel.

When he walked into his room the phone was ringing, but he didn't answer it. When it stopped, he called the operator and told her not to put any calls through. He had a bottle of Scotch in his bag, and he poured himself a stiff one. Shortly, he was asleep on his bed. He didn't wake up until the following morning.

He ordered breakfast and read the *New York Times* and the *Washington Post*, both of which had fairly complete summaries of the hearings. He was about to start packing for his return flight when someone knocked on the door. "Who is it?" he shouted.

"Special delivery letter, Mr. Brooks," a young voice replied.

"Shove it under the door." He picked up the letter and looked at the return address. It was from Higgins & Reed, a Los Angeles law firm he had never heard of. He opened it and began reading and thus learned that his wife had filed for divorce; that she had removed his belongings from their home and sent them to an empty apartment in the Santa Monica building that they owned; that a key to the apartment was enclosed; that she would decline to speak to him directly in the future and that all their communications must be conducted through their respective attorneys.

Sid sat down on the bed, picked up the phone and placed a call to his Beverly Hills home. Five minutes later, the operator rang him back and told him that the number had been disconnected. Then he noticed a second page of the letter which said that the locks and telephone number of his home had been changed. In addition to the key to the Santa Monica apartment, a receipt from a dry cleaner's was enclosed, listing a suit and a sport jacket.

Sid finished packing in a daze and went downstairs, carrying his own luggage. He was waiting for a taxi when another writer who had been an unfriendly witness got out of a cab. "Sid, did you hear that after Bertolt Brecht testified, he went straight to the airport and left the country?" The playwright had been one of the unfriendly witnesses.

"No, I didn't."

"They're calling the rest of us the 'Hollywood Ten.'"

"Swell," Sid said and got into the vacated cab. "National Airport," he said.

The airplane took off on time, and because of strong headwinds, stopped short of its normal refueling point, Witchita, and landed instead in Little Rock. He spent the night there and, at the crack of the next dawn, continued his journey west. After refueling at Albuquerque, the airplane arrived in L.A. after dark.

At Los Angeles Airport he took a taxi to Beverly Hills and rang his doorbell. No answer. He walked around to the side of the darkened house and peered into the garage through the little window in the door. His car was not there. He got back into the taxi and gave the driver the address of the Santa Monica apartment building.

When he arrived he saw his Buick convertible parked in the little parking lot. He let himself into the vacant apartment and found a pile of suitcases and cardboard boxes neatly stacked in the living room. There was plenty of room for the stuff, since there was no furniture in the apartment, not even a bed.

Sid got into his car and drove to a diner, had some supper, then returned to the apartment. He slept on the floor that night, under his overcoat.

The following morning he rose early and had breakfast at the diner. He visited a furniture store and ordered a bed and a comfortable chair, then stopped at his bank in Beverly Hills to cash a check for a hundred dollars. The woman in the teller's cage went to a ledger and looked something up, then returned.

"I'm sorry, Mr. Brooks, but your account balance is seventy-six dollars and twenty cents. Would you like to cash a smaller check?"

Sid laughed. "There's a mistake here; I have in excess of a hundred and fifty thousand dollars in that account."

She handed him back his check. "Please go and speak with Mr. Merrill, at the first desk on the platform," she said, pointing to a middle-aged man.

Sid approached the man. "Mr. Merrill? I'm Sidney Brooks; we've met before."

"Of course, Mr. Brooks. Please have a seat."

Sid took the chair next to the desk. "I've been out of town for a couple of weeks, and when I tried to cash a check just now, the teller told me my balance was less than a hundred dollars."

"Well, that's substantially less than your usual balance, isn't it?"

"It certainly is. A month or so ago, I deposited a check for a hundred and fifty thousand dollars, and there was already around ten thousand in the account."

"I'm very sorry, Mr. Brooks," the man said. "Please wait a moment while I investigate." He got up and was buzzed through a door to the area behind the tellers' cages. Five minutes later, he returned. "Mr. Brooks, our records show that Mrs. Brooks recently transferred a hundred and sixty thousand dollars from your joint account to an account in her name at the Bank of America. I took the liberty of checking the balance of your savings account with us, and found that she has also transferred forty thousand dollars from that account, leaving a balance of less than ten dollars. Were you not aware of that?"

"I was not. Can you cancel the transfer?"

"I'm afraid not. You see, you and Mrs. Brooks are joint owners of your account here; she's not just an added signature. She was legally entitled to made that transaction."

"You mean she can just steal all that money from me?"

"Legally, it's not stealing. I'm afraid your only recourse would be a civil action to recover some portion of the funds."

Sid grappled with this for a moment. "Mr. Merrill, my wife has announced her intention to divorce me and has moved my things out of our house into an apartment building we both own. This . . . action of hers has left me without funds; may I borrow ten thousand dollars from the bank for thirty days?"

"I can certainly take a loan application, Mr. Brooks, but it would require collateral, and approval would have to go to the loan committee, which would take a week. Do you have any stocks and bonds?"

"I do, but those are in a joint account, too, if you see what I mean."

"Ah, yes. I suppose . . . Mr. Brooks, I can approve a loan of a thousand dollars immediately, if that will help while you are sorting out these affairs."

"Thank, you, Mr. Merrill, that would be very helpful."

Sid signed the note, opened a new account, deposited the loan proceeds and left the bank in a white-hot rage.

25

S id drove up to his house, hoping to speak to Alice, but there was no one there but the embarrassed maid, who said that Alice had gone to New York and she didn't know when she'd be back. Sid left and drove over to Wilshire Boulevard to Hyman Greenbaum's office building and went upstairs.

"Good morning, Mr. Brooks," the receptionist said. "Is Mr. Greenbaum expecting you?"

"No," Sid said, "but it's important that I see him right now."

She made the call. "Please go right in, Mr. Brooks."

Hy was on his feet to greet him as he walked into the big corner office. "Sid, I'm glad you're back," he said, shaking his client's hand warmly.

"Thanks, Hy, but I'm not sure I'm glad."

"Yeah. I know things went badly in Washington. I always thought you fellows had bad legal advice."

"That's not what I'm talking about," Sid said, handing him the letter from Alice's lawyers.

"Yeah," Sid said, reading the letter, "these guys are a top firm, but they only occasionally handle divorce; Alice must have a connection there."

"That's not all," Sid said. "I went to my bank this morning to cash a hundred-dollar check, and it bounced."

Hy's eyebrows went up. "Uh-oh."

"I had deposited your check from Centurion, and I had at least another twenty thousand in that account. I haven't even paid the taxes on the Centurion money."

"She cleaned you out?"

"Yes, she certainly did."

"Joint account?"

"All our accounts are joint."

"That means she probably cleaned out the brokerage account, too."

"Probably. I'm afraid to call them."

"I'm sorry, Sid."

"You warned me she might leave, and I ignored it. Is this legal, Hy?"

"I'm not a lawyer, but I don't think she can do all that. Trouble is, you'll have to go to court to get anything back."

"I'm going to need a lawyer, a specialist."

"Just a minute," Hy said. "Let me make a call." He dialed a number. "David? Hyman Greenbaum." He explained the situation briefly, then listened. "Good. I'll send him to you now. All right, half an hour." He hung up. "Sid, I'm going to send you to a young lawyer I know who will know how to help you."

"Young? Does he specialize in divorce?"

"He's young, but he's very smart, and he has all kinds of connections. He's not a divorce lawyer per se. He's more of a generalist, but when you meet him, I think you'll feel comfortable. Believe me, if he can't handle it, he'll know exactly who can."

"All right, Hy. I'll go see him. Where is he?"

"He's on the second floor of this building, and don't be put off by his offices."

"All right. Next thing is, I've got to make some money."

"I understand," Hy said, "but we're in a new kind of ball game, Sid. Nothing like this has ever happened before, and we're going to have to feel our way."

"Do we have the rights to the novel yet?"

Hy opened a drawer. "I've got the contract right here. Sign it, and we'll have the rights; they've already executed."

Sid signed the agreement. "Oh, God, I've got to give them five thousand dollars. I borrowed a thousand from the bank, but I've already spent, maybe, three hundred."

"Don't worry about it; I'll cut a check and send it with the executed contract by messenger. You can reimburse the agency when you get some things worked out."

"Thank you, Hy. I appreciate that. Did you get a chance to read the treatment of the novel?"

"I did, and I love it. Whoever reads it is going to love it, but we've got to face reality here, Sid."

"Tell me the reality."

"If we put your name on this, nobody's even going to read it, let alone buy it."

"How about Centurion? I think Rick Barron would buy it."

"It'll be Eddie Harris's decision, and he's a party, however unwilling, to the statement the studio heads issued in New York a couple of days ago. Let's use a pseudonym. I'll tell him I've signed a new writer."

"They would want a meeting to discuss the script."

"I'll say the writer lives in New York. No, not New York; Maine— Portland, Maine. Nobody is going to travel up there to talk with a writer. We'll do conferences by phone."

"So I have to give up my name?"

"This is temporary, Sid. I don't know how temporary, but it'll blow over eventually, believe me."

"Can you get my price for the treatment, Hy?"

"I don't think you should count on that; after all, we're talking about a new writer, not an established one, like you. I'll have the treatment retyped, so it won't look like your usual submission."

"Thank you."

Hy stood up. "I'll be in touch in a few days, Sid. Do you have a phone in the new place?"

"I forgot. I have to call the phone company. There's a phone there; it's just not hooked up to the exchange."

"Call me with the number when you have one. Now go see David Sturmack."

D avid Sturmack was tall and slender, with thick, dark hair and a prominent nose. He appeared to be in his early thirties. His office was a mess: the furniture was battered, and there were a lot of unfiled documents. He greeted Sid warmly. "Just kick that stuff off the sofa and have a seat," he said. "You want some coffee?"

"Thanks."

He pointed to a coffeemaker in the corner. "You pour while I read that letter from your wife's lawyers." He held out his hand.

Sid gave him the letter and poured the coffee.

"Black for me," Sturmack said.

Sid poured another cup and handed it to him.

"This is shitty," Sturmack said, holding up the letter. "And she cleaned out your bank and brokerage accounts, too?"

"Probably."

"How much?"

"Over a hundred and fifty thousand in the bank account—I had deposited a big check, hadn't even paid the taxes yet—and, maybe a quarter of a million in the brokerage account."

"You did well during the war, then."

"Yes, we did."

"Too old for the draft?"

"Yes. Where were you?"

"France and Germany. I commanded an airborne regiment."

"You made colonel?"

"Yes, at the very end; they wanted me to stay in."

Sid was impressed.

"I'm twenty-nine," Sturmack said, reading his mind. "Have you had any contact with your wife, other than this letter?"

"No. I went by the house straight from the airport to get my car, but the house was dark. I went there again an hour ago, and the maid said she had gone to New York and she didn't know when she'd be back."

"Uh-huh." Sturmack walked behind his desk, picked up the phone and, checking the letterhead for the number, dialed. "Pick up and listen," he said to Sid, pointing to the phone on the coffee table.

Sid picked up the instrument.

"Higgins and Reed," an operator said.

"Thomas Reed. David Sturmack calling."

"Mr. Reed's office. Can you hold, Mr. Sturmack?"

"For a brief time."

"David? Tom Reed. How are you?"

"I'm depressed, Tom. It always depresses me when I have to take an ethics complaint to the bar association, especially when it's a lawyer I like and admire. I thought better of you, Tom."

"Whoa, David. What are we talking about, here?"

"I'm representing Sidney Brooks, that's what we're talking about, and I've never seen a more outrageous list of actions against a client with no legal basis whatever."

"Now, David . . ."

"She orders him out of his home, then leaves for New York? She expects him to move out, even when she's not living there?"

"David, I'm sure we can . . ."

"And she confiscates his funds and investments with no notice, funds on which taxes have not yet been paid."

"Listen to me, David . . ."

"No, Tom, you listen to me. I'm going to file the ethics complaint even before I go to a judge for an order to restore the funds, which you know I'll get. Did you think you would be negotiating from a position of strength by doing this?"

"David, what do you want?"

"My client moves back into his home today; if Mrs. Barron wishes to visit L.A. she can stay at a hotel paid for with marital funds. She restores seventy-five percent of the funds taken from the bank account and all of the funds taken from the brokerage account, and we both stipulate that no investment transactions be made without mutual consent. Before close of business today."

"I think I can do that."

Sid held up a key and pointed to it. "She changed the locks," he mouthed.

"And I want keys to the house delivered to my office before lunch, and I eat early."

"All right, all right."

"When all that has been accomplished we can convene a settlement conference. Call me back and confirm." Sturmack hung up. "I think that'll do for now," he said to Sid.

"I certainly think so," Sid said, stunned. "All that from the threat of an ethics complaint?"

"Oh, there was a subtext to that conversation," Sturmack said. "Clients of mine are involved in something very big with clients of his; he didn't want to make me angry. When the keys come, I'll send them over to the house with my secretary. She'll put them under the doormat, so you should be able to move in by, say, three o'clock? Give me the address."

Sid wrote down the address.

"Phone number?"

"She changed it; I don't know what it is."

"I've got a friend who can deal with that. You'll have your old number back by suppertime."

"David, I can't thank you enough. We haven't discussed your fee."

"Nothing, so far; it was just a phone call. I'll bill you for my time while we negotiate the settlement; I won't need a retainer. I doubt if

the divorce will come to more than two, three grand; she can pay
Higgins and Reed herself."

S id left David Sturmack's office with the feeling that, for the first
time in a couple of weeks, his head was above water.

26

The days in Wyoming were growing shorter, and there was frost on the ground in the mornings now; they had to wait for the temperature to rise before filming, so that the actors' breath could not be seen. Rick accelerated the shooting schedule, and they wrapped the final exterior scene four days early.

That night there was what Rick thought of as a professional amateur show in the dining hall, where the cast of the picture provided the entertainment. The highlight of the evening was the finale, when the two costars, in hobo costumes, performed "Burlington Bertie from Bow," accompanied by three other actors on piano, bass and guitar. They brought the house down and had to do another chorus as an encore. Rick began thinking about putting them into a musical.

It was nearly midnight when Rick and Glenna returned to the ranch house, where there was a note to Rick from Eddie Harris to call him at home, no matter how late.

"Yes?" Eddie's voice said.

"Hi, it's Rick. You're back from Washington and New York?"

"Got home not much more than an hour ago. Have you heard the news?"

"I haven't heard any news for at least a week."

"The meeting with the other studio heads was appalling," Eddie said. "They've instituted what amounts to a blacklist, though they avoided using that word. Sam Goldwyn, Harry Cohn, Dore Schary and I fought it, but we lost. There was a public announcement this afternoon saying that no studio would employ anyone who is or was a party member or refused to answer that question before Congress. They're starting with the 'Hollywood Ten'—that's the ten guys who testified as unfriendly witnesses—and Sid Brooks is one of them."

Rick was flabbergasted. "You mean we can't hire Sid again?"

"We've got to talk about that when you get back. When will you wrap up there?"

"We wrapped this afternoon; I'll be back tomorrow afternoon."

"Call me from the airport, and we'll decide whether to meet at the office or at home. This is going to be a mess, Rick."

"I believe you."

"Sorry to be the bearer of bad news, but there it is."

"I'll see you tomorrow."

Rick hung up, called the pilot and told him he wanted to take off at eight A.M., then he told the other passengers as they returned from the party. Leo Goldman, Vance Calder and Susie Stafford would be joining him and his family.

Rick went upstairs. "I just talked to Leo." He told Glenna the substance of the conversation.

"I don't understand. Is it just these ten who are being made scapegoats?"

"I think it's going to go a lot farther than that," Rick said.

"Good God."

"Let's don't get too worried about this yet; I'm meeting with Eddie as soon as we get home tomorrow to talk about how this is going to affect Centurion."

They landed at Clover Field at midafternoon. Rick called Eddie, then Glenna dropped him at Centurion on her way home.

Eddie was waiting for him when he got to his office. "Come on," he said, leading the way. "The newsreel department has put together some footage for you, so you can catch up on what's been happening in your absence."

They sat down, and the film clips rolled: testimony by Jack Warner, Adolphe Menjou and Robert Taylor, among the friendly witnesses, then John Howard Lawson, Ring Lardner Jr. and others. Sid Brooks's testimony was the shortest. Finally, they saw film of Eric Johnston of the Motion Picture Producers' Association, reading the joint statement of the studio heads at the Waldorf.

They went back to Eddie's office, and he poured Rick a drink.

"That was awful," Rick said. "What are we going to do about it?"

"I'm not sure how this is going to unfold on a day-to-day basis," Eddie said, "but something has happened that will give you an idea of the sort of problems we're going to encounter."

"What's that?"

"This morning I got a call from our distributors, asking for a meeting."

"What did they want?"

"They had good news, at least for us."

"Go on."

"Alan James's picture, *Dark Promise*, was scheduled to open at the Radio City Music Hall at Christmas, but after the hearings, and given the circumstances of his death, it's been cancelled. It's a pity, because the word around town is that Alan is a sure thing for an Oscar nomination and the favorite to win."

"That's sad."

"The upside of this is they asked to see what footage we had of *Bitter Creek*, and I showed them your rough cut."

"But, Eddie, it's not . . ."

"I know, I know, but it's fairly complete, and they certainly saw how beautiful it's going to be and how good the performances are."

"And?"

"And they want to substitute it for *Dark Promise* at the Music Hall, for Christmas."

"Jesus, Eddie. That's not much more than a couple of months away, and we haven't even shot the interiors."

"I went through the script, and if you work through the week-end, you can have them in the can in ten days."

"And it's still got to be scored."

"We'll get the composer started tomorrow. It's amazing how well the rough cut works with no music; if we keep it spare, we can do it. It'll be right down to the wire, but it's the Music Hall for God's sake. It'll be wonderful for the careers of Vance and Susie, wonderful for the director and wonderful for the studio."

"I don't question that; I just hope we can do it."

"This is thrilling news, Rick. Don't let the cancellation of Alan's picture bother you; we had nothing to do with that. We were presented with a fait accompli."

"You're right, I guess; I should be thrilled."

"There's something else, though."

"Uh-oh."

"Yeah, it's like that. They want Sid Brooks's credit taken off the screen."

"What are you talking about, Eddie? We can't do that to Sid."

"We're not doing it to him, Rick. Other people are."

"I won't do it. Tell him they take the film with the credits intact, or they can't have it. We'll open next year, the way we planned."

"I've already shaken hands on the deal, Rick; I can't go back on my word."

"What about our word to Sid? He has a contract that specifies a single-card credit; he could sue us. *I* would, if I were in his place."

"I think I have a solution to that problem."

"What solution?"

"Get Sid in here and tell him what's happened; get him to agree to have his credit dropped. We'll insert a pseudonym."

"And why would he agree to do that? It's the best thing he's ever written; he's sure to get nominated."

"Even if he does, he'll never get the Oscar, not the way things are now. He'll see how great this will be for Vance and Susie and you; he won't want to stand in the way of that."

"I don't want to do that, Eddie. I can't do that to Sid."

"Rick, even if we open it next year, we can't have Sid's credit on the screen."

"Why not? I thought you disagreed with the studio heads on the blacklist."

"I did, and I do, and I'll do whatever I can to subvert it, but other forces are at work here."

"What forces?"

"The American Legion, for one, and other organizations are being formed as we speak. They're going to picket the theaters where any film is shown that has Communist actors, writers or directors and that stars any of the Hollywood Ten. We've got more money tied up in this picture than anything we've ever made, and we can't just flush it down the toilet."

"I hate this," Rick said, "and I won't do this to Sid."

"There's something else," Eddie said.

"What?"

"You can offer Sid another fifty thousand, if he'll agree."

"And you think he'd accept that? He'd spit in my eye."

"No, he won't."

Rick looked at Eddie. "What do you know that you're not telling me?"

"Alice Brooks walked out on Sid right after he testified. She's filed for divorce, and she's tied up everything: real estate, bank accounts, the works. Sid has moved into a little apartment building that he and Alice bought in Santa Monica, and for the moment, at least, he's flat broke. Fifty grand would save his life right now."

"He's not going to take his own life; he told me that himself."

"Was that before or after he testified and was cited for contempt? Before or after Alice left him? Before or after the blacklist? Sid is in a bad place right now, worse than the place Alan was in. He might do anything. He needs our help, and having his credit on this picture won't help him. Fifty thousand dollars will."

Rick slumped. "All right, I'll see him, but I won't take his credit off the film without his agreement. I'll resign, first."

Eddie went and put a hand on Rick's shoulder. "I've been over this a hundred times, Rick, and this is the best thing to do for all of us, including Sid. Please believe that."

"I hope you're right, Eddie."

"I'll dictate a one-page addendum to his contract and have a check cut," Eddie said. "See you tomorrow, kiddo."

Rick took his drink back to his office and sat in the darkening room, wondering how he could ever say to Sid what he had to say.

27

When Vance Calder arrived at Centurion after the trip from Wyoming, a letter was awaiting him at the front gate.

Vance,

We're delighted with your work on Bitter Creek, and it seems appropriate that you have better accommodation on the lot. Accordingly, we've moved your things to the bungalow at 1 A Street; I think you'll be more comfortable there. Also, your agent already has a bonus check from us for ten thousand dollars, and your price for the next two pictures will be fifty thousand dollars each. Your contract has been amended accordingly.

We'll be working very quickly on the interiors, so plan on working straight through the weekend. I'll tell you why when I see you and the rest of the cast at nine o'clock tomorrow morning at the ranch house set on Stage One. Again, you have the thanks of everyone here for a very fine job.

Warm regards,
Rick

Vance, a grin on his face, drove to A Street and made a right. There on the corner was number 1, the bungalow that had been

Clete Barrow's dressing room. He guessed that this meant he was now the number one star on the lot. Then he remembered Susie.

He drove quickly to his old half-bungalow and found her waiting on the front porch. "Get in your car and follow me," he called out, then he led her back to his new digs, and they got out of their respective cars.

"This is the old Clete Barrow bungalow," she said. "What are we doing here?"

"The landlord has upgraded me," Vance replied, holding up the key. "Come on, let's get your stuff."

"Wait a minute. You mean *your* stuff, don't you?"

He put his arms around her. "Listen, why should you go on sharing that tiny apartment in Hollywood, when I have all this room? Anyway, I've grown accustomed to sleeping with you in my arms. You don't want to make an insomniac of me, do you?"

"Let's take a look inside," she said.

Vance opened the door and switched on some lights. The place had been newly painted, and the furniture looked new, too. There was a big living room, with a kitchenette and bar in a corner, a bedroom, lots of closet space and a makeup room with a barber's chair and a lighted mirror.

"Wow," Susie said.

"How about it, Hon?"

She smiled and kissed him. "You're on."

He went to their respective cars and hauled in their things, then he picked up the phone and called the studio commissary and ordered dinner for two. "We'll be dining in an hour," Vance said to Susie. He opened the fully stocked bar. "In the meantime, let me fix you a drink."

"I'll have a Scotch and water," she said.

He handed her the drink and made himself one, on the rocks. "To a mutual new era of stardom," he said.

They drank.

"When did they tell you about this?" she said.

"There was a letter waiting for me at the front gate."

"Wait a minute," she said, going to her purse, "there was one for me, too." She opened the letter and giggled. "They've given me a bungalow, too—your old one—and I got a bonus!"

"I don't want you to feel that you have to occupy it," Vance said.

"Well, I'll occupy it some of the time. After all, we don't want to become an item in the columns."

"I think we're going to have to get used to that sort of thing," Vance said.

She giggled. "Let's hope so."

Dinner arrived in a van, and a waiter set Vance's dining table, opened their wine, poured some and left them alone. Vance held her, chair, then sat down.

"You know," Vance said, "we've been so busy working and . . ."

"Fucking," she said, finishing his sentence.

"Well, yes, fucking, and it's been wonderful. I want it to go on and on. But my point was we don't know much about each other."

"You want my studio bio?" she asked.

"I'd like the unexpurgated version."

"All right. I was born in a little town in Georgia called Delano that neither you nor anybody else has ever heard of. Its claim to fame is that it's five miles from Warm Springs, where Mr. Roosevelt had his Little White House and died."

"Did you know him?"

"Of course not. Did you know Winston Churchill?"

"I met him once, when he came to a performance of a play I was in in the West End and visited backstage."

"Well, I saw Mr. Roosevelt drink a chocolate milk shake, once, while sitting in his car outside the City Drug Company. He used to drive himself around the county and stop for refreshments."

"So we're both politically well connected. What were you like as a little girl?"

"I was bright, pretty, got good grades and studied dancing from the time I was three, because my mother had a dance studio. I got all the best parts in the school plays, and then I went to college at the University of Georgia and got all the best parts there, too.

"After college I went to New York and got into the Neighborhood Playhouse, which got me a couple of supporting roles on Broadway; then a talent scout spotted me, offered me a screen test and I came out here nine months ago. I had a small part in a picture at RKO; then I got *Bitter Creek*. The rest will be history."

"It certainly will."

"Now you."

"I was born in London, but since my father was an Anglican vicar, we moved around the southeast of England several times, mostly in Kent. My mother would take me to the theater in London sometimes, and I was enthralled. When I was fourteen, I made up a fake résumé and ran away from my boarding school, joining a repertory company that was passing through town doing *She Stoops to Conquer*.

"I painted scenery, ran errands, ran the lights, pulled the curtain then finally started getting juvenile roles. I looked older than I was, so I was playing early twenties. I was also taken into the bed of the leading lady, who was instructional."

"So that's how you got so good in the sack!" she said, delighted. "I thought maybe you had worked as a gigolo!"

"I never gave up my amateur status," Vance said. "Anyway, I went to London to audition for the Royal Academy of Dramatic Arts, failed to get in, but instead someone who saw my audition offered me a supporting role in a new play. We had a good run in London, then the Schuberts brought it to New York, where we had only a middling run. The rest of the cast went back to London, and I stayed on in New York, where I—not to put too fine a point on it—starved.

"Finally, in the dead of last winter, I hitchhiked to L.A., got a job with a construction crew and found a room in a boarding house in Santa Monica. One of the jobs I worked on, fortunately, was the beach house that Rick and Glenna are building in Malibu. Glenna came over to talk to me, introduced me to Rick and the next day I had a screen test that got me *Bitter Creek*. I believe you are acquainted with the rest of my résumé to date."

"Two such all-American stories," Susie said.

"One all-American, one all-English," he corrected.

She poured herself some wine. "There's something else you'd better know about me; you may already have heard it, but I'd prefer you had the real story from me."

"All right."

"When I was in New York, after college, I roomed with a beautiful girl who, well, preferred other beautiful girls to men. I also saw men, on the sly, but she and I were a couple, sort of, and I liked the sex. Then, just before I came out here, she surprised me by telling me that she was getting married. To a man, by the way."

"Were you upset?"

"Not really. I knew I was, basically, heterosexual, though I doubt that she was. It came at a good time, since I was coming out here, anyway."

"I'm glad you told me, but . . ."

"There's more," Susie said. "When I got the part at RKO, I was staying at the Studio Club—a kind of dormitory for aspiring actresses—and a script girl on the picture offered to share her apartment with me. I moved in, and we had pretty much the same sort of relationship that I had had in New York, except I was not as comfortable with it. I resolved to move out when I got back from our location shoot, and I had planned to do so tomorrow."

"Anything else?" Vance asked.

"Nope, that's it. I wanted you to know." She laughed. "I don't ever want anyone else to know, though, so promise me you'll keep it to yourself."

"Of course I will."

"Any questions?"

"Will you move in with me? Just you, no girls. Unless we share them, of course."

She laughed. "You betcha I will, starting right now. I do want to keep the pretense of having my own place, though, which will be easy, now that Rick has given me the little half cottage."

"That's fine with me. I don't want to live on the lot forever. I'd like to buy a house as soon as I can afford one."

"Let's cross that bridge when we burn it behind us," she said. "Now can we go into the bedroom and fuck each other's brains out?"

"Oh, yes."

And they did.

28

Rick called Hyman Greenbaum when he couldn't reach Sid Brooks by phone, then Sid called him back, and they made a dinner date at a little place on Santa Monica Boulevard.

Rick went into Eddie Harris's office. "I have a dinner date with Sid Brooks," he said.

"I'll get that check cut," Eddie replied, picking up the phone.

"Can you raise that much cash?" Rick asked. "If Sid's in the middle of a divorce, I think he'd rather not deposit it into a bank account."

"Not to mention avoiding taxes," Eddie said.

"I'll spread it among the production costs of *Bitter Creek*."

"Okay, but don't make a habit of this. My girl will bring it to you." He held out an envelope. "Here's what Sid needs to sign. Don't forget to ask him what pseudonym he wants to use."

Rick arrived at the restaurant on time, and Sid was already sitting at the bar. They shook hands and were led to a booth.

"How are you doing?" Rick asked.

"Better," Sid replied. "I had a few bad days, especially when I learned that Alice was leaving and that she had taken everything I had with her. Hy sent me to a lawyer named David Sturmack; one phone call from him to her lawyer and my part of the money is back in the bank, and I'm living in my own house again. The phone number will be the same."

"I'm glad to hear it, Sid. Who is this Sturmack? I've never heard of him."

"Somebody Hy recommended; they're in the same building. He's only twenty-nine years old, and he came out of the war a colonel, and Hy says he's very well connected, whatever that means."

They ordered drinks and got menus. When their order was in, Rick got down to business. "Have you and Hy talked about what working is going to be like after the hearings?"

"Yes, at some length. What it boils down to is that I'm going to have to work under pseudonyms, and I won't get my usual price."

"I don't want to know the pseudonyms, Sid, but I want to see whatever you want to write. We'll have to keep it at arm's length, just in case I get subpoenaed, or if questions arise from other studios."

"I understand, Rick. I certainly don't want to cause you and Eddie any embarrassment in the industry."

"Eddie and I would just as soon tell all of them to go to hell, but there's another consideration: the American Legion and some new groups plan to boycott and picket any films that have blacklisted writers, directors or actors associated with them."

"All the more reason for pseudonyms," Sid replied.

"This means we're going to have to put a pseudonym on your credit card for *Bitter Creek*, too."

Sid looked taken aback but nodded. "I guess that was inevitable."

"Sid, you have a contract with us that guarantees your single-card credit on this picture, so you can sue us if you want to and probably win. It's what I'd do in your position."

"It's what I would have done a couple of weeks ago, but it wouldn't be in my interest to do that. I'm just going to have to lump it until things change."

"I hope they change quickly, Sid. I really do."

"Look, I'm the architect of my own fate, here; I'm not looking to blame anybody else."

Rick nodded. Their food came and they ate quietly, making only desultory conversation. When the plates had been taken away and coffee served, Rick spoke up again. "I have a couple of pieces of good news, though."

"I'll take all the good news I can get," Sid said.

"First, the bad news: Alan James's picture, *Dark Promise*, was scheduled to open at Christmas at Radio City Music Hall, but because of the circumstances surrounding his death and, of course, because of the hearings, it was cancelled. Yesterday the distributors came to see Eddie, saw the incomplete rough cut of *Bitter Creek*, and offered us the slot at the Music Hall."

"That's wonderful!" Sid said. "I'm delighted."

"It makes removing your credit all the more painful."

"Don't worry about that; it'll be great for everybody who worked on it. Anyway, a lot of people around town know I wrote it; I'll get a few pats on the back even if I don't get a nomination."

"Oh, Eddie wants you to sign this." He gave Sid the envelope and watched as he read it and readily signed it.

Rick put a thick manila envelope on the table and shoved it across. "Here's the other good news: we're paying you another fifty thousand for your script. The envelope is full of cash, hundreds and fifties. We cleaned out the vault at the studio."

Sid opened the envelope, peered inside and grinned. "I've never seen this much money before."

"Neither have I. Of course, you don't have to mention this to Alice or the IRS. If you want to pay Hy his commission, that's up to you."

"Of course I'll pay Hy, but Alice can whistle for it; this is *not* marital income." He patted the envelope as if it were a puppy. "Thank you, Rick, and thank Eddie for me, too. This will go a long way toward keeping me on my feet after the divorce."

"Do you know what that's going to cost you?"

"I had a second meeting with Doug Sturmack this afternoon, and he tells me, since Alice and I were married for twelve years and all during the time I made any money, I'd better get used to the idea of giving her half of everything. In the end we'll have to sell the house and the apartment building in Santa Monica and split the proceeds."

"Can't you just buy her out of the house?"

"The idea is that we'd have the real estate appraised and each of us could buy the other out, but the fact is neither of us would have the cash. I couldn't get a mortgage under the present circumstances, since I'm technically unemployed, and she couldn't either, as a divorced woman with no job. Sturmack has already gotten their agreement to put both properties on the market."

"I'm sorry; I know you love that house."

"The house is a thing; it wasn't very big, but it had everything we needed. When things change I can buy another one. I don't mind letting it go just to get out of the marriage."

Rick thought of something. "Do you have any idea what it's worth?"

"I don't know, maybe eighty or ninety grand. A house a couple of doors down went for a hundred grand, but it's bigger than ours."

"Do me a favor. Get it appraised, but don't put it on the market for a few days. I know a potential buyer, and it would save you paying a broker's commission."

"All right, Rick."

"Is there a mortgage on the house?"

"No. Both properties are free and clear."

"Right. There's something else I'd like to ask you about, Sid."

"Shoot."

Rick told him about receiving the two party cards in the interoffice mail, but he didn't mention Glenna's name. "Do you have any idea who at Centurion might have sent those cards?"

Sid shook his head. "No, I can't imagine who would do that."

"Sid, who would have access to membership records of the party in New York?"

"The chapter officers, I imagine."

"Would they have kept your card, or was it issued to you?"

"Actually, they showed it to me, then kept it. They apparently didn't want members showing their cards around."

"So any officer of the branch could take the card, have it photostated, then replace it in the files?"

"Any officer or, I suppose, any clerical employee. I would imagine, though, that the cards would be kept under lock and key, and lately I doubt if they would have been kept on the premises of the party offices, since they are liable to be served with a search warrant."

"One other thing: could a party member sign somebody else up for membership and pay his dues?"

"I've never heard of that being done, but somebody with the right access might be able to do that."

"Without the person's knowledge?"

"Yes, I'd think so."

"That's what I need to know, I guess. Thank you."

"Let me know if there's anything else I can do, Rick."

The two men parted in front of the restaurant, Sid with the manila envelope under his arm.

29

Rick gathered the cast of *Bitter Creek* in his office, gave them coffee and addressed them. "Something's come up," he said. "Something good."

They all looked expectant.

"*Bitter Creek* has been chosen to open at Christmas at Radio City Music Hall."

There were smiles and applause all around.

"But that leaves us with only a very short time to complete the interiors, cut it and insert the opticals and titles and score it. We had scheduled three weeks to shoot the interiors, but in light of this good news, we're going to have to shoot them in ten days, and that means working right through the weekend. I'm going to need the help of every one of you to get that done, and I know you'll do your best. The sets are complete and are being assembled and dressed, and we're ready to shoot the ranch house interiors, starting today, so let's get over there, get costumed and made up, and we'll start before lunch."

Everybody got up and shuffled out of Rick's office, chattering excitedly.

Eddie Harris came in. "How'd it go with Sid last night?"

"He was happy to cooperate, Eddie." He handed him the executed addendum to Sid's contract. "And happy to have the cash, too."

"What pseudonym does he want to use?"

"Jesus, I forgot to ask him. I'll call him later today."

"Good."

"Eddie, I know you're interested in keeping Vance Calder at the studio over the long term."

"I certainly am."

"Something came up last night: Sid and Alice are going to sell their house and split the proceeds. Vance, you know, is living in his bungalow, but he's interested in buying a place. I think he might like Sid's house, but he doesn't have that kind of cash yet."

"How much are we talking about?"

"Sid's having it appraised, but he thinks it's worth eighty or ninety thousand."

"And we just gave Vance a ten-grand bonus, so he's holding some cash. If he wants the place, tell him we'll loan him ninety percent of the purchase price for, what, two years?"

"Give him three; we want him to owe us for a while, don't we?"

"Sure. Three is good. We don't need to do anything more for Susie right now, do we? I mean, we gave her the bonus and the new dressing room."

"My guess is Susie's star is tied to Vance's right now. If she wants a new place to live, it will probably be with him."

"Yeah, you're right. You're starting the interiors this morning, aren't you?"

"Yeah. I'm going over there in a few minutes; the cast is getting ready now. They're pumped up about the Music Hall announcement."

"Great. I'll look forward to the rushes." Eddie took his leave.

Rick buzzed his secretary. "Please get hold of Tom Terry and ask him to come see me. Now, if it's convenient." Tom Terry had worked on the Beverly Hills police force with Rick, and when Rick was promoted to producer, he hired Tom to replace him as head of studio security.

T om Terry came in and sat down. "Hi, Rick. I heard about the
Music Hall thing; congratulations."

"Thanks, Tommy. Listen, there's something I want you to do
for me."

"Sure, anything."

"Write this down. I want you to find out everything you can
about a Harold Schmidt of Milwaukee, a.k.a. Hal."

"Lot of Schmidts in Milwaukee, Rick."

"Fewer Harolds, though. This one is probably a member of the
CP and seems likely to be involved in left-wing activities in the city
or state. That's all I know about him."

"Okay, I'll get on it. Best thing is to make some calls and get a
name on the Milwaukee force."

"Go to Milwaukee, if you have to."

"You want me to talk to Schmidt about anything?"

"Locate and research him first, then call me. I'll decide then
whether I want you to see him, or if I do it myself."

"I'll get right on it," Tom said, then left.

R ick asked his secretary to forward any calls from Sid Brooks to
Stage One, then he got into his little electric cart with his shooting script and drove over there.

Basil was finishing up lighting the ranch house set, and various
members of the cast were standing around. He was headed for his
canvas chair, next to the camera, when the script girl came to him.

"There's a call for you, Rick," she said. "Your secretary's on the
line."

Rick walked over to where a phone stand stood against a wall
and picked up the instrument. "Rick Barron."

"Sidney Brooks is on the line," his secretary said. "I'll put him
through."

"Sid?"

"Yeah, Rick. I'm sorry to disturb you on the set."

"Not at all. What's up?"

"David Sturmack got an appraiser over to the house first thing this morning, and he says the house will sell for ninety grand. He'll work up a detailed report later, but that's going to be the number. If your friend wants to see it, have him call me."

"Thanks, Sid. I'll get back to you. Oh, by the way, what do you want to use for a pseudonym for your credit on *Bitter Creek?*"

"How about Mark Twain?"

"That would be rubbing their noses in it. Something more anonymous."

"Oh, you pick something, Rick. Whatever you like."

"Okay, Sid. Talk to you later." Rick hung up, walked farther along the soundstage to Vance Calder's stage dressing room and rapped on the door.

"Coming!" Vance called back.

Rick opened the door. "Not quite yet, Vance; it'll be a few minutes. Got a moment?"

"Sure, Rick. Come on in."

Rick took a chair. "Vance, you said something to me once about wanting to buy a house someday, didn't you?"

"Yes, I did. Maybe in a year or two, when I get some money saved up."

"You may have heard that Sid and Alice Brooks are getting a divorce."

"Yes, I did."

"They want to sell their house. It's a very nice place on a good street in Beverly Hills, lots of privacy. Not too big but very comfortable. They renovated it and did it up very nicely."

"Well, it sounds great, but I'm not in a position to buy something like that yet."

"Tell you what, Vance. Give Sid a call at this number"—he wrote it down—"go take a look at it, and if you like it, the studio will loan you ninety percent of the purchase price for three years. That'll give you time to pay off the loan, or you could get a mortgage, if you want to."

"That's a very nice offer, Rick. What does Sid want for the place?"

"It was appraised this morning for ninety thousand dollars, and, for what it's worth, I think that's a fair price."

"All right. I'll call Sid and take a look at it. Is it furnished?"

"Yes, but I don't know what they want to do about that. Alice seems to have moved back to New York, so they might want to sell some or all of it. My guess is, you could be in the place in a week, if you and Sid agree."

"But where would Sid go?"

"He owns an apartment house in Santa Monica, and he can move in there."

"Okay. I'll call him later today."

Somebody came and knocked on the door. "Five minutes, Mr. Calder."

"Be right there," Vance said. "By the way, Rick, you said you would sell me the Ford convertible. How much?"

"Don't buy it; it's yours for as long as you like. When you get tired of it, give it back to Hiram."

"Thank you, Rick."

Rick left him and headed for his chair. "Call 'places,'" he said to the assistant director.

"Places everyone!" the man yelled. "Places!"

Rick reminded himself to ask Eddie who David Sturmack was; he kept hearing that name.

30

Rick got two scenes and five setups done that day, finishing at seven that evening. He called Glenna to let her know he was on his way home, then walked to his electric cart. As he reached it, Tom Terry pulled up in his own cart.

"Hang on, Rick," he called.

Rick sat in his cart and waited for Tom to turn his around. "You got something on Schmidt?" he asked.

"Turned out to be easy," Tom replied. "I got connected to a source in the Milwaukee department, and as soon as I mentioned Schmidt's name, the guy knew who I was talking about."

"Is he a criminal?"

"Labor organizer. He put together a strike at a brewery in Milwaukee, and after a few weeks the whole thing blew up; big fight: scabs and hired cops against the strikers. Schmidt was convicted of inciting a riot, got two years in the Wisconsin State pen. He got out three days ago."

"Can you find him?"

"I believe so. I could get a plane to Milwaukee in the morning."

"Do that, please, Tom. This is on me, not the studio."

"It's personal?"

"Yes."

"What do you want me to talk to him about?"

"Back before the war—this would have been '38, or so—Schmidt went out for a while with a girl named Louise Brecht. A few weeks ago, somebody at the studio sent me an interoffice envelope with a photostat of a CP card with that name on it. She acknowledges knowing Schmidt but denies ever joining the party or even attending a meeting, though she says she did go to a couple of cocktail parties with Schmidt during the time she was seeing him. A knowledgeable source has told me it would have been possible for Schmidt to enroll her in the party without her knowledge. I want to know if he did and, if so, exactly how and if it exists, I want the record of that card expunged. It's possible the local party never issued the card to her but hung on to it in their files."

"You want me to get Schmidt to get the card and expunge the record?"

"I'm going to leave that to your judgment, Tom. You can offer him a thousand dollars to do that, but you're going to have to decide if you can trust him."

"And if I don't think I can?"

"Then I want somebody to go in there, wherever it is, and take care of it. You can do it, and I'll give you the thousand, or you can hire somebody, and I'll pay for it. I want it clean and quiet, Tom, and I don't want you to get caught with your hand in the cookie jar. Got it?"

"Got it. One other thing: do I need to know who Louise Brecht is?"

"She's Glenna, and you're to keep that entirely to yourself."

"Of course."

"Come back to the office with me. There's some cash in my safe."

"I'm right behind you."

It was nearly nine before Vance was able to leave Susie and meet Sid Brooks at his house. He drove up the street, past the address, checking the neighborhood. It was beautiful. He turned around and pulled into the driveway, and Sid met him at the door.

"Hi, Vance," Sid said, offering his hand. "Come in."

"Hello, Sid. First of all I want to say how sorry I am for your problems, and I don't want, in any way, to take advantage of your difficulties."

"Actually, Vance, if you buy the house you'll be easing my difficulties considerably by hastening the day when I'll have this behind me. I'm not offering the house at a knockdown price, and I'll actually get more money by not having to pay a broker. Come on, let me show you around."

Vance followed along while Sid showed him the handsome living room, then the study with the walnut paneling and custom-made cabinets and bookcases. He led him upstairs and showed him two bedrooms, then the master, which included two baths and two dressing rooms. Then he took him down the back stairs to the dining room and kitchen, which was fitted with new, postwar appliances, including an electric Hotpoint dishwasher.

"There's a laundry room at the back and a three-car garage. The previous owners, who built the place, had three. There's a three-room flat over the garage if you want a live-in couple. We've never used that; we have a housekeeper who comes daily, and I recommend her to you."

"How many square feet?" Vance asked.

"About forty-two hundred, and the lot is an acre. The houses on either side have bigger lots and big gardens so this lot seems bigger."

"What about the furnishings?"

"Alice wants some of the pictures but no furniture; I need a few pieces to furnish the apartment I'm moving into. You can have everything else for another five thousand."

"I'd like to buy it," Vance said. "The furniture, too. When do you want to close?"

"The sooner the better. Will it be all cash?"

"Yes."

"Good. That will make things go faster. I'll tell my lawyer to get a title search done and to draw up the sales documents. I should think we could close in a week or ten days."

Vance took out his new checkbook and wrote one for ten thousand dollars. "This and a handshake will secure the deal, as far as I'm concerned." He handed the check to Sid, who put it into his pocket.

The two men shook hands.

When Rick got home there was a messenger-delivered envelope from Hyman Greenbaum waiting for him on the front hall table. He opened it and found a hardback copy of a slender novel, *Greenwich Village Girl*, and a neatly typed treatment by someone he'd never heard of, Wesley Hicks. He put it back in the envelope to read later.

After putting the girls to bed and having dinner, he and Glenna lay in bed, propped up on many pillows, Glenna reading the novel, Rick reading the treatment and making notes in the margin. Rick finished first. "What do you think?" he asked.

"I'm not finished."

"Yeah, but what do you think so far?"

"I think I'm too old for the girl."

"Any other thoughts?"

"Vance and Susie, of course. They're perfect for it, and it's perfect for them."

"That's what I think, too," he said. "I'll call Hy in the morning."

31

Tom Terry got out of Jack Barron's Beech Staggerwing at Milwaukee's General Mitchell Field and grabbed his suitcase and briefcase. He and the pilot got a cab into the city and went to a medium-sized hotel recommended by the driver, one that specialized in traveling salesmen. They registered under false names, and Tom paid for both rooms in advance. Tom had a room-service dinner and got a good night's sleep.

The following morning Tom took a taxi to the address given him by his Milwaukee P.D. contact and told the cab to wait. The house was a duplex in a working-class neighborhood. No one answered the bell, and the mailbox was full; Tom went through everything, finally striking gold: among the letters was a bill, in a plain brown envelope, for dues from the Milwaukee Communist Political Association. Tom wrote down the address in his notebook, stuffed the mail back in the box and rang the doorbell on the other side of the duplex. A small woman in a house dress and apron came to the door.

"Good morning," Tom said, "I'm Jim Fellows from the Central States Insurance Company. I just want to deliver a check to Mr. Harold Schmidt. Does he still live next door?"

"I don't think so, sir," the woman replied. "He got arrested for his union work and did some time for it. He got out a couple of days ago and came back here to get his stuff and moved out."

"I noticed he has a lot of mail piling up in his box. Do you have any idea of his forwarding address?"

"He told my daughter he was moving to sunny California," she said.

"Did he say where?"

"Hollywood."

Tom knew that a lot of people outside California thought of all of Los Angeles as Hollywood. "What's he going to do out there, I wonder?"

"Well, I don't know, but all he knows about is unions and trouble, far as I can tell."

"Thank you, ma'am," Tom said, tipping his hat. He went back to the cab and gave the driver the address of the Communist Political Association. The building was in a light industrial part of the city, and the CPA was a doorway next to a printing shop.

Tom opened the door and went up a long staircase to the second floor, where he found another, fogged-glass door with the name lettered on it. He opened it and stepped into a small reception room, manned by a thin, primly dressed young woman at a desk.

"May I help you?" she asked, looking at him suspiciously.

"Yes, miss," Tom said. "I'm Jim Mitchell, and I'm new in Milwaukee, looking for work. I went to some meetings back in Buffalo, New York, and I was kind of interested in the party. I wonder if you could give me a pamphlet about it, or something."

She brightened. "Why yes," she said. "Please wait for a minute; we just had a new supply delivered from the printers this morning, and they're in Mr. Warchovski's office." She got up from her desk and went into the next room.

Tom could hear her tearing open a box. He brought his attention to bear on four two-drawer filing cabinets behind her desk, neatly labeled. One of them said "Membership." All of them had built-in locks.

The woman came back and handed Tom two envelopes. "There you have a pamphlet explaining our principles and also a membership application."

"Thank you, Miss . . ."

"Wilson," she said.

"And Mr. Warchovski is . . ."

"He's the local representative of the national party."

"I wonder if I could speak with him for a moment?"

"I'm sorry. He's out of the city all day, today. May I make an appointment for you tomorrow?"

"Could I call you later in the day? I'm not sure of tomorrow's schedule just yet."

"Of course. I'm here all day, except between twelve and one."

"Thank you so much, Miss Wilson."

"Would you like a copy of yesterday's *Daily Worker*?" she asked, handing him the newspaper. "I'm afraid we get it a day late."

"Why, thank you very much," he said. Downstairs, he checked his watch: 11:40 A.M. He walked to the corner, leaned against the building and opened the *Daily Worker*. At one minute past noon, Miss Wilson emerged from the building, crossed the street and walked half a block to a café. The moment she was inside, Tom went back to her office.

The fogged-glass door was locked, but Tom produced a zippered manicure kit from a pocket that contained, in addition to the normal tools, a set of lock picks made for him by a burglar of his acquaintance. It took him half a minute to open the door, and he went straight to the membership filing cabinet, prepared to pick that lock, too. Fortunately, Miss Wilson had not bothered to lock the filing cabinets before she left for lunch.

For a long moment, Tom couldn't remember Glenna Gleason's original name, but finally it came to him: Louise Brecht. He went through the Bs three times, worrying until he found a manila folder with her name on it jammed down behind a lot of other B names. The folder contained an application and, stapled to it, a membership card.

He was about to leave when he had another thought. He opened the M drawer and found a neatly typed mailing list. Louise Brecht's name was there with the notation. "Hold all mail."

Hers was the last name on the page, so Tom found a pair of scissors in Miss Wilson's desk drawer and snipped Louise's name off the paper.

He went into Mr. Warchovski's office and went through his desk, looking for other related documents, and found another copy of the mailing list. He snipped Louise's name off that, too, and replaced it, stuffing both strips of paper into a pocket.

Tom tucked the manila folder into his belt in the small of his back and left, taking the time to lock the door behind him. A quick check of the nearly empty street, and he was out of there.

He had to walk a dozen blocks before he found a cab, and on the ride back to the hotel he read the slim contents of the file. The application was filled out in block capitals and signed "Louise Brecht," but the signature was simple script without the flourishes or scrawling that usually came with a person's signature; it looked written rather than signed.

Back at the hotel he found the pilot in the coffee shop, had a sandwich himself, then they checked out and headed for the airport. It was after midnight before, after a fuel stop in Denver, they landed at Clover Field.

T he following morning Rick was in his office when Tom Terry was announced. He came into the office and handed Rick a manila folder. "This is all they had on her," he said, "and it looks to me as if Schmidt filled out the application and signed her name. It doesn't look like a signature, you know?"

"No," Rick said, "it doesn't."

"I also cut her name off two copies of a mailing list of members I found. There was a notation next to her name, saying to hold all mail. I couldn't find any other evidence of Louise Brecht in the office."

"Did you speak to Schmidt?"

"I missed him by a couple of days; a neighbor said he left Milwaukee for sunny California. It might be interesting to know if he turns up in L.A."

"It might at that. Please look into it."

"Might take a few days; give him time to get a phone number."

"No rush. Thank you, Tom. Did you have any additional expenses?"

"No, you've already covered it. The pilot and I stayed at a commercial hotel and registered under other names. Nobody will ever know we were in Milwaukee."

"That was good work, Tom. Thank you again."

The two men shook hands and Tom left.

Rick read the application carefully, then locked the file in his safe.

32

Rick yelled, "Cut! Print it! Wrap!" and everybody on the set cheered and applauded. *Bitter Creek*'s interiors were complete, and within twenty-four hours the entire picture would be in the can, ready for final editing, opticals and scoring.

Eddie Harris yelled for quiet and made a graceful little speech, thanking everyone for their extra efforts, then food and drink from the studio commissary were wheeled onto the soundstage, and the wrap party began. It was nearly midnight.

After everyone had had some food and a couple of drinks, Eddie pulled Rick, Vance and Susie aside. "Some more good news," he said. "We're going to have simultaneous openings, one at Radio City and the other at the Chinese Theater, here. Vance, you're going to New York, and Susie, you're going to headline the L.A. opening." He saw Vance and Susie exchange a regretful glance. "Don't worry, kids, the next day the studio will fly Susie to New York, and you'll do a ton of publicity together there." The two appeared to relax at that news.

"That's great, Eddie," Rick said. "We'll get lots of radio time and a double shot at the newsreels, too."

"Now," Eddie said to Vance and Susie, "don't you two kids disappear anywhere, because you're going to be doing wall-to-wall press interviews, some together, some alone, between now and the opening. We open on Saturday, the thirteenth, twelve days before Christmas, and all these interviews are going to release the following day in newspapers and magazines all over the country. This will be the biggest publicity push in the history of Centurion Studios. That means we have to get everything right. The publicity department is going to brief you both on the points to make in the interviews and on how to handle things like your relationship with each other, your living arrangements, etc. You have to do this the way publicity tells you, so that there's no slipup. One important point: Sidney Brooks is not to be mentioned; you never heard of him. This film was written by a man called Harlan Rawlings, who lives in Wyoming. You met him once; he was a quiet fellow, a typical westerner. Got that?"

Both the actors nodded.

"Okay, go have some fun." Eddie pushed them toward the party.

"They'll do well," Rick said. "They're charming people, and the press will love them."

"I had a call from Hyman Greenbaum yesterday; he wants to renegotiate Vance's contract."

"Of course, he does," Rick said. "Are you going to do it?"

"Yes. If this picture does anything like the business I think it will, Vance would be resentful if we held him to the terms of his original contract, even with the bonuses we gave him and the loan for the house. What I want is for us to lock Vance into Centurion for his whole career, and that means binding him to us emotionally as well as financially. If we're anything but generous with him, that would damage the relationship. There isn't a smarter agent in town than Hy, and he's going to want a deal structured so that Vance participates from dollar one."

"Jesus, Eddie."

"Don't worry; everything will depend on grosses, so if any picture tanks, we'll be protected. What's new in all of this is that Hy wants stock options for Vance."

Rick laughed. "Somewhere our beloved founder, Sol Weinman, is spinning in his grave."

Eddie laughed. "You're not kidding, pal, but Sol never ran into anything like this. When Gable came along around, what, 1930, they paid him a weekly salary, and although he's making, what, five grand a week now, it's still a weekly salary. But not Cary Grant; he went independent, and he's going to make a lot more money in his career than Gable will in his. That's what Hy is going for, and it's exactly what I would be doing if I were Vance's agent. We're going to have to be a lot nicer to Susie, too, since we only have her for this picture. I love the *Greenwich Village Girl* treatment you sent me, and we certainly want her for that. We'll do a three-picture deal, something like Vance's original contract. If she turns out to have drawing power on her own, we can always work it out later."

"Eddie, I could never fault you on the big picture," Rick said. "By the time we're ready to ship prints of *Bitter Creek*, we'll have a first draft of *Greenwich Village Girl*."

"You want to direct it?"

"Maybe. I'll let you know."

"Listen, kiddo, if you're thinking that you want to be a full-time director, I can live with that."

"God knows, I love doing it."

"Well, if you're leaning that way, what would you think of grooming Leo Goldman for head of production?"

"Grooming Leo? He's been grooming himself for that job since he was in the mail room at Metro."

Eddie laughed. "He reminds me of me."

"He reminds me of you, too. If I go that way, Eddie, I still want to keep a hand in management, and I will *not* work for Leo. We'd have to arrange things so that he's still reporting to me."

"I can do that," Eddie said.

"Another thing: I know that you and I are of the same mind about the blacklist, but Leo definitely is not. He's in bed with Cecil

DeMille and Duke Wayne and that crowd, and I don't want him making decisions for us in that regard."

"You've talked with Leo about this?"

"Yes, while we were in Wyoming."

"I'll keep that in mind," Eddie said. "Leave it to me, kiddo."

"I always do," Rick replied.

L ate in the day, Rick got a call from Glenna.

"You about done at the office?" she asked.

"Just about. I'll be through here in half an hour."

"Then meet me at the beach property."

"How's it coming?"

"Meet me there," she said, then hung up.

A n hour later Rick arrived at the property and pulled into the driveway, which, to his astonishment, had been paved with cobblestones. Even more astonishing, a house stood where once there had been only pilings. The place had been shingled in cedar, which was a bright tan that would weather into gray.

Glenna came out the front door. "What do you think?"

"I think it looks fabulous."

"There's still a lot of finishing work to be done, but come look around. The workmen are gone for the day, so we won't bother them."

She led him from room to unfinished room, and it was better than he had pictured it in his mind.

"We'll be in in a month," she said.

"It can't happen fast enough for me," he replied, kissing her.

They sat on boxes on the rear deck and watched the red ball of the sun sink into the Pacific.

33

The day after finishing the interiors for *Bitter Creek*, Vance Calder closed on his new house. All he did was take a check for eighty-five thousand dollars to David Sturmack's office, sign some documents and watch while Sid Brooks signed them as well. Alice Brooks had already sent a power of attorney from New York, so her attorney signed for her. He rode the elevator downstairs with Sid, and they chatted in the parking lot for a moment.

"The house is ready to move into," Sid said, "and the housekeeper has spent the last three days cleaning it thoroughly and washing the windows. She can tell you anything you need to know about how the place works. You've got her number. And here's the Japanese gardener's number, too; you'll need him, since the property is heavily planted."

"Thanks, Sid," Vance said. "When will you take the things that you and Alice want?"

"Already done," Sid replied. "Now all I have to do is sell the apartment house in Santa Monica, and I'm done with Alice. I've already signed a lease for my apartment there."

"We finished shooting *Bitter Creek* yesterday, and I want to thank you again for that experience."

"Rick showed me the rough cut, and I think it looks great," Sid said. "It's certainly my best work so far. Rick sent me a publicity bio of Harlan Rawlings, which is the pseudonym they're using for my screen credit. Seems Harlan is a first-time screenwriter who lives alone on his ranch in a remote part of Wyoming and doesn't give press interviews."

Vance laughed. "Oh, I've met Harlan."

"It's funny, especially when the writer is a nice Jewish boy from the Lower East Side who's never been on a horse."

Vance held out his hand. "I hope things work out so that I can work in a lot of other Sid Brooks scripts. Good luck to you, Sid."

"Thanks, Vance, I hope for that, too. Oh, here are your keys." He held out a clump of half a dozen, all tagged.

The two men parted and went their separate ways.

Vance found a pay phone and called Susie Stafford at her cottage at the studio. "Got a pencil?"

"Yep."

"Write down this address." He dictated it. "The place is a couple of blocks above Sunset Boulevard. I'll meet you there in half an hour."

"Okay, but why?"

But Vance had already hung up. He had told her nothing about the house.

Vance arrived first and unlocked the front door with his new key. He walked into the house and found everything in pristine order. He noticed a couple of blank spaces on the walls where pictures had hung, and some furniture was missing from the living room, but the place looked just great. He went and sat on the little front porch to wait for Susie.

Susie parked her car beside Vance's in the circular drive, ran up the front steps and gave him a kiss. "So what's the big mystery, and whose house is this?"

"It's mine," Vance said. "Come on in, and I'll show it to you." He led her into the living room.

"You bought this place?" she asked, her eyes wide.

"We closed half an hour ago."

"But you haven't been looking at houses; we've been too busy shooting."

"I bought it from Sid Brooks. He and Alice are divorcing and decided to sell."

"But you said you'd never go into debt for anything, not even a house."

"I won't be in debt for long," Vance said. "My agent and Rick are already working on a new deal for me after we finish two more pictures."

"Wow. It's beautiful, Vance."

"Come on. Let me show you the master suite." He led her upstairs and showed her the sunny bedroom and the two dressing rooms and baths. "Think you can fit your stuff in here?" he asked, waving an arm at the shelves and closets.

"Are you kidding? I'd have to shop for a month to half fill it."

"You'd better get started, then."

She turned and looked at him. "What does all this mean, Vance? You're not asking me to . . . I mean, it's way too soon to . . ."

"I'm not suggesting anything permanent; we have a lot to learn about each other. I just thought we'd learn it faster if we moved in together full time." He kissed her.

"We can't let anybody know about this. If the columnists ever got hold of it they'd be telling the world we're living in sin, and my parents would read about it in the Atlanta paper."

"The studio publicity department will handle all that. You think we'll be the only couple in pictures living together?"

"Come on," she said. "Show me the rest."

He showed her the two guest rooms. "Plenty of room for your parents to visit."

"Are you kidding? They'd take one look and return me to Delano under armed guard!"

"Okay, okay. I get the picture."

They looked at the study, the dining room and the kitchen.

"I can cook here!" she enthused.

"You cook? I thought you were only good at acting and sex."

She punched him in the stomach. "Come on, let's see the backyard."

They went out the kitchen door, rounded a hedge and were confronted with a pool and a tennis court.

"Holy cow!" Vance said. "I didn't see this before!"

"Who's going to keep the place looking like this?"

"Oh, it comes with a housekeeper and a Japanese gardener."

"I'm going to have to take tennis lessons," Susie said.

"So am I. I've been working since I was fourteen, so I've never had time to learn."

"By the way, buster," she said, "I got a look at your passport the other day."

"Uh-oh."

"I got the shock of my life. Do you know I'm five years older than you?"

"Well, if it's any consolation, it's only four years, because today is my birthday."

"I know it is," she said, reaching into her handbag and coming out with a small, beautifully wrapped gift. "I saw your passport, remember?"

Vance took her back into the house, they sat on a living room sofa and he unwrapped it. "A Cartier watch!" he said, surprised. "It's beautiful."

"It's called the 'tank' watch, because it was designed for the tank corps in the first war or something like that. Now, will you please throw away that ratty thing you've been wearing since I met you?"

Vance unbuckled his five-dollar watch, tossed it into a nearby wastebasket and put on the new one. "Gorgeous."

"Now the watch is as nice as that one suit of yours," Susie said. "By the way, it's time you went shopping for clothes; you can't rely on the Centurion wardrobe department to dress you for every occasion forever. I'll go with you, if you like."

"That one I can handle on my own," Vance said.

"Well, if the one suit is any example, I guess you can."

Vance scooped her off the sofa, carried her upstairs and tossed her on the bed. "Let's christen the place," he said, peeling off her sweater.

"You betcha," she replied, working on his buttons.

34

As *Bitter Creek* was being completed, Vance's and Susie's days were largely taken up with meeting newspaper editors from all over the country who were flown to L.A. for individual meetings and big press conferences. They were all housed at the Beverly Hills Hotel, and Vance and Susie had suites reserved where they did the interviewing. Once, they had nearly been caught in bed together by an editor who arrived early for his interview.

Vance had moved his things into the house, including new clothes he had bought or had had made, but Susie had not yet moved in. They had been sleeping at the Beverly Hills, anyway, for convenience's sake. Vance was a little troubled that Susie had not yet moved into the house, and he asked her about it.

"Oh, I've been too busy, just like you. Anyway, we're living at the hotel for the moment. I thought I'd wait until you leave for New York, then I can move in and take my time doing it, without you looking over my shoulder."

"Have you taken your things out of the flat you were sharing with . . . the script girl from RKO?"

"Hank. Henrietta Harmon. No, not yet. She's not going to like my moving out, and I don't want a scene if I can help it. I plan to go by there one day when she's working and get all my stuff. I'll do it while you're in New York."

"New York should be fun," Vance said. "We'll have adjoining suites at the Plaza, and we'll be on the expense account the whole time."

"And I can get my Christmas shopping done, too. I can send my parents' presents home directly from there. I'm giving them a big television set; they don't have one, and Daddy loves college football and baseball."

"It occurs to me that we don't have one for the Beverly Hills house," Vance said. "I'm not sure there's anything worth watching. What do you think?"

"I think it would be nice to have one for the times when something special comes on. And there's more and more programming all the time."

"All right. I'll order one. Where do you want it placed?"

"How about the bedroom?"

He smiled. "As long as it doesn't replace other bedroom functions."

"Don't you worry your head about that," she said, laughing.

Sid Brooks found his posthearings life radically changed from what he had been accustomed to. He wasn't being invited to dinner parties and cocktail gatherings by his non-Communist friends, although he had kept his old phone number, and he didn't really feel like seeing the old leftie crowd, not that he heard much from them, unless they needed money. He had stopped going to Chasens and other places popular with movie people, doing most of his dining in Santa Monica, not far from his apartment. He was working twice as hard, making a third of the money he was accustomed to, and with the divorce now final, he was having to pay Alice five thousand dollars a month in alimony for ten years. After taxes and his agent's commission were paid he found himself subsisting on about twenty percent of his former disposable income, and yet he worked constantly, cranking out treatments and screenplays and polishing or adding dialogue to the work of others, in addition to his own output—anything that would bring in a few hundred dollars.

Hy Greenbaum called him and invited him to meet at the Brown Derby, where Hy habitually lunched. Sid arrived at the restaurant and was greeted warmly by the headwaiter but hardly anyone else. Heads turned away and eyes shifted as he made his way to Hy's table and sat down. "How are you, Hy?"

"I'm okay, but I know you're not so good, Sid, and I'm worried about you."

"I'm getting by," Sid replied.

"I'm sorry I can't get you more money for scripts and treatments, but that's just the way it is at the moment."

"It's not your fault, Hy; you've been great all the way. I'm hearing that some other agents are not being so great to their clients. I heard a story about Paul Kohner running into Duke Wayne at a bullfight in Tijuana, and Wayne wouldn't shake his hand. Allegedly, he said, 'I don't shake with people who represent Commies.'"

"That's a true story," Hy said. "Paul himself told me about it. Times like these don't bring out the best in people."

"Well, I hope things will get better after we get our Supreme Court hearing; then, at least, we won't have to worry about the contempt of Congress citation. I certainly don't want to go to jail."

They ordered lunch, and when it came, Hy leaned in closer and spoke quietly. "Sid, I've been talking to some people, and there may be a way to make all—well, most of this—go away."

"Well, I'd certainly like to hear about that," Sid said.

"There's a kind of process you can go through that would . . . what's the word?"

"*Rehabilitation?*"

"Right."

"What would I have to do?"

"You'd meet with an investigator from HUAC and agree on your testimony; then you'd go back before the committee, be contrite and give your testimony. Then the committee would thank you—that's the code word—and you'd be able to work again under your own name."

"You mean I'd have to crawl."

"I guess there's no other word for it."

"And my testimony would entail naming names?"

"You wouldn't have to name anybody the committee doesn't already know about."

"I could name the five names Al James was going to name?"

"Well, no, since they were all among the Hollywood Ten. You'd have to name others from your past, people you saw at Party meetings and other events, but they would all be known Communists. It's not like you'd be ratting anybody out."

"I'd be ratting just the same, Hy, and nobody would ever speak to me again."

"Who's speaking to you now, Sid? You getting a lot of support from your Party acquaintances?"

That stung. "Well, not so's you'd notice it."

"I'll tell you who would speak to you, if you do this: the studios would speak to you; the directors and producers would speak to you. These are the people who've always given you the opportunity to earn a good living. What have the fucking Communists ever given you?"

"Not a lot," he admitted.

"So you're going through this hell to protect a bunch of people who can't even benefit from your loyalty, because they've already been exposed for what they are. And these are people who've never done anything for you, except give you bad advice on how to defend yourself."

"The Supreme Court is going to fix this," Sid said.

"Do you read the papers? Have you noticed that Truman has recently made two new appointments to the court and that those two gentlemen are a lot more conservative than their predecessors and a lot less likely to rule in your favor?"

"That remains to be seen."

"You're taking a big risk, Sid. What happens if you win in court? Well, you might feel vindicated, but that's not going to change what the producers' association has said about not employing Communists; it's not going to change what the American Legion and Red Channels and a dozen other outfits are doing to enforce the blacklist. Can't you see how difficult your situation is?"

"Hy, that's a very clear delineation of my position, I know, but . . ."

"One other thing: if you spend a year or two in prison they're not going to let you write screenplays there. All the while you're inside, repairing roads or making license plates, the payments to Alice will still have to be made, and nothing will be coming in. It's going to eat up your part of the divorce settlement, and by the time you get out, you'll be in a deep hole."

"Do you think I haven't thought about that, Hy?" In fact, he had not thought that far ahead; he had been dreaming of a favorable Supreme Court decision, which was now in doubt.

"Promise me you'll think about this some more, Sid."

Sid sighed. "All right, Hy. I promise to think about it." He would, in fact, think of little else.

35

V ance flew to New York with Rick, Glenna and the Radio City print of *Bitter Creek* a week before the opening. By the time the airplane was off the ground, he was missing Susie. They broke the flight in Chicago, landing at Meigs Field on the lake, and he attended a screening for the midwestern critics and answered questions from the group at a late supper. The following morning they continued their flight to New York and landed at LaGuardia.

The suite at the Plaza was high on the north-facing side of the hotel, with spectacular views of Central Park. Rick and Glenna took him to "21" for dinner and introduced him to the management there. Beginning the following morning, daily showings of the film for the press took place at a rented screening room, followed by the group question-and-answer session. He had at least two interviews daily with selected press: those with columns, like Ed Sullivan and Walter Winchell, or feature writers with the New York papers. Since he was, invariably, asked the same questions each time, his answers became more and more polished, funnier and, thus, more quotable.

B ack in L.A., Susie was undergoing the same procedure with the West Coast press, and she found it tiring. She kept meaning to go to Hank Harmon's apartment and pack her things, but there were more and more demands on her time. She and Vance talked daily, usually in the early evening.

"How are you, Sweetheart?" Vance asked on Friday evening.

"Exhausted, to tell you the truth; I never knew what hard work it is, being a movie star. In fact, I'm going to postpone my flight until Monday, just to have a day to rest. Do you mind?"

"Of course, I mind," Vance replied, "but I understand. I don't want you to have to spend your first days here in bed, except with me, of course."

"I'll rest up on Sunday and be ready for the long flight on Monday, but let's don't go out on Monday evening. Let me get one more night's rest."

"Have you moved into the house yet?"

"I haven't had a moment. I'll do it Sunday afternoon, when there won't be anybody clawing at me for an interview."

"I'm beginning to think you're having second thoughts about moving in."

"Of course, I'm not. In fact, I can't wait until we're back from New York and away from all this craziness and can have some uninterrupted time together at home."

"Did Rick send you the treatment and pages for *Greenwich Village Girl?*"

"Oh, yes, and I just love it! What about you?"

"I think it's very funny, and it will be fun to make."

"I don't suppose we can make *all* our pictures together, but I'm glad we're doing two in a row."

"So am I. Maybe, between the time we get back from New York and the start of the picture, we can get down to Mexico for a few days. Rick tells me there's a wonderful little fishing village there called Puerto Vallarta that's beautiful and peaceful."

"It would be fun to lie on a beach for a few days."

"I'll get Rick to loan us the airplane to take us down there."

"Lucky you, getting to fly to New York on the Centurion airplane, when I have to fly commercial."

"Lucky me!"

They murmured affections for a minute or two, then said good night.

Susie attended the Chinese Theater opening of *Bitter Creek* on the arm of Eddie Harris and had a wonderful time being the center of attention. There was a late supper with the top press afterward, and she didn't get to bed until nearly three A.M.

V ance had a nearly identical experience at Radio City, arriving with Glenna Gleason on his arm and Rick following close behind. He slept late and was awakened at one P.M. by Rick and Glenna banging on his door, bearing the New York papers.

He tied a robe around him and opened the door. "Come in." He ordered brunch for them, then sat down to read the reviews.

"They're spectacular," Glenna said, handing him the *Times* review, "especially for you and Susie."

They read them aloud to each other, then they had a leisurely brunch of eggs Benedict and mimosas.

Vance glanced at his watch. "Nearly three," he said. "Time to call Susie; she's slept enough." He sat down on the bed and placed the call.

"I'm sorry, Mr. Calder," the operator said. "There's no answer at that number."

"Will you try every half hour until you reach somebody, please?"

"Of course."

Vance hung up the phone. "No answer," he said.

"Is she at the house?"

"She should be."

"Call the studio and see if she's at her bungalow."

Vance tried that with the same result. "She's supposed to move all her things this afternoon from the flat she shared with a friend."

"She's probably doing that right now," Rick said. "The operator will get her as soon as she returns."

Susie had left the house moments before Vance's call and headed for West Hollywood and Hank Harmon's apartment. She had planned to take care of this when Hank was working, but her schedule had kept her from doing that, and she was uncomfortable with the idea of seeing Hank. Susie had not been returning her phone calls, and she felt guilty about that.

She drove around to the rear of the little Spanish-style apartment building and parked her car, then entered through the rear door and went upstairs, carrying some cardboard boxes she'd gotten from a liquor store the day before. She rang the bell and got no answer. Susie was relieved; maybe she'd be able to get everything out of the place without a confrontation. She unlocked the door with her key and went inside.

She packed and carried down the boxes, until there was only a remaining suitcase, and then she would be gone. She went back to the apartment and packed the case, then, as she was about to leave, she thought it would be best if she left a note. She went to Hank's desk, took some of her stationery and wrote a two-page letter, intending to be both kind and grateful to Hank, while making clear that their relationship was over. She sealed it in an envelope, wrote Hank's name on it and propped it up on the hall table.

Susie went back to the bedroom, picked up her suitcase and started out, then she heard the front door open and someone enter. She heard the envelope being ripped open. She could get out through the service door in the kitchen while Hank read the note. She took off her shoes, held them in one hand and her suitcase in the other and ran lightly down the hall.

36

After Rick and Glenna left, Vance sat alone in the suite, listening to some music on the radio and trying to read the Sunday papers. He thought of going out, but he wanted to be there when the hotel operator reached Susie.

He had dozed off on the sofa when the phone rang. He sat upright and reached for it. "Susie?"

"It's Rick."

"Oh, sorry."

"You haven't heard from her yet?"

"Not a word. I've checked with the operator twice, and she's still calling every half hour."

"I'm sure there's a perfectly good reason she's not at home. Maybe she had to do some last-minute shopping."

"On Sunday?"

"Well, there is that. Look, why don't you come out for dinner with us. We've been invited to a dinner party at some friends' place in the Waldorf Towers. You can have the hotel operator forward any calls there."

"Thanks, Rick, but I'm a little tired, and I want to be here when Susie calls."

"All right. I'll talk to you in the morning."

"I don't have anything in the morning, do I?"

"No, just lunch with some people from *Life* magazine at a restaurant called He Voisin, on Park Avenue and Sixty-third Street. It's on your schedule. A car is coming for us at twelve-thirty."

"All right. I'll meet you downstairs at twelve-thirty." He said good-bye and hung up.

Vance tried to read, then gave up and ordered dinner from room service. He was in bed by ten, after a final call to the operator. It took him a long time to get to sleep.

The phone in Rick and Glenna's suite rang at ten-thirty the following morning, and Rick answered.

"Rick, this is Barry Feldman from studio publicity. I'm at L.A. Airport. The studio driver went to pick up Susan Stafford at Vance Calder's house half an hour ago, and she wasn't there. He paged me at the airport."

"Maybe she forgot about the driver and took a cab," Rick said.

"I don't know why she would do that; she's been driven to every appointment all week by the same driver, and she had asked him to pick her up at the house at six-thirty. Her plane takes off in twenty minutes, and I don't know if I should try to hold it. I mean, if I knew she were on the way I could throw myself on the runway in front of it, but I've no reason to think that."

"Did the driver ring the bell at the house?"

"Repeatedly and at every door. He said her car was parked out front with a lot of boxes and a suitcase in it, and the keys were in the ignition."

"She was moving some things from her old apartment yesterday afternoon, so she must have come home. Can you reach the driver?"

"Not until he calls me back."

"When he does, tell him to break into the house, if necessary, and if the cops come, to call me here for an explanation. She could be ill and unconscious."

"I'll go over there myself."

"No, Barry. You stay there, in case she arrives."

"Shall I try to hold the airplane?"

"What time is the next one?"

"Twelve-thirty, and she'd get to New York very late, what with the time change."

"Don't try to hold the plane. Just book her on the next one and wait to hear from either her or me. What number do I call to page you?" Rick wrote down the number and hung up. He called the studio and got the front gate.

"Hello?"

"This is Rick Barron. Have you seen Susan Stafford either come or go this morning?"

"No, sir."

"How about yesterday?"

"I'll check the log." There was a moment's pause. "No, sir, she wasn't logged in or out yesterday."

"Transfer me to the studio police line." He waited, and a man answered.

"This is Rick Barron. You have pass keys to all the bungalows, don't you?"

"Yes, sir, we do."

"I want you to go first to Susan Stafford's bungalow, open it and see if she's there. If she is, she's not answering the phone. Then go to Vance Calder's bungalow and check there. I'm in New York; call me at this number from Vance's bungalow." He gave the man the number.

"Yes, sir. It should take me ten or fifteen minutes."

Rick hung up.

Glenna, who had heard his side of the conversation, came and sat on the bed. "What do you think is going on?"

"I have no idea, but I'm worried."

"Susie doesn't seem like a prima donna. She wouldn't just disappear, would she?"

"I don't think she would; she's always seemed very level-headed."

"I'm going to shower while you wait for the call."

"Go ahead." Rick picked up the *Times* and tried to read it. Ten minutes later, the phone rang. "Hello."

"Mr. Barron? This is studio security. I'm at Mr. Calder's bungalow. Miss Stafford isn't here, and she's not at her own bungalow, either."

"Thanks."

"Anything else you want me to do?"

"Tell the front gate if she turns up at the studio to call me at this number."

"Yes, sir."

Rick hung up and called Vance's room and brought him up-to-date.

"Something's happened," Vance said. "Susie wouldn't do this."

"I agree. Do you have the name and address of the girl whose apartment she was supposed to visit?"

"Her name is Henrietta Harmon, and she's called Hank. She's a script girl at RKO. I don't know her address, but it's in West Hollywood; she could be in the book. Shall I call there?"

"No. Let me handle it. I'll call you when I know something."

"Is our lunch still on?"

"I don't want to cancel an interview with *Life*, then find out there's some simple explanation for all this."

"All right, I'll get dressed and wait to hear from you."

Rick hung up, got out his address book and called Tom Terry at home.

"Hello?"

"Tom, it's Rick. We've got a problem."

37

Tom Terry checked the phone book and found Henrietta Harmon in West Hollywood, off Sunset. He made a note of the address and phone number, then got dressed, got into his car and drove quickly to Vance Calder's house in Beverly Hills. As he pulled into the driveway he saw two cars ahead: a prewar Chevrolet coupe and a big Packard sedan. That would be the studio car.

He pulled up, and the studio driver got out to meet him. "Good morning, Mr. Terry," he said.

"Morning, Jerry. I've heard what's going on. Have you been in the house?"

"No, sir. I just rang the bell."

Tom went to the front door, rang the bell, then tried the knob. It was unlocked. He turned to the driver. "Jerry, follow me, and stay in my tracks. Don't touch anything."

"Yessir."

Tom went from room to room and found everything in order. He went upstairs, found the master bedroom and looked in both dressing rooms and baths. In one dressing room he found several pieces of a woman's clothing and underwear in the drawers. On the floor there was a cardboard box containing sweaters and blouses. In the bathroom, there was makeup in the medicine cabinet and on the sink.

"There's more boxes and a suitcase in the coupe," Jerry said.

"Yeah? Then it looks like she unlocked the front door and brought one box inside, then went back for more, then . . ."

"It don't make any sense," Jerry said.

"No, it don't," Tom replied. "Something must have happened before she could bring in more boxes."

"What?"

"I don't know." Tom went back downstairs and checked the interior of the car and the trunk, which was unlatched and contained more boxes. The car keys were in the ignition, and there was what looked like a couple of house keys on the key ring.

"What do you want me to do?" Jerry asked.

"Who are you reporting to today?"

"One of the publicity guys. He's at the airport waiting for Miss Stafford to show for her plane."

"I don't think she's going to make the plane, Jerry. Go back to the studio and report back to your boss. He can get in touch with the publicity guy."

"All right, Mr. Terry." He got into the Packard and drove away.

Tom got into his car and headed for West Hollywood, stopping at a corner pay phone to call Henrietta Harmon's house. No answer; the girl must be at work.

Tom found the building and parked out back. He ran up the main stairs and rang the doorbell: no answer, so he got out his kit and picked the lock. Inside, he closed the door softly behind him and looked around. He was standing in a small entrance hall. On a table in front of him was an envelope that had been torn open, and on the front was written one word: *Hank*. He replaced it, then tiptoed into the living room. It was nicely furnished and perfectly neat. He found the only bedroom, and it was in the same condition. The walk-in closet had a full rack of jackets and trousers on one side, but they looked more like the clothes of a slender man than those of a woman. There was nothing but hangers on the opposite rack.

He checked the bathroom and found some empty spaces in the medicine cabinet, as if some bottles had been cleared out, but there was no makeup of any kind—strange for a woman's bathroom. He checked the kitchen: the dishes were all put away and the countertops were clean. He looked for signs of blood everywhere but found none. He opened the service door and looked down the back stairs, then closed it. He went back to the front door, let himself out, relocked the door and went back to his car. He sat there for a moment, thinking, then he started the car and drove to the studio.

At his desk, he called Rick Barron in New York.

"Hello?"

"Rick, it's Tom."

"What did you learn?"

"Miss Stafford appears to have moved out of the Harmon apartment yesterday and then drove to Mr. Calder's house with a car full of boxes. She unlocked the front door and went upstairs to her dressing room, deposited one of the boxes there, then went back downstairs. Then she disappeared."

"Disappeared?"

"Well, no one has seen her, have they?"

"No."

"Oh, I let myself into the Harmon apartment and found that Miss Stafford had left a note for Miss Harmon on her front hall table. The envelope was still there but not the note. Everything in the apartment was in order, though it was obvious that one of the two roommates had moved out. The remaining clothes were of a mannish nature, and there was no makeup in the bathroom, which is odd for a woman's apartment."

"Where are you now?"

"Back at the studio. There are only two further things I can do: go to RKO and interview Miss Harmon, or call a lieutenant we both know at the LAPD and report Miss Stafford missing. If I call him, then he should probably interview Miss Harmon. One other thing:

the LAPD is leaky with situations like this, so if we call them in, you'd better be prepared to read about it in the morning papers, probably even the New York papers."

"I think it's too early to call the police, don't you?"

"I'm not sure it is. I'm disturbed that Miss Stafford was going about her business in a normal way, then suddenly disappeared in the middle of moving into Calder's house, abandoning her car. Something else odd: after unlocking the front door of the house and taking a box of clothes upstairs, she replaced the keys in the car's ignition."

"I suppose that's a little unusual, but hardly a reason for calling in the police."

"Are you thinking maybe the girl just got overloaded with publicity appearances and bailed out? Went home to mama?"

"It crossed my mind."

"Then either somebody picked her up at Calder's, or she's on foot. Have you talked to her agent? She might confide in him. And somebody ought to call her family, if you know how to reach them."

"Her agent's name is Marty Fine, at William Morris. You call him, and if you think it's a good idea, go interview Miss Harmon. I'll deal with Susie's parents if that becomes necessary. I have to go to a luncheon with Vance and some people from *Life*; when I get back, I'll call you at the office. If you need to reach me urgently, I'll be at a restaurant called Voisin." Rick gave him the number.

"All right, Rick." Tom hung up, called William Morris and got Marty Fine's secretary on the phone.

"Who shall I say is calling?"

"Tom Terry, head of security at Centurion. It's urgent, and if he's with somebody, tell him to take the call on another phone."

"Just a moment, please."

"This is Martin Fine," a voice said.

"Mr. Fine, this is Tom Terry, from Centurion. Rick Barron asked me to call you. Have you spoken with Susan Stafford during the past twenty-four hours?"

"No. I last saw her at the opening of *Bitter Creek* on Saturday night. She told me she was going to rest on Sunday and leave for New York this morning, so she should be on a plane."

"She missed her flight. Can you think of anyone she might go to if she's . . . upset about something, or if she just wants to get away from it all?"

"The only people I know that she's close to in L.A. are Vance Calder, who should be in New York, too, and a woman named Hank Harmon; they used to share an apartment."

"No other men, no other girlfriends?"

"She lived at the Studio Club when she first came to town, but she never mentioned anyone's name there."

"No relatives out here?"

"No. Her parents live in a place called Delano, Georgia. You want their number?"

"Yes, thanks." Tom wrote it down.

"I'm surprised she didn't make the plane this morning," Fine said. "She was looking forward to going to New York."

"Did she show any signs of personal strain on Saturday night?"

"She was just a little tired, I thought, but she'd had a pretty full schedule all week. I'm concerned about this. Will you call me if you learn anything?"

"Sure."

"And if there's anything else I can do to help you, please let me know."

Tom thanked him, then headed for his car and RKO Studios.

38

T om drove over to RKO Studios and identified himself to the
front gate guard. "I'm looking to talk with an RKO script girl
named Hank Harmon," he said to the guard.

"Sure, I know Hank," the guard said, "but she's not working
here today. She's over to the Culver lot, where they're shooting a
western."

"Thanks." Tom turned around and drove out to the "forty acres,"
as it was known, the back lot where many films had been shot, including a lot of the exteriors for *Gone With the Wind*. He gave the
gate guard his card and talked his way onto the lot, following directions to the western street set. He parked some distance away and
walked over, not wanting to make car sounds when they might be
shooting. In his time at Centurion, Tom had learned how to move
around a movie studio without disrupting production.

He found the western street and saw the production grouped at
the far end, shooting a street fight. Staying out of camera range, he
moved closer down the street.

Hank Harmon was not hard to spot. She was sitting in a folding
canvas chair a few feet from the director, a notebook in her lap, her
face partly obscured by large sunglasses. She was handsome rather
than beautiful, but striking nonetheless. She was wearing a western
shirt and boots, and a buckskin jacket was draped over the back of

her chair. Tom waited twenty minutes or so while they finished with the setup, and when they broke to move the camera, he approached Hank Harmon.

"Miss Harmon?" He extended a hand and smiled. "I'm Tom Terry from Centurion Studios."

She returned his smile and his handshake. "How are you, Tom?" She seemed a very pleasant person. She was very tall—Tom estimated six feet or more, with the high-heeled boots—and slender but athletic-looking.

"Just fine, thanks. I wonder if you can help me. I'm looking for Susan Stafford. Do you know where I can find her?"

"Why no. She shared my apartment for a few months, but yesterday she came by and removed her things. The last time I spoke to her, she said she planned to move into her bungalow at Centurion."

"Did you see her yesterday when she came by?"

"No, I was out. I went to the farmer's market, which I do every Sunday, and when I came back she had come and gone. She left a note."

"I wonder, may I have a look at the note?"

"What's this about, Tom?"

"No one has seen Susan since she left your house yesterday, and we're concerned."

"Who's 'we?'"

"The studio. Susan was supposed to take a flight to New York this morning, but she missed it, and we haven't been able to locate her. Maybe there's something in her note that could give us some indication of where she went or, at least, her state of mind."

"There was nothing like that in the note; what she had to say was more of a personal nature. I don't have it with me, anyway. But her state of mind was just fine. She said she was moving in with Vance Calder."

"I'm sorry, I thought you said she told you she was moving into her bungalow when you last saw her."

Hank blinked rapidly. "I guess things must have progressed with Mr. Calder in the meantime."

"What was there about the note that made you believe her state of mind was 'just fine,' as you put it?"

"It was just normal Susie stuff. She didn't seem upset or anything."

"When was the last time you saw Susan?"

"Oh, it was some time ago, before she went away on location for her picture."

"Was she living in your apartment up until the time she went on location?"

"Yes."

"And after she came back?"

Hank looked away. "No, she didn't return to my place after that."

"Did you two break up before she left?"

Now Hank began to look wary. "Break up?"

"What was the nature of your relationship with Susan?"

"I beg your pardon?"

"How many bedrooms are in your apartment?"

"One."

"And how many beds in that room?"

"Excuse me. I thought you said you work for Centurion, but you're beginning to sound like a policeman."

"I used to be a cop; I apologize if I sounded that way, but we're very concerned about Susan. What was the nature of your relationship?"

"We were friends."

"Were?"

"Obviously, if she moved out, we're not as close now."

"She had quite a few of her things at your apartment, didn't she?"

"She had everything there."

"But you haven't seen her for a period of many weeks, and she only moved her things out yesterday. What did she do for clothes?"

"Well, I assume the studio supplied her with western wear in Wyoming."

"Costumes, yes."

"Perhaps she went shopping. I don't know."

"Did you drive her car to Vance Calder's house some time yesterday?"

"Why, no."

"So if we go over her car for fingerprints, we won't find any of yours in the car?"

Now Hank was looking just a little flustered. "Well, I have been in her car in the past."

"Have you ever driven it?"

"No. Susie always drove."

"Then your fingerprints wouldn't be on the steering wheel or the gearshift or the keys."

"Well, I . . ."

"Hank!" an assistant director yelled from a few yards away. "We need you."

"You'll have to excuse me," Hank said, looking relieved.

Tom gave her his card. "Will you call me if you hear from Susan?"

"Of course," she said, then walked away.

Tom walked quickly back to his car. He drove back to the studio, lost in thought, and not good thoughts. Back in his office he checked his watch and called the restaurant Voisin in New York. A woman with a French accent answered, and he asked her to find Rick Barron and bring him to the phone. It took several minutes.

"Hello?"

"It's Tom."

"What's up?"

"I spoke with Hank Harmon half an hour ago."

"And?"

"All sorts of warning signs in the interview. You know what I mean." Rick had been a cop, too.

"Yes, I do. What's your best judgment, Tom?"

"I think Susan Stafford never left Hank Harmon's apartment alive."

"Tom," Rick said, "call in the police."

39

Rick left the phone booth and walked slowly back to the table, forcing himself to seem calm and unconcerned.

Vance leaned over and asked, "What's up?"

"Just some studio business," Rick replied and resumed his conversation with the *Life* people, while a photographer circled the table, looking for good angles on Vance.

In the car after lunch, Rick turned to Vance. "That was Tom Terry on the phone. He's talked to Hank Harmon, and he's suspicious."

"Suspicious of what?"

"You have to understand how cops think. When questioning people they look for small signs of discomfort that shouldn't be there. They try to trip up the people they're questioning, get them to contradict themselves."

"And after questioning Harmon, what does Tom think?"

"He suspects foul play; I told him to get the police involved."

"Just what kind of foul play?"

"He can't know that for sure; he's just hoping for the best and doing everything he can to find Susie."

"He thinks she's dead, doesn't he?"

"He thinks that's a possibility. The other possibility is that she just had too much pressure on her last week, what with all the interviews and the opening, and she just felt she had to get away."

"Susie is a strong girl," Vance said, "and a responsible person. She wouldn't just walk away from her work on the picture, especially since the worst was over. She was looking forward to coming to New York."

"I can't argue with that, Vance. I'm as much in the dark as you are."

"I want to go back to L.A. Is the Centurion airplane still here?"

"No, it's on the Coast. I'll have the travel department get you on the first flight tomorrow morning."

"Is there a night flight?"

"I'll find out as soon as we get back to the Plaza."

"Someone should speak with Susie's parents."

"I have their number; I'll do that. We don't want them to find out about this from the press."

Vance left the hotel at eleven P.M. to catch a midnight flight from LaGuardia with a studio PR man who arranged for them to drive through a gate directly to the airplane, where Vance and his luggage were deposited at the steps to a TWA Constellation. He was the first aboard and was given two seats in the first row of first class.

As the other passengers got on board he began to notice something different: some of them were obviously recognizing him, perhaps having seen something in the papers or even having seen the picture. A couple of them complimented him on his performance. In the circumstances, he felt uncomfortable about this; he was unaccustomed to being recognized by anyone, and this was a new experience.

After a refueling stop, the airplane arrived at L.A. airport in the late morning, and another studio PR man came aboard to escort him to a car waiting next to the airplane.

"Has anyone heard from Susan Stafford?" he asked the man. He had a sick feeling in his stomach.

"No, nothing. I think you may want to go to the studio," the man said. "The police are at your house with Tom Terry, our head of security, and sooner or later the press is going to start showing up there, if they haven't already."

"All right," Vance said, "I'll go to my bungalow."

"Tom has promised to get in touch with you as soon as he knows anything."

Having gotten little sleep on the airplane, Vance arrived at his bungalow exhausted. He ordered some soup sent over from the commissary and as he finished it, Tom Terry arrived and introduced himself.

"Have the police learned anything?" Vance asked.

"They've taken two sets of fingerprints from the driver's side of Susan's car, but as yet they have nothing to compare them with. Susan's prints are not on record anywhere, and neither are Hank Harmon's, and without evidence connecting her to a crime, they can't force her to give them her prints."

"Rick said you talked to Harmon yesterday. What do you think about all this?"

"I think Harmon is hiding something, that she knows more than she's willing to tell."

Vance was more frightened than ever. "Do you think she's harmed Susie?"

"I don't know, but in Susan's absence, it's something we have to consider. It's fortunate that you were in New York when this happened."

"What?"

"In a disappearance like this, the boyfriend is always the first suspect. Tell me about your day on Sunday."

"I had brunch in my suite with Rick and Glenna, and we read the reviews in all the papers."

"What about after that?"

"I tried to call Susie at my house, and when there was no answer, I asked the hotel operator to try her every half hour, so I waited there, in case she called back."

"Did you wait with Rick and Glenna?"

"No, they left around one o'clock, I think. They called later . . ."

"What time did they call?"

"Around five o'clock. They asked me to go with them to a dinner party at the Waldorf Towers, but I declined and had dinner in my suite alone."

"Did you speak to Rick again on Sunday?"

"He called when they came back from dinner, around eleven, I think, to find out if I'd heard from Susie."

"That's good; it means we can place you in New York until eleven on Sunday night, and that eliminates you as a suspect. Susie's agent was apparently the last person to see her after the opening on Saturday night, except for the studio driver who took her to your house afterward, so whatever happened to her happened between, say, midnight on Saturday and Monday morning, when the driver went back to the house to drive her to the airport. We assume that sometime on Sunday she went to Hank Harmon's apartment to pick up her things. Harmon says she was out at the farmer's market for most of the afternoon, and when she came back, Susie had gone and left her a note."

"What did the note say?"

"Harmon became defensive when I asked her about it, said it was of a personal nature. The police are talking to Harmon, and they'll find out exactly what hours she was away from her apartment, so we can pinpoint when Susan was there."

"Tom, tell me the truth. Do you think Susie is dead, that Hank Harmon killed her?"

"I'm sorry to tell you that I think that's what happened. I hope to God I'm wrong."

Vance buried his face in his hands. Panic was rising inside him.

Tom went to the bar and poured Vance a drink. "Here, get this inside you; it'll help."

Vance took a slug of the drink and barely got it down. He ran to the bathroom and threw up.

"Vance, are you all right?" Tom called from the living room.

"Yeah." Vance put cold water on a facecloth and came out of the bathroom with it pressed to his face. "I'm sorry, Tom. I just don't feel very well. Will you excuse me? I think I want to lie down for a while."

"Of course, Vance. Get some rest. In the unlikely event that anyone from the press gets in touch with you, just tell them you don't know anything and refer them to the publicity department."

"All right, Tom." Terry left, and Vance went into the bedroom, stretched out on the bed and draped the cool facecloth across his forehead. He had never felt anything like this: frightened and helpless.

40

Rick and Glenna got back to L.A. on Wednesday, and on Thursday morning Rick was in a meeting with Eddie Harris, Tom Terry and the studio's publicity chief, Bart Crowther. Tom brought them up-to-date on the investigation.

"The police are at a dead end," he said. "They have Susie's car and her boxes of belongings, and, except for a few clothes in her bungalow, that's all that exists of her. They have two different sets of fingerprints from Susie's car and no one to compare them to. Hank Harmon has got herself a lawyer, and he won't allow her to be fingerprinted. I personally think Susie is dead, but my guess is until her body is found there aren't going to be any breaks in this case."

"Tom, what's your time line for all this?" Rick asked.

"Harmon told the police she was out of her apartment from around two to four on Sunday afternoon, and the cops tell me a couple of witnesses have put her at the farmer's market during that time. My guess is that's when Susie went to the apartment, packed up her stuff, then wrote Hank Harmon a note, which Harmon now says she can't find, and was about to leave when Harmon came home. There was probably an argument, and Harmon either hit Susie with something or strangled her.

"After that, I think she waited until the wee hours, put Susie's body in her car, disposed of it—God knows where—then drove the car to Vance Calder's house. She used Susie's key to get in and leave a box of clothes in an upstairs dressing room, then put the keys back in the car's ignition and walked home."

"How long a walk would that be?"

"I clocked it at about three and a half miles, perfectly doable in the middle of the night without being noticed. Sunset is deserted at that hour."

"Any other way it could have happened?"

"Only if she had an accomplice, and who the hell do you call up and say, 'I've just murdered somebody and I need help in getting rid of the body and getting her car out of here'?"

"That all makes sense to me," Rick said. "Is anything else being done?"

"I've got two private detectives, experienced men, going over everything about Henrietta Harmon with a fine-toothed comb. We'll know more about her in a day or two."

"Has anybody talked with her family?" Eddie asked.

"I called them from New York," Rick said. "They wanted to come out here, but I discouraged that."

Bart Crowther spoke up. "I speak to them daily."

"I see the papers have got this now," Eddie said.

"It's been pretty mild, considering," Bart said. "They're concentrating mostly on Hank Harmon, and she's hiding out somewhere. She hasn't been to work since the first of the week."

"Have the press found Susie's parents yet?" Eddie asked.

"Yes, but a relative is answering their phone and giving out 'no comments.' Vance has spoken with them, too."

"How's Vance doing?" Eddie asked.

"I haven't seen him since I got in, but I'm going over there when we're done here," Rick said.

"I'll go with you," Eddie said.

Tom spoke up again. "He was very shaken right after he got back. He was going to lie down for a while."

"Bart," Rick asked, "do you have any other recommendations on how we should be handling this?"

"It's under control right now. If the police find a body, then everything will explode, but my people are ready for that."

"Why don't you come over to Vance's bungalow with us and get him ready for it?" Eddie said.

They broke up the meeting, and Rick, Eddie and Bart went over to Vance's bungalow and found the actor sitting on the living room sofa, looking pale and drawn. They all sat down in the bungalow's living room.

"How are you managing, Vance?" Rick asked.

"I'm all right," he replied. "I'm getting a little cabin fever here, though. I'd really rather be at my house."

Bart shook his head. "Vance, if you go back there before there's some resolution to all this, the press will be all over you, and we don't want that."

"I suppose that at some point I'm going to have to address this publicly."

"No, you're not," Bart said. "We'll issue a press release with a quote of two or three sentences from you, and that will be it. I don't want you to talk to *anybody* about this, except the police."

"Vance, did Hy Greenbaum get you a lawyer?" Eddie asked.

"Yes, a fellow named David Sturmack. I spoke to him at some length on the phone. After I told him what little I knew he told me to tell the police everything. They came here and talked to me for an hour, and I followed David's advice."

"Vance," Rick said, "you were talking about going down to Puerto Vallarta for a few days with Susie; maybe it would be a good idea if you went now."

"No," Bart said. "The press would find him there. *Confidential* magazine is trying to get together a story on Susie, and they'd pay anything to get to Vance."

"Vance," Eddie said, "would you like to go to the ranch in Jackson Hole for a while? You wouldn't be molested by all these news hounds."

"Yes!" Vance said emphatically.

"There's snow on the ground," Eddie said, "but the Coopers are still in the main house, and I'm sure they'd be glad to see you."

"Yes, please," Vance said.

"I'll arrange for you to be flown up there," Rick said. "Nobody will ever find you there."

"How soon can I leave?"

"Tomorrow morning. Early, say, seven o'clock at Clover Field?"

"Good. I'll be there."

"I'll have wardrobe fix you up with some warm clothing," Rick said. "If you need anything, you have only to call me." Rick handed him a manila envelope. "Here's something to read, when you feel like it."

"A script?"

"Yes, and we can go to work on it the minute you feel like it."

"I'll read it."

"Oh, we'd like to assign a permanent secretary to you," Eddie said. "There's already a lot of fan mail about Susie."

"The steno pool sent a girl over earlier. I'd be happy to have her stay on permanently."

"Good. Phone her every day, and if we need to speak to you, we'll leave a message with her."

The group left, and Rick went back to his office to make the arrangements for Vance's travel. An hour later, Tom Terry called.

"Remember our friend Harold Schmidt from Milwaukee?"

"Yes," Rick said.

"He's turned up in L.A."

41

V ance Calder took off at half past seven from Clover Field in Jack Barron's Beech Staggerwing with a hired pilot. He persuaded the man to let him fly the airplane for long periods, and he learned to operate the radio and the radio direction finder. By the time he reached Jackson, Wyoming, he had resolved to learn to fly.

W hile Vance was still in the air four county garbage trucks and a dozen workers showed up in the farther reaches of Mulholland Drive, closer to Malibu than to Beverly Hills, to clear a part of the remote area that had been used for months as an illegal garbage dump. Twice before the county had cleaned up the place, but people were still coming out there and dumping old furniture, dead pets and whatever else they no longer wanted. This time, the county employees were determined to end this, and they planned, after clearing the area once more, to fence the approaches to the informal dump and make it impossible for people to reach the area by car or on foot.

They began by removing the larger objects—sofas, chairs and kitchen appliances—and loading them onto the trucks. They planned, after removing anything larger than a bread box, to bring equipment to scoop up the remaining trash.

Two men were struggling with an old refrigerator, complaining about its weight, when the door came open and the naked corpse of a woman spilled out. The foreman sent a man in search of a telephone and the sheriff.

L ater the same day, Tom Terry answered his phone at the studio security office.

"Lieutenant Morrison of the Los Angeles Police Department to speak to you," his secretary said.

Tom picked up the phone. "Ben?"

"Hello, Tom. I may have some news for you."

"Shoot."

"This morning, a cleanup crew from the county was clearing an illegal dump way out on Mulholland, and they found a woman's body in a refrigerator."

"Any identification?"

"No, the body was naked and, of course, in poor condition, but the height and hair color and maybe the weight match your girl, Susan Stafford. Can you round up some photographs of her?"

"Sure, I can. I'll messenger them to you."

"Something else: the medical examiner found a small gold ring—pinkie ring—on her left little finger. There was a lot of swelling, and he had to cut it off. It's two hands shaking, you know what I mean?"

"Yeah, sort of a friendship ring."

"Like that. Was your girl wearing anything like that?"

"I don't know, but I'll try and find out. Anything else you need?"

"Just the photos, not that they'll be of all that much use. She's pretty much unrecognizable."

"Are you taking fingerprints and dental impressions?"

"Sure."

"There's a dentist near the studio that we send a lot of actors to for cosmetic work; I'll find out if she's been to him."

"Thanks, that would be a big help."

"I'll call you when I know more." Tom hung up and called Bart Crowther in publicity.

"Hi, Tom. What's up?"

"You said you're in daily touch with Susan Stafford's parents, Bart?"

"That's right. I talked to them about an hour ago."

"A body has turned up, way out on Mulholland. There was a ring on the left little finger, a gold ring with two hands shaking."

"I've seen rings like that."

"Will you call her parents and ask if Susan wore anything like that?"

"Sure, I will."

"I'd call Vance, but he's on his way to Wyoming."

"I'll call the parents right now."

"One more thing, Bart: do you know if the studio sent Susan to our dentist for any work?"

"Yes, we did; not much, though."

"Will you call him and ask if he made any impressions of her teeth? It would be a big help in identifying the body. Also, I need some photographs of Susan."

"Sure. I'll get back to you."

Tom waited impatiently for half an hour before the phone rang.

"It's Bart. Bingo on the ring. Her mother says it had her initials and another girl's, somebody she roomed with in New York, but she couldn't remember her name."

"Did you tell the folks about the body?"

"Of course not. I just asked her to describe any jewelry that Susie wore; told them the police forgot to ask."

"How about the dentist?"

"He made full mouth impressions, even though he was only doing a couple of caps. Thorough guy."

"Thanks, Bart. Can you send the photos over? Call the dentist and tell him I'm sending a messenger for the impressions and to wrap them up good. And get somebody to walk the photos over here, will you?"

"Sure thing. Be sure and let me know if an ID is made; we need to get out ahead of this story."

"Sure." Tom hung up and called Ben Morrison.

"Lieutenant Morrison."

"It's Tom. Susan Stafford wore a ring like the one you described. It will have her initials and the initials of another girl, name unknown, engraved inside. Her dentist also has full mouth impressions, and I'm sending them and the photos to you by messenger; you'll have them in less than an hour."

"That's great news, Tom. Thank you."

"Ben, I'd like to be the first to know if you make the ID, and our publicity guy would like to know about it before you make an announcement to the press."

"Of course, Tom. I'll get back to you, but it might be late; the body is at the sheriff's office on ice."

"I'll wait for your call." Tom hung up and called Rick Barron.

"Hello?"

"Rick, it's Tom. A body has been found, and it was wearing a ring like one her mother said Susan wore. We're sending photos and dental molds from the studio dentist to Ben Morrison, and we may have a confirmed ID sometime tonight."

"Where was the body found?"

"Way out on Mulholland at an illegal trash dump. Height, weight and hair color match Susan's, but, of course, we need to know for sure."

"Call me at home when you hear, Tom."

"Will do. Shall I call Eddie?"

"I'll take care of that."

Tom hung up, ordered some dinner sent over from the studio commissary and settled in for the wait.

42

Tom Terry was asleep on the sofa in his office when the telephone rang. He checked his watch: twelve-fifteen A.M. He grabbed the phone. "Tom Terry."

"It's Ben, Tom."

"What have you got?"

"It's your girl; no doubt about it. The initials on the ring match, and the dental impressions made it final."

"Have they got a cause of death?"

"Manual strangulation; no sign of a ligature. She was beaten around her head and body with some sort of instrument; not enough to kill her, though. There were defensive wounds, and her fingernails were all broken. She didn't go easy. She was probably beaten unconscious, then strangled. The condition of the body confirms Sunday afternoon, more or less."

"When will you make a public announcement?"

"Not until tomorrow morning, when it's too late for the morning papers."

"We appreciate that, Ben."

"The body will be ready for release to a funeral parlor by midday."

"I'll see that's dealt with."

"I'm sorry we didn't have a better outcome."

"Me, too. Are you going to pick up the Harmon girl?"

"We don't have enough evidence, I'm afraid. We went through her apartment thoroughly and found nothing, and we haven't had a chance to talk to her again; she's disappeared."

"I think I know why. You said Susan fought for her life; I'll bet Harmon has scratch marks and bruises on her arms and chest. When I talked with her, her face wasn't obviously marked, but she had her hands stuffed in the pockets of her dungarees, and she was wearing a long-sleeved shirt. She's not going to come out of hiding until she's healed up. If you can find her quick, you might be able to nail her."

"I'll pass that up and see if we can get some more people on it."

"I've got a couple of private guys working on her background. If they come up with a relative or a friend who might be hiding her, I'll let you know."

"Thanks, Tom."

Tom thanked him again and hung up. It was twelve-thirty now, and he didn't see any point in ruining a lot of people's sleep, so he locked up his office and went home.

Early the following morning, Rick got a call from Tom Terry. "It's confirmed, Rick. The body is Susan Stafford."

"Tell me everything you know."

Tom did. "The body will be ready for release from the county morgue around noon."

"I'll see to it. Thanks for your good work on this, Tom."

"Sure."

Rick hung up and made the call to Eddie Harris, telling him everything.

"Shit," Eddie said. "I hate this."

"We all do."

"Have you told Vance?"

"I'll call him now."

"I'll deal with the funeral parlor; you deal with him. Get him to stay at the ranch for a while, until the papers are tired of this."

"I'll try."

Rick hung up and called the ranch. Mac Cooper answered. "Hi, Mac. It's Rick Barron. How are you?"

"Pretty good. Vance isn't, though. He's a different boy."

"Can I speak to him?"

"I'll get him."

Two minutes passed, then Vance picked up the phone. "Rick?"

"Yes, Vance. You sitting down?"

"I am now."

"A body was found early yesterday morning at a makeshift garbage dump up on Mulholland. Late last night it was positively identified as Susie's. She's gone, Vance."

Vance was quiet for a moment. "I've been getting ready for this, but I'm not."

"I know how you feel; we all loved her."

"Give me all the details."

"There's plenty of time for that later."

"Give it to me now; I want to get this over with, and I can't as long as I have questions in my mind."

Rick told him everything Tom Terry had told him. "That's it, that's everything, and I'm told there's not likely to be more."

"Have you spoken to Susie's parents?"

"Not yet."

"I'd like to do that. I spoke with them once before, so they know me, and they know I was her friend. It would be better than having the publicity guy do it."

"All right. I'll give you the number."

"I have it. Will you send the airplane back for me?"

"There won't be an airplane available for a few days."

"I'll find one up here, then."

"Vance, don't come back just yet; there's absolutely nothing you can do here. The body will likely be flown back to Georgia, and her parents will handle the funeral arrangements there."

"I really feel that I should be there, Rick."

"For what? Tell me what you want to do when you get here."

Vance thought about that. "I guess you're right; I can't think of anything."

"There's going to be a big thing in the press, and you don't want to be here for that. Get some rest, some fresh air and some exercise. Read that script I gave you. Read some books."

"Rick, they've got a nice little movie theater in Jackson, and Ellie Cooper wants to show *Bitter Creek* to raise money for a local charity. Can you do that?"

"Of course. I'll have a print to you the first of next week, so tell her to set a date."

"She'll be very grateful to you."

"Call me if you need anything at all. And when you feel you're ready to go back to work, just let me know, and I'll send the airplane."

"Thanks, Rick."

Vance hung up, and, without waiting, placed the call to Susie's parents. He got her mother on the phone and broke the news. He was surprised how calm Mrs. Stafford was.

"Vance, did they tell you about the ring?"

"Yes, some sort of friendship ring."

"A girl she used to live with in New York gave it to her; it meant something special."

"She told me about that."

"Did she tell you about Hank, too?"

"Yes, she did."

"Susie was always like that. Boys came and went pretty quick; it was the girls who were the constant. She was just born that way, I guess."

"She didn't seem that way with me. I think we would have been married, eventually."

"Maybe it's better that you weren't, Vance; I don't think it would have lasted, not the way you would have wanted it to. The pull of the other side of her nature was too strong."

"I suppose you could be right."

"We saw the picture when it opened in Atlanta, and we thought you were just wonderful. Susie, too, of course, but then we're prejudiced. You're going to have a wonderful career, Vance. Remember Susie, but don't let her memory be a burden to you. She wouldn't have liked that."

"Thank you, Mrs. Stafford." He gave her his number in L.A. "Please call me if you ever need anything."

"I don't think we'll need anything further. We've decided to have her body cremated in Los Angeles, probably tomorrow. A friend is arranging it."

"I see. Please give my best to Mr. Stafford. The two of you brought up a wonderful daughter." He hung up and went back to the breakfast table and told the Coopers everything.

"You need to get out of the house today, Vance," Mac said.

"I thought I'd take a couple of horses and some grub and ride up to that line shack you told me about," Vance said. "Maybe stay a few days."

"Good idea, Vance."

43

Tom Terry waited outside the building of the Screen Extras Guild, a blowup of a Milwaukee P.D. mug shot his only reference. It was a little after seven, and Harold Schmidt had not yet come out of the building. Tom began to wonder if the mug shot was a good enough likeness.

Then two men appeared at the entrance to the building and stood talking for a moment. One of them was the head of the extra's union; the other, clearly, was Schmidt, dressed in a decent suit and a tie. They finished their brief conversation and parted in opposite directions, Schmidt walking toward where Tom was parked at the curb. Tom got out of the car.

"Hal?" he said as the man drew abreast of him.

Schmidt turned and looked at him, askance. "Were you speaking to me?"

"You're Hal Schmidt, aren't you?"

Schmidt looked at him narrowly, then knowingly. "Who wants to know."

"My name's Tom. I'm not a cop; I'm a friend of Louise Brecht."

"Yeah? How is Lou?"

"I'd like to talk to you about that. Can I buy you a drink?"

Schmidt looked at his watch. "I guess so."

"Hop in."

The two men got into Tom's car and pulled away from the curb. "There's a decent joint down here around the corner," Tom said.

"Nice car."

"Thanks, but it's not mine."

"How do you know Louise?"

Tom parked the car near the saloon. "Let's get that drink, and we'll talk about that." He led Schmidt inside, and the two men found a booth and both ordered bourbon. "Your health," Tom said, raising his glass.

"Bottoms up. Now enlighten me."

"You and Louise were fairly close for a while, back in Milwaukee, weren't you?"

"Yeah, we were."

"Were you two of one mind politically?"

"Lou didn't have a political mind; she wanted to be in show business. And she made it, didn't she? You see, I know who Lou is now."

"I expected you would. If she wasn't politically inclined, why did you sign her up for the party?"

"What party was that? Democratic? Republican?"

"We both know which party, Hal."

"What makes you think I signed her up for anything?"

"Well, she didn't sign herself up, but she got signed up, anyway. You were the only party member she knew."

Schmidt smiled a little. "You're a fed, aren't you? You work for the committee."

Tom shook his head. "Wrong. I told you. I'm a friend of Louise. Of the family, you might say."

"Yeah, I saw something in a magazine, pretty picture: husband and a kid."

"Two kids, now. They're very happy."

"I'm glad to hear it; Lou was always a good sort."

"You bear her no ill will, then?"

"Why would I? She was always decent to me."

"If that's so, why would you try to get her involved in the party?"

"It's not like it's something dirty, you know; it's a political movement with an idealistic agenda."

"I know all about that, but you've already said Louise wasn't political."

"I guess I looked at it as doing her a favor. After the revolution, party membership would stand her in good stead."

"I guess you know that, in Hollywood, party membership has turned out to be something of a problem for a lot of people, people who are mostly out of work these days, some of them facing prison."

"Look, it's not my fault or the party's fault that the political system in this country screwed them."

"Let's not get into the rights and wrongs of what's happened; my only concern is Louise. I don't want any of these bad things to happen to her, especially since she's a complete innocent in all this."

"Nobody's innocent; you're on one side or the other."

"Do you want to hurt her?"

"Of course not."

"Do you want to help her?"

Schmidt shrugged. "Sure, but how do I do that?"

"By giving me some information."

"What do you want to know?"

"First of all, you admit that you signed her up for the party, and without her knowledge or consent?"

"Now you sound like a lawyer."

"Wrong again. The first thing I need from you is a written statement saying that you did this without her knowledge or consent."

"You want me to admit, in writing, that I'm a party member? You've just told me what happens to party members in this town."

"Hal, you've never made any secret of your party membership; why start now?"

"I'm being cautious."

"I don't want this statement so I can give it to the newspapers. I just want some protection for Louise, if it ever comes up."

"What else do you want?"

"I need a little inside knowledge of how the party works."

"You must have a screw loose, pal. I'm not here to be your political tutor."

"You misunderstand; let me explain."

"I'm listening."

"When you signed up Louise, the party office in Milwaukee kept her membership card in their files; she never saw it."

Schmidt shrugged. "Sometimes they do it that way."

"Well, a few weeks ago, somebody here in L.A. sent her employers photostatic copies of two party membership cards: one belonged to a man who has since been exposed as a party member and blacklisted; the other had Louise's name on it. Now, here's the interesting part: the guy who's been blacklisted was a member of the New York chapter or den or whatever you call it, and they kept his card on file. What I'm trying to get at is how two people from Milwaukee and New York—two different branches—have photostats of their membership cards turn up on the same desk at a movie studio in L.A.?"

Schmidt stared at Tom for a long time before he spoke. "That's a very interesting question, Tom. You work for the studio in question, is that it? That's why you drive such a nice car?"

"Yeah. I'm a regular capitalist tool."

Schmidt laughed.

"Look, I'm just a working stiff who's trying to keep a friend— one who used to be *your* friend—from getting hurt."

"Let me look into it. You got a phone number?"

Tom took out a notebook, wrote down his direct office number, tore it out and handed it to Schmidt. Schmidt tore the page in half and gave Tom his own number. "I'm there nights," he said. "Don't call me at the union office."

"Okay. Look, I'm happy you're willing to look into this, but don't roil the waters, okay? Be discreet."

Schmidt tossed off the rest of his drink and stood up. "Don't worry; I want answers just as much as you do. I'll call you, and thanks for the drink."

"Thanks, Hal. Maybe I'll be able to do you a favor one of these days."

"I doubt it," Schmidt said. He turned and walked out of the bar.

44

V ance Calder walked his struggling horse through the last yards of flank-deep snow, towing a pack mule. He pulled up in front of the little cabin, or perhaps shack would have been a better description. He dismounted and tried to open the front door, but snow prevented it from moving.

The handle of something protruded from the snow next to the door, and a few yanks revealed it to be the handle of a snow shovel. He used the tool to clear the area around the door, then got the door open and walked inside. He found a box of matches and lit a kerosene lantern hanging over a small table. The resulting light revealed the place to be more comfortable than he had imagined.

He went outside again and used the snow shovel to clear the doors of an attached shed. He led the animals inside, unsaddled them, rubbed them down, clearing the snow and ice from their hooves, then fed them and watered them from a pump. He closed the shed doors so the place would warm up from their heat, then returned to the cabin and began making himself comfortable. He got a fire going in the iron stove, using wood the previous occupant had chopped, and the one room began to warm up. He pumped some water and made coffee, setting the pot on the stove to boil when it got hot enough.

He opened the three-paned windows, pushed back the heavy wooden shutters, then closed the windows again. Now he had decent light. An hour later, when it was dark, he lit another lantern for light to read by.

He made his bed, and by the time he had heated a can of stew for his dinner, the cabin was toasty warm, its log walls sweating from their thawing. Dinner finished and the dishes washed and put away, Vance settled into the one comfortable chair and opened a book, taking a moment, since it was New Year's Eve, to wish himself a happy new year.

Then he began to weep, and he wept until there were no tears left. He dragged himself to the bed and pulled a blanket over him. He replayed the moments of his time with Susie in his head until he finally slept, then he dreamed of her.

When he woke the following dawn he felt better, and he began to try to draw a curtain on the recent past and think about the future instead.

Rick and Glenna arrived at Eddie and Suzanne Harris's home for the Harrises' annual New Year's Eve party, which had become a regular event for a hundred or so of their closest friends. It was a pleasantly warm L.A. evening, and dinner was from a huge buffet on the back terrace of the house, overlooking the pool, the tennis courts and the extensive gardens.

Rick was getting a drink from the bar when he bumped into Tom Terry, decked out in a new tuxedo. "Happy New Year, Tom," he said. "Are you partying or working?"

"I'm working," Tom said. "I've got a dozen guys here doing security, watching the front door and watching the valets." He pulled Rick away from the crowd at the bar. "Yesterday I had a drink with one Hal Schmidt, who turns out to be not such a bad guy."

"And what was the result of that?"

"Hal thought he might be able to find out something about how those party cards made it to your desk. I'm going to leave him to it until he calls me back or until a week has passed, whichever comes first. He admitted applying for membership in Glenna's name, and I think he'll give us a written statement to that effect, which we can put in the bank until it might become necessary to show to somebody."

"Don't waste any time getting that statement, Tom."

"Let's let it ride for a few days; I'd rather not push him, because I don't think he's the type to push easy."

"What's he doing in L.A.?"

"He's working for the extras' union."

"Doing what?"

"Well, we know about his background as a strike enforcer."

"But we have a new contract with that union."

"Maybe Hal has other talents I haven't discovered yet. Anyway, he could be a valuable guy to know; I intend to cultivate him."

"I guess it can't hurt."

"Well, I'd better get back to work," Tom said. "Happy New Year, Rick." He vanished into the crowd.

On the way back to the terrace Rick met Leo Goldman.

"This is my wife, Amanda," Leo said. "Amanda, this is one of my bosses, Rick Barron."

Amanda Goldman was small, pretty and smart-looking in a gown worthy of a movie star. "How do you do, Mr. Barron?" she said.

"It's Rick, please. We're all family at Centurion, aren't we, Leo?"

"Oh, sure," Leo said.

"How's my husband doing?" Amanda asked.

"He's doing very well," Rick said. "In fact, he impressed me so much with his work on *Bitter Creek* that I'm promoting him to production manager for the studio."

Leo nearly dropped his drink. "What did you say?"

"You heard me, Leo. Come see me Monday morning, and we'll work out your deal." He shook Amanda's hand again. "A pleasure to meet you, Amanda. Happy New Year to you both." He continued his walk to the back terrace, leaving a flabbergasted Leo Goldman in his wake.

Eddie and Suzanne Harris were talking with Glenna, and Eddie pulled him aside. "Some interesting news," he said. "I talked with Susie Stafford's mother this morning, and she's not bringing Susie's body back to Georgia for burial."

"That's surprising."

"Instead, she's instructing the funeral home here to have the body cremated and to turn the ashes over to a family friend."

"Anybody we know?" Rick was thinking Vance.

"The funeral director said it was confidential."

"I don't understand that; you'd think they'd want to bring her home."

"Someday, my friend, in the Great Beyond, all will be revealed to us. But probably not until then."

45

On the Monday morning after New Year's, Vance split logs to replace those he had burned, then cleaned the cabin, packed his mule, saddled his horse and made his way back down the trail. The ranch was spread out before him, and in the clear Wyoming air he thought he could see a hundred miles.

His mind was as clear as the air. He had read his book and Rick's script, explored the countryside on horseback and done what he could to place Susie's death in a different part of his head, one that did not occupy all his thoughts. The trip back to the ranch house took four hours, and he was there in time for lunch. After he had eaten, he called Rick Barron.

"Vance, how are you?"

"I'm very well, Rick. Coming up here was the perfect thing to do, and now I'm ready to come back."

"I'll have the Staggerwing at Jackson Airport in the early afternoon, tomorrow" Rick said.

"I read the script for *Greenwich Village Girl*, too, and I liked it. Who do you have in mind for the girl?"

"Eddie and I think a lot of a girl who's under contract to the studio. Her name is Hattie Carson. I'll show you a test she made when you get back."

"Fine. I'd like very much to see it. Who's producing?"

"I am, but I don't think I'll direct this one. We can talk about that when you get in. Why don't we have lunch in my office the day after tomorrow?"

"I'd like that."

"I don't know if you've heard from Hy Greenbaum, but he and Eddie have reached agreement on your new deal. You might want to speak with him before our lunch, so we can have that out of the way."

"I haven't talked to him, but I'll call him this afternoon."

"Great. The pilot will call the ranch tomorrow as soon as he lands. Oh, and I've dispatched a print of the film to the Coopers."

"I'll let them know, Rick."

"I'll see you on Wednesday, then."

"I look forward to it."

Vance hung up and started to think about work again.

E ddie came into Rick's office and sat down. "All hell has broken loose in the papers and the trades," he said.

"I know; they've been calling me all morning. I just had my secretary refer all the calls to Bart."

"He's issued statements, one for us and one for Vance, and told them that will be all."

"The LAPD will follow up with the press and keep them posted on leads. I think it's best if the studio just stays out of it."

"So do I. By the way, Leo and I have had our talk, and I think he has a thorough understanding of his place here. He knows he still works for you, although I'm sure he still covets your job."

"No," Rick said. "Leo covets *your* job."

"This is a big jump for such a young guy. He'll be our Irving Thalberg," Eddie said, referring to the former production head at MGM, who had died in his thirties.

"I didn't know Thalberg, but from what I've heard he and Leo have a lot of stylistic differences."

Eddie grinned. "I think you could say that."

"I heard from Vance. He'll be back tomorrow night, and we're having lunch on Wednesday. You want to join us?"

"Nah. You two have a lot to talk about. Did he read the script?"

"Yes, and he liked it."

"I was worried he wouldn't want to do it without Susie."

"He didn't mention Susie, but he asked who I had in mind. I think when he sees Hattie Carson's test, he'll like her."

"Good. We go into wide release on both *Bitter Creek* and *Times Square Dance* today. I can't wait to see our first week's grosses."

"Well, we've certainly milked every ounce of nationwide publicity; what with that and the reviews, we ought to do well."

"I'm counting on it," Leo said. "I want the profits from that picture to finance our move into television, and I hope the other picture will help, too."

"You really think it's not too early for that, Eddie?"

"Listen, kiddo, I'm told that industry-wide ticket sales were off twenty percent last year, and you can blame TV. The number of sets has doubled in the last year, and it's going to do even better next year. We did okay last year, with our ticket sales up about six percent, but we've got to catch the wave at the right moment, and that's now, while the other studios are still in denial and are dragging their feet."

"I had an idea for a show," Rick said.

"Tell me."

"I think we should get space in New York for a production facility and do live dramas of two hours. We can buy Broadway plays, maybe even do some classics. And I think we should commission original stuff, too. It might be a good testing ground for later feature pictures."

"I think that's a terrific idea, kiddo. I'm going to be in New York in a couple of weeks, and I'll feel out the networks. Have you given any thought about who should run it?"

"Yes, I have. I was thinking, maybe, Sid Brooks."

Eddie's eyebrows went up. "Have you talked with him about this?"

"No."

"Good, because the blacklist is in force in TV, too."

"Hy Greenbaum has managed to get some of his blacklisted clients rehabilitated."

"Yeah, I've heard about it. Are you thinking that after what Sid went through he would change his mind and do that?"

"Hy has told me he's trying to talk him into it. Maybe with something like this for an incentive, he'd do it. Also, maybe he doesn't want to go to prison."

"Does he know anything about TV?"

"No, but who does? They're making this up as they go along. Sid knows drama, and he's directed a couple of times on Broadway, and I've heard he's very good with actors. Certainly, his name on the show as, say, executive producer would attract a lot of good New York talent, actors and playwrights, too."

"Maybe you should have a discreet lunch with Sid sometime soon."

"Maybe I should," Rick said.

46

Rick stood up and walked around his desk to greet Vance Calder. "It's good to have you back, Vance," he said. "You look wonderful: tanned and rested."

Vance smiled, his new dental work set off against his tan. "I think that about sums it up."

"Before we sit down, I've got Hattie Carson's test put up in my screening room. Want to take a look?"

"Of course."

Rick led him into the little room; they sat down and Rick picked up the phone next to his chair. "All right," he said.

The test, consisting of three scenes, began to run. Once in a while Rick glanced at Vance, but he got no reading. Then it was done, and the lights came up.

"What do you think?" Rick asked.

"I think she's awfully good; I'd love to have her on the picture."

"Great," Rick said, relieved. Vance was now in a position to insist on a big star opposite him, and the studio would save a lot of money by using a contract player. "Let's have lunch."

They went back into Rick's office, where the studio commissary had set up a table, and sat down. A waiter began serving them. When he had gone, Rick asked, "Did you speak with Hy about your new contract?"

"Oh, yes," Vance replied, "I almost forgot. I signed it this morning, and Hy is messengering over all the copies. I'm very pleased."

"I'm glad, Vance."

"I was particularly pleased that you and Eddie forgave the loan on the house. That's a big load off my mind."

"Do you think you'll be happy there?"

"I think so, but my ultimate ambition is to build somewhere. When I worked in construction I liked seeing other people's houses go up, and I thought I'd like to invent my own place."

"That's a great idea. You'll enjoy it," Rick said. "Our place at the beach will be ready to move into soon, and we're looking forward to it." Rick took a more serious tone. "Vance, I'm sure that Hy has told you that this is an extraordinarily rich deal for an actor who's made one picture."

"I understand that."

"The reason we did it is that we not only like your work, but we admire the seriousness with which you approach it. We think you have a long and successful career ahead of you, and we want it to take place at Centurion."

"I'd be very pleased if I never made a picture anywhere else," Vance said. "All you have to do is keep Hyman Greenbaum happy."

"We'll try. What we want to do for the next couple of years is create properties for you that are not only quality pictures but also ones that show your versatility."

Vance grinned. "How do you know I'm versatile? I've just made the one."

"I know," Rick said. "Your test showed me your versatility, and I liked it that a lot of the press who interviewed you during our recent publicity blast were surprised to learn that you are English. I mean, other actors with accents, like Errol Flynn, have made westerns, but they never sounded American. The press and the critics loved that."

"I'm glad. Tell me, Rick, why don't you want to direct *Greenwich Village Girl*?"

"Two reasons: first I don't think I have the background and experience to direct a fast-paced comedy; second, I've promoted Leo Goldman to production manager for the whole studio, working under me, and I want to be around to help him find his feet. It won't take Leo long, believe me, and by the time you're done with this picture, I should be ready to direct the next one."

"Any idea what you want that to be?"

"Glenna read a novel that she liked, and I agree with her. It's a serious drama, very suspenseful, and I think it might be the perfect follow-up to the comedy. It's called *Deep Night*, by a first-time novelist. Hy Greenbaum is touting a new writer of his up in Maine to adapt it."

Vance managed a small smile. "Maine, huh?"

Rick smiled, too. "We all know it's Sid Brooks, but under the present circumstances, we mustn't know. Hy has hopes of persuading Sid to purge himself in a second appearance before the committee and get off the blacklist."

"I hope he'll do that," Vance said.

"So do I. I'm having dinner with him tonight to talk to him about it."

They met at Bennie's and sat in a rear booth, out of sight of the bar. They shook hands warmly and ordered drinks.

"I'm glad to see you looking well, Sid," Rick said.

"Thanks, Rick. I'm getting by, but at a time in my life when I thought I wouldn't be just getting by."

"I hope that will improve," Rick said.

They ordered the steaks.

"So," Sid said, "why are we having this dinner?"

"Oh, I just wanted to be sure you're eating, Sid."

Sid laughed. "Come on, Rick; we both know what this is about: you're in league with Hy."

"Why do you suppose that is, Sid? I mean, Centurion can go on buying your scripts from Hy, all written under assumed names, and for half what we'd usually pay you. You think we have ulterior motives? Just the opposite, I can tell you. Eddie and I want you back working under your own name, winning Oscars and prospering."

"Leo Goldman doesn't," Sid said.

"Have you had some kind of contact with Leo?"

"No, the only kind of contact people like me have with Leo is when we feel the back of his hand. I hear you've given him a big new job."

"I gave Leo the job because he'll be good at it, not because I agree with his political views. I don't want to go on supervising every production; I want to produce and direct my own projects. I've learned that I'm happiest doing that, and I want some of them to be your projects."

"Thank you, Rick. I know you're nothing like Leo."

"Listen, Leo is the kind of guy who, once you've put all this behind you, will be delighted to work with you again."

"Yeah, he just goes with the flow."

"Let me give you something new to think about, Sid."

"What's that?"

"We're going to make a big push in television, starting this year."

"I think that's smart, Rick. The Supreme Court decision that made the studios sell their theaters is going to wreck the business as we know it."

"Well, since we didn't own any theaters, it can only help us. But let me tell you what I'm thinking about."

"All right."

"I want us to produce a series of live two-hour dramas in New York, with top actors and writers. Eddie is going to be talking to the networks about it soon, when he's in New York."

"I think that's a great idea, Rick, to have some quality entertainment, instead of the schlock that's on TV now."

"This is all speculative at the moment, but if it happens, I think it will happen fast. What I'd like is for you to run the thing as executive producer and to write some things for it as well as direct from time to time."

"But, Rick, the blacklist is, if anything, worse in TV than in pictures. I would . . ." Sid stopped talking. "Oh, I get it."

"Do you?"

"If I purge myself before the committee and get off the blacklist, then I can do it openly, using my own name."

"You get it."

"Yeah. I not only have a stick behind me—the possibility of going to prison—now you and Hy have given me a carrot out front."

"I haven't even talked to Hy about this, but yes, and it's a pretty good carrot, don't you think? It's a way to produce a lot of good work in a comparatively short time . . ."

"And to rehabilitate myself in the eyes of the studios."

"Right. I think it might even be a good idea if you could find an anti-Communist property you could write and direct, one that you could live with, morally."

Sid poked at his steak. "Well, if nothing else, Rick, you've shown me what I'm missing by sticking with the party crowd."

"What I want for you, Sid, is what you once had, plus a great deal more. You have a fine talent, one that shouldn't be squelched, and you have the capacity to do even better work."

"I'm going to have to think about this, because I won't be able to get it out of my mind. It's a big step, and a complete break with my past."

"It's going to cost you some friends, Sid, but eventually make you some new ones. Why don't you do this: talk with Hy, and let him meet with these people and see what kind of a deal he can come up with. Once you know exactly what's expected of you, then you can make an informed decision about what to do."

Sid sighed. "All right, Rick. I guess I can do that without committing to anything."

"Good. By the way, I'm sending Hy a novel I'd like that client of his in Maine to adapt. It's called *Dark Night*."

"I'm sure he could do that; dark night is where he is right now."

"There's a sunrise around the corner, Sid."

"We'll see."

47

Tom Terry pulled into a parking space in front of Jimmy's, a cop bar on Melrose, hopped out of the car and walked into the joint, looking for Lieutenant Ben Morrison.

"I'm right behind you," Ben said, poking him between the shoulder blades with a finger.

"Don't shoot until I've had a drink," Tom said. They found a booth and ordered.

"How's the picture business?" Ben asked.

"I think it must be okay, but somehow I don't think of myself as being in the picture business. I'm something else; I'm not sure what."

"Private eye? Philip Marlowe?"

"Hired gun, jack-of-all-trades . . . I don't know. Every day is different."

"That can't be bad; it's what I've always thought was the best thing about being a cop."

"Don't get me wrong; I'm not complaining. I really like the work. I just never know what it's going to be. At least, they haven't asked me to kill anybody."

"Well, you may have to kill Hank Harmon, if you want justice for your girl."

"What are you talking about, Ben?"

"I'm talking about having no case against her. I can't prove she's not telling the truth."

"Have you talked to her again?"

"She came in yesterday with her lawyer and allowed us to print her."

"And?"

"And her prints are not a match for the ones we got out of Susie's car. One set was Susie's—we got them off her corpse—but the other? Who knows? Close your mouth; it's hanging open."

"Did you check her arms and chest for scratches or scarring?"

"Yep. Nothing there."

"I don't believe it."

"Neither did I. Like you, I made her for the crime right off."

"Holy shit. I pretty much promised my people that Harmon would go up for murder."

"Not unless we get a major break. A witness that saw her dump the body would do nicely."

"How about a witness that saw her walking home from Vance Calder's house?"

"That would be a big help, but we've come up dry there. None of our patrol cars or the Beverly Hills department's saw anybody like her. We even talked with the garbage truck drivers on that route. Nothing."

"Ben, it's not like she planned every detail of this. She came home, found Susan there and went nuts: beat her up, hit her over the head and strangled her. Spur-of-the-moment murders are untidy; the killer *always* makes a mistake, usually several mistakes."

"You're reading from my book," Morrison said. "I'm with you all the way. I'm just telling you that, if that's the way it happened, the Harmon girl, once she'd killed her girlfriend, did absolutely everything right. Or maybe she's just very, very lucky."

"Nobody's that lucky," Tom said. "Was there anything at Calder's house besides the prints in Susan's car?"

"We got Harmon's permission to search her place, and we had a dozen guys go over it; didn't find a thing."

"What about at Vance Calder's place?"

"Same there. Oh, there was one odd item that cropped up."

"Tell me."

"The place is beautifully gardened, you know? Lovely plantings, everything kept in tip-top shape by a Japanese gardener."

"Yeah. I saw it."

"Well, there was one anomaly: around to one side of the house, next to the garage doors, there was a thick bed of ferns. It looked like something big had wallowed in it, like a deer had slept there."

"A deer? In Beverly Hills?"

"All right. Maybe a bum caught a night's sleep there; what do I know? Something mashed down the ferns, messed them up good. The gardener replaced them after we released the premises; it looks like before, now."

"Makes no sense."

"You're telling me."

"It's a shame Harmon went for a lawyer; I'll bet she would have broken, if you'd sweated her."

"Maybe, but she's a very cool customer." He paused. "Or she's innocent."

"My money's on cool."

"It's your money."

"Ben, the papers haven't said much about Harmon; maybe it's time her cover was blown."

"Cover?"

"She's a dyke, for Christ's sake. She's got stuff to hide."

"I guess, but maybe your girl Susie had stuff to hide, too. I mean, she lived with Harmon for several months, and I'm sure you noticed there was only one bed in the apartment. You think your studio would want that sort of thing brought out about their dead movie star?"

Tom sighed. "You're right; any heat we brought on Harmon would land on Susan, too, and my studio definitely would not like that. Her picture just went into wide release."

"What's wide release?"

"Sorry, that's studio speak. The picture opened at Christmas in four cities, so it would be eligible for Academy Awards. 'Wide release' means it opened all over the country, probably a couple of thousand theaters."

"Look, Tom, even if Harmon did it, it's not like she's a danger to the public. She had her heart broken when her girlfriend jumped ship for a guy, and she reacted badly. She's not going wild in the streets. She's gainfully employed at RKO, and the people she works with like her."

"Management wouldn't like her if they knew she was a dyke."

"Aw, c'mon. If any studio started firing three-dollar bills, they wouldn't have any people left to make the pictures. The last thing they'd want is to have a spotlight thrown on who's queer in the business, and that's all firing her would accomplish. As it is, even the scum at *Confidential* haven't managed to scrape up enough for a story, let alone a cover. I hear they've given up."

"Was there anything new in the final M.E.'s report?"

Morrison shrugged. "There were some signs of sexual assault. There was some bruising in the anus, and something that might have been a human bite on her vulva. They can't be sure about that; it might have been an injury when the body was being disposed of."

"You mean she had something up the ass, and somebody bit her pussy? Is that a dyke thing?"

"Well, I'm told the girls use dildos from time to time, but we found nothing of that sort in Harmon's apartment. As to biting, I've seen that a fair amount in regular folks."

"Did you talk to any of her other girlfriends?"

Morrison shook his head. "It's a tight-knit sisterhood," he said. "Nobody talks about nothing. All we got was what a great gal ol' Hank is."

"Well, shit," Tom said.

"Yeah," Morrison replied.

48

Sidney Brooks and Hyman Greenbaum arrived at the Beverly Hills Hotel half an hour early for their appointment.

"Let's get a cup of coffee," Hy said and led Sid into the Polo Lounge.

Sid had not set foot in the place since his appearance before the committee, and he did not particularly want to be seen there today, but it was midmorning, between the breakfast and lunch crowds, and the room was nearly deserted. They ordered coffee.

Sid was very uncomfortable about what was coming; he had wrestled with himself about it, and finally he had been able to rationalize what he was doing. Hy had already talked to the Motion Picture Industry Council, a committee that was the first step in the rehabilitation of a blacklistee. Hy said that some of its members had known Sid and thought well of him and that they were all decent men.

"Sid," Hy said, "I've been talking with these people for weeks now, on the behalf of one client or another—sometimes on behalf of just friends—and I've found them to be reasonable. They're FBI agents, for the most part, or ex-agents; they're just doing a job, and they're not anti-Communist nuts."

"I'm glad to hear it," Sid said.

"When you talk to them, don't be confrontational."

"I'm not normally a confrontational person, Hy."

"I know that, but it won't do your case any good to get angry and upset."

"Are they going to try to upset me?"

"Probably not. Try and give complete answers to their questions without running off at the mouth. Don't give them just yes and no; that would make it seem like you had something to hide."

"Okay. I can do that."

"If they ask you a question you don't know the answer to, just say that, but if you know the answer, tell it truthfully. You're not going to be under oath, that's part of the deal I worked out, but if you lie to them it could well come back to haunt you."

"I understand."

Hy looked at his watch and called for the check. "This is not going to be all over today; this is just the next step, but it's a big one. These people have to be able to go back to the committee with an outline of the testimony you're going to give. After your testimony, we'll still need to do some PR. You're not going to wake up the next morning off the blacklist; it will take time, but it will happen."

They walked into the back garden of the hotel, where the hotel's most private quarters, the cottages, were located, and Hy led him to a door and rang the bell. The door was opened by a man in shirt sleeves and a tie and suspenders.

He smiled, "Good morning, Hy. Thanks for coming."

"Good morning, Roy. May I introduce Sid Brooks?"

"Hi, Sid. How are you?" Roy said. "Come on in. Would you fellows like some coffee?"

"We've just had some, thanks," Hy said. "I see you're comfortably quartered here."

"Oh, we've just been loaned the place for the day."

Roy led them into the living room, where three other men were seated. They all stood up and shook hands politely when introduced. Sid immediately forgot their names.

"Have a seat, fellows," Roy said. When they were all settled, Roy began. "Sid, Hy has told me that you're ready to talk to us as part of the rehabilitation process. What we want to do this morning is to listen to your story and let you know what's expected of you."

"Thanks," Sid said. "I'd certainly like to know that."

"We realize that you may feel that you're informing on your peers, but I hope by the time we're through, you'll feel better about it. Your testimony before the committee last time was very brief, and that's a good thing, because you won't be in danger of contradicting yourself. Now, let's begin by asking you some of the questions that you might be asked during your testimony. You're not under oath; this is all very informal. From time to time, we may interrupt you with suggestions about the way you couch your answers."

"All right."

"Sid, when and where did you first join the Communist Party?"

"In 1935, in New York."

"What were your reasons for joining?"

"Well, we were in the depths of a terrible depression, and things were very bad. I suppose I had the feeling that things weren't working as well as they should in the country, and the party seemed to offer an alternative to the Republicans and the Democrats. Their proposals seemed to me idealistic. For instance, I was attracted to their position on racial equality."

"All right, Sid. Let's remember that some of the committee members, like Congressman John Wood of Georgia, are not going to be receptive to comments about the lack of racial equality in this country, so in answering, you might want to avoid mentioning that."

"All right."

The questioning continued for more than an hour, with occasional comments from the men present. Sid found their suggestions helpful. Finally, Roy handed Sid a sheet of paper with six names typed on it.

"As Hy has no doubt told you, you're going to have to identify some of the people you met at party functions," he said. "We'd like to suggest these names, all of which are already known to the committee."

Sid looked at the list. Three of the names were New Yorkers, and another three were living in California. "All these names are familiar to me," he said. "I met the first three in New York at party-sponsored social events; the last three were all among the nineteen who were originally subpoenaed."

"Are you personally acquainted with them all?"

"Yes, though I've never been close to any of them."

"Are they all members of the Communist Party?"

"You have to understand that when you meet people at party-sponsored events, no one ever says to you that he's a Communist."

"Have you ever attended a formal party meeting where any of these people were present?"

"I was at a meeting where the first man was present," Sid said.

"Are you willing to testify to that?"

"I suppose so."

"What about the others?"

"The other two New York names were commonly thought of by the people I knew as party members, but remember, no one ever flashed a membership card. In fact, I was never given my party card; it was held in the local organization's files."

"All right. We understand that. In fact, we've seen a photostat of your party card; don't ask how."

This surprised Sid, but he didn't say so.

"What about the three from California? Were you ever in a party meeting with them?"

"Yes, all three, but the meetings were held after we were subpoenaed, for the sole purpose of discussing our legal defense. Actually, after I came to California, I never attended a regular party meeting. I drifted away from the party."

"All right, let's do this; give us an account of each party-sponsored function—cocktails, even—where you saw any of these individuals."

Sid wracked his brain and managed to come up with some answers. "Some of these things were fund-raisers for Soviet relief during the war, when the Russians were our allies. Sometimes petitions were circulated."

"Sid, were you acquainted with the actor Alan James before his death?"

"Yes. We were in the theater together in New York; he appeared in leading roles in two of my plays there."

"To your knowledge, was Alan James a member of the Communist Party?"

"Yes. He was. We both joined at the same meeting."

"Did you continue to be close to him after he came to California?"

"No. Alan came before I did and established himself sooner. We didn't often work on the same productions, and we just drifted apart, I guess you'd say."

"Was Alan James a hard-core Communist?"

"No. I'd call Al more of a social Communist. I think he joined mostly because people he knew were party members."

"Did you have occasion to see him shortly before his death?"

"Yes. We had dinner the evening before he died. He called and suggested we meet for dinner."

"What was the subject of your conversation that evening?"

"Alan had decided to become a friendly witness, but he was very conflicted about it."

"Was he considering not testifying in a friendly manner?"

"No. I think he was fully committed to testifying, but he felt badly about naming friends of his."

"Do you know if you were one of the friends he would have named?"

"Yes. He told me that. I think he felt he owed me an explanation before he named me."

"Did you part on good terms?"

"Al got very drunk at dinner, and I had to drive him home and put him to bed. He was in no condition to be on either good or bad terms. Apparently, he woke up the following morning and ended his life."

"Do you think he felt guilty about becoming a party member, or guilty about naming people he knew?"

"I think he was guilty about both."

"The committee would probably prefer it if you emphasized his guilt over party membership."

"I'm sorry, I can't do that."

"Why not?"

"Because I don't think he felt all *that* guilty about joining. I believe he took his own life because he didn't want to be thought of as an informer by his friends."

"Can you shade that a bit in your testimony?"

"I was told not to lie to you today; I haven't."

Roy made a note on a pad, then he leaned forward, his elbows on his knees. "Sid, was your wife, Alice, a party member?"

"No. She was not."

"Was she a sympathizer?"

"No. She attended one or two of the fund-raisers with me, but she never approved of the party. She tried very hard to get me to be a friendly witness before the committee. When I failed to do so, she filed for divorce."

Roy smiled. "That's pretty much what she told our investigators in New York."

Sid was stunned. "I had no idea your people had talked with her; we've been out of touch since we separated. All our conversations have been through lawyers since that time."

Roy smiled. "All right, Sid. I'm pleased to tell you that all of the answers you've given us today are consistent with the information we have from other sources. If you're willing to testify before the committee again, along the lines of what you've said here today, I and my colleagues are willing to submit your name to the committee as a friendly witness."

Hy spoke for the first time. "That's good news, Roy. Thank you all for your help."

After a round of handshakes and good-byes, Sid and Hy left the cottage.

"That wasn't so bad, was it?"

"It could have been worse," Sid said.

49

Tom Terry walked into the restaurant and looked around. A man waved at him from a table, and he walked over and shook his hands. "Hello, Jake. I'm Tom Terry."

Jake Connor shook the hand. "Sit down, Tom." Connor was Tom's opposite number at RKO, their head of security. "Have a drink?" There was a glass of brown whiskey before him.

"Sure. I'll have a Wild Turkey and water."

Jake waved down a waiter, ordered the drink and asked for menus. "How are you enjoying life at Centurion? You've been there a while, haven't you?"

"I like it a lot," Tom replied. "I replaced Rick Barron when he left for the navy in '42."

"You didn't get caught in the draft?"

Tom shook his head. "I was a flatfoot who really had flat feet. How about you?"

"I joined the Marines, but I blew a knee in basic training and got a medical discharge. I guess we were both lucky, eh?"

"Well, we're both alive."

They ordered lunch.

"You've got a good reputation around town, Tom."

"So do you."

"So, we're both good at our jobs. I guess the blacklist is giving you problems, just like me."

"It hasn't been too bad; Centurion has fewer people under contract than most studios, so maybe that's helped."

"Yeah, I guess it would."

"Were you ever a cop, Jake?"

"Yeah, I was a detective with the Long Beach department, burglary and vice mostly. You were with Beverly Hills, weren't you?"

"Yeah, I was in a patrol car."

Lunch came, and they began to eat.

"What did you want to talk about, Tom?"

"First of all, this is off the record, under the table, whatever you want to call it. You can use what I tell you, but you can't tell *anybody* where it came from."

"I guess I can live with that. What's up?"

"One of your studio's employees is a murderer."

Connor's eyebrows went up. "Only one?"

"Only one, that I know of, who's both a murderer and a lesbo."

"Well, Tom, I guess you know that the picture business, in general, is pretty loose about who puts what, where, in the sack. Unless she wears a crew cut and carries a whip, or makes a major pass at a female star who doesn't share her inclination, her dykeness is likely to be overlooked."

"Is murder likely to be overlooked?"

"Is this about the Susan Stafford case?"

"Yes, it is."

"And Hank Harmon?"

"Yep."

"I don't really know the girl, but I've seen her around the lot. Ben Morrison at the LAPD made a courtesy call on me when he first questioned her, but it's my understanding that she has been eliminated as a suspect."

Tom shook his head. "Don't you believe it. I had lunch with Ben a couple of days ago, and she's still right at the top of the list. In fact, hers is the only name *on* the list."

"I thought she had an alibi."

"Not one that covers the time in question. Her story was that she went to the farmer's market, and that was confirmed by witnesses, but the case theory is that she returned to the apartment in time to catch Stafford there. Do you know the story of their relationship?"

"You mean that beautiful girl was in the sack with Hank?"

"Stafford lived with her for four or five months. I took a good look around Harmon's place, and there was only one bed. When Susan came to work on *Bitter Creek,* she took up with her leading man, and, by all accounts, they fell in love. She was moving her stuff out of Hank's apartment and into her costar's place when Hank came home and caught her leaving. She beat up Stafford, knocked her unconscious, then strangled her. Late that night she drove the body, in Stafford's car, way out Mulholland and dumped it on a trash pile, then she left the car at the leading man's house and walked home. She did a good job of cleaning up after herself, too."

"You've been following Morrison's investigation, then?"

"He's been following mine; I was the first person to talk to Hank. I made her as guilty in a ten-minute interview, and if she hadn't lawyered up so fast, Ben would have sweated it out of her."

"But there's no physical evidence to put her in Hank's apartment, is there?"

"We don't need that evidence; Hank *admits* the girl was there and left her a note, but says she was already gone when she got home."

"Have you seen the note?"

"Nah. She says she threw it away, but you can bet your ass it was a 'Dear Mary' letter. The fact that Susan was leaving her for a *man* pushed Hank over the edge."

"But Morrison doesn't have any hard evidence?"

"No witnesses, no blood on the floor, no prints in Susan's car. Let me ask you something, Jake: when you were working in Long Beach didn't you learn to read a suspect?"

"Yeah, I did, and I don't think I was ever wrong about one. Couldn't always prove it, but I knew."

"I knew right away that Harmon killed Susan Stafford, and so did Ben Morrison; we just haven't been able to prove it yet."

"What are you asking me to do about this, Tom?"

"I'm not asking you to do anything, Jake. I just want to give you something to think about."

Jake toyed with his food.

"Talk to Harmon yourself; see what *you* think."

Jake shook his head. "Nah. She's had plenty of time to get her story straight."

"Yes, she has. Look, I don't know what your management is like, but I can tell you that if *my* management knew that there was a homicidal dyke working on our lot, she wouldn't be there another minute, and she wouldn't walk away with a fulsome letter of recommendation."

"I don't think my management would like it much, either," Connor said.

"There's another factor."

"What?"

"If Harmon was out on the street and unemployable, she'd be pretty pissed off, wouldn't she?"

"Sure. I expect so."

"And in that frame of mind, with pressure on her, she'd be more likely to make a mistake, maybe cry on somebody's shoulder."

Connor nodded. "Probably so."

"Jake, my people at the studio are really hurting about this situation. The girl has parents back in Georgia, and she was the light of their life. She's gone from being a brand-new movie star to being dumped, dead, on a trash pile, and from her family's point of view, nobody's doing anything about it."

"Shit," Connor said, "if I were in your shoes I'd probably take her out somewhere and put a slug in her head."

"Believe me, that crossed my mind, and I haven't ruled it out yet, but I want to give the system a chance to work."

"I see your point."

"Well, Jake, it was good to meet you," Tom said, putting down his napkin "Let me get lunch."

"Nah. It's on me," Connor replied. They shook hands. "Let me see what I can do."

"It's probably better if we don't speak again for a while," Tom said, rising from the table. "But after some time has passed, I'll buy lunch."

"We should keep in touch, anyway," Connor said.

Tom walked back to his car, knowing he had planted a ticking bomb under Hank Harmon.

50

Rick was working on the budget for *Greenwich Village Girl* when Eddie Harris came through their connecting door, through their shared screening room, holding a newspaper in his hand.

"Have you seen this?" he asked.

"I read it at breakfast."

"Then you saw Hopper."

"Saw her column; didn't read it."

"It's written as a news story under Hopper's byline. Listen to this, Rick: 'A script supervisor at RKO, linked by police to the brutal murder of Susan Stafford, the beautiful young costar of Centurion's huge hit, *Bitter Creek,* has been unceremoniously fired by RKO. No one in management there would confirm the reason for the firing, but speculation has increased that the LAPD is closer to an arrest. Henrietta Harmon, known as "Hank," was escorted off the RKO lot by security officers at the close of business yesterday.

"'Harmon was the first person investigated by police after Susan Stafford disappeared, and after Stafford's body was found at a garbage dump, a search warrant was obtained and detectives searched Harmon's apartment. They found no evidence of the murder, but a source at the LAPD has told this reporter that the place had been thoroughly cleaned before their arrival. This reporter has also learned that Harmon disappeared after initially being questioned, and police believe that she did so in order to allow cuts and scratches that she would have received during the killing to heal. The coroner's report states that Stafford fought for her life.

"'When Harmon returned to Los Angeles she hired a criminal lawyer who refused to allow police to question her further. Knowledgeable sources tell me that new evidence is being developed that will further link Henrietta "Hank" Harmon to the killing of Susan Stafford, and that an arrest is imminent.'"

"You know anything about this, Rick?"

"First I've heard of it."

"Well, I didn't plant it, either, but I'm glad there's nothing about a lesbian affair. Did you get a call from Hopper, asking for confirmation?"

"No, but there isn't anything in that story that I could have confirmed, except that Susie is dead."

"This thing smells planted," Eddie said. "I asked Bart Crowther if he had anything to do with it, and he denied planting the story."

"It could very well have been planted by somebody at RKO or somebody at the LAPD."

"Well, I hope it's true."

"So do I."

V ance Calder packed the last of Susie's clothes in a cardboard box and stacked it on top of the box she had left in her dressing room the day she went missing. He carried the two boxes downstairs to the kitchen, where his housekeeper, Maria, was sewing a button on one of his shirts, and set them on the table.

"Maria, these are some things that belonged to Miss Stafford," he said. "If there's anything you want, or if you know anyone who might need the clothes, please take them. Anything else you can drop off at a Salvation Army store on your way home tonight."

"Thank you, Mr. Calder," Maria said. "And I'll put your shirt back in your dressing room in just a moment."

Vance walked through the house to the study; his new desk had arrived the day before, Sid Brooks having taken the old one, and he began putting office supplies that he had brought from the studio into the drawers. With the help of the studio's design department he had replaced the furniture that Sid or his ex-wife had removed, and the living room had been painted a warm yellow. He had begun to feel that the place belonged to him and no one else.

Maria knocked at the door.

"Yes, Maria?"

She walked in and handed him a blue-velvet jewelry box. "This was in the bottom of the carton with the sweaters, Mr. Calder."

"Thank you, Maria." She left, and Vance opened the box. It contained a pair of small, diamond ear studs, along with a Bulova wristwatch and a couple of brooches. Also in the box was a gold, heart-shaped locket on a matching chain.

Vance picked up the locket and pressed the clasp. Inside, was a photograph of Susie with another girl, who Vance assumed was Hank Harmon. Both women appeared to be naked, at least from the waist up. Susie was leaning against Harmon, wrapped in her arms. One hand was resting on Harmon's left breast. On the other side of the open locket was engraved an inscription: "Susie and Hank, one forever."

Vance closed the locket and put it back in the box. He thought for a minute, then he picked up the phone and called Centurion Studios. "This is Vance Calder," he said to the operator. "Will you please connect me with Tom Terry in security?"

"Of course, Mr. Calder."

A moment later, Terry was on the line. "Hello, Vance. Can I help you?"

"I need some advice, Tom. I gave some clothes that belonged to Susie Stafford to my housekeeper, and in one of the boxes she found a jewelry case that contained, among other things, a locket holding a rather . . . affectionate photograph of Susie and a woman I assume to be Hank Harmon. I don't think I want to send the photograph to her parents. My question is: what should I do with it?"

"You should give it to the police, Vance. I'll call the detective in charge of the investigation and let him know about it. I expect he'll send someone over to get the locket."

"Thanks, Tom. Did you see the item in the paper this morning by Hedda Hopper?"

"Yes, I did, and I think it's a good one."

"Do you think they're near an arrest?"

"If they are, they must have some new information I'm not privy to. I'll call Lieutenant Morrison now; I expect you'll hear from him soon."

"Thank you, Tom. I'll wait to hear from him."

B en Morrison was at his door half an hour later. Vance let him in and shook his hand.

"We met once before, Mr. Calder," Morrison said.

"I remember; at my bungalow at the studio. Come into the study; the jewelry box is there."

Morrison followed him into the study, and Vance handed the velvet box to him. He sat down, opened the box and examined the locket carefully. "This is very interesting," he said.

"It doesn't seem like a crucial piece of evidence, does it?" Vance asked.

"It could be valuable, in that it helps establish the relationship between the two women."

"I'd hate for that photograph to be displayed in open court; so would her parents, I think."

"I can keep it out of the papers, but when we go to trial, I'm sure it will be placed in evidence. There's nothing I can do to prevent that, except extract a confession from Miss Harmon, and I don't think her lawyer is going to let her do that."

"I saw something in the papers this morning that implied you are close to an arrest."

"I saw that, too, Mr. Calder. It didn't come from me, and I doubt that it came from any of my people. My best guess is that it came from RKO."

"Are you close to arresting Hank Harmon?"

"No, sir, we're not, but please don't tell anyone I said that."

"Do you feel any need to correct the newspaper account?"

"Oh, I don't think so," Morrison said. "Maybe it will stir the pot a little. You never know."

"I hope so," Vance said. "When you're finished with the jewelry, would you return it to Susie's parents? Not the photograph; I don't think they should see that."

"Of course, I'd be glad to." Morrison stood and offered his hand. "I'll let you know if we come up with anything new."

"Thank you, Lieutenant." Vance showed him to the door, then returned to his study and sank into a chair. Once again, he drove the recurring thought from his mind that he should buy a gun and shoot Hank Harmon. He made himself calm again, as best he could.

51

Tom Terry sat in his car across the street from Hank Harmon's apartment house and watched a passel of photographers and reporters mill around. The shades were drawn on Harmon's windows upstairs, and there was no sign of life.

Then Tom saw a prewar Chevrolet convertible, with the top up, edge out of the parking lot behind the building, driven by a woman. He wasn't sure it was Harmon, but he was going to find out.

The Chevy turned up the hill, away from Sunset and the photographers, and accelerated. Tom started his car and followed, staying well back. The car made a couple of turns, then headed back toward Sunset. Tom made a note of the plate number and followed. The convertible turned up Coldwater Canyon and began climbing the mountain. As it crested the ridge at the top, it pulled over, and the top went down. Hank Harmon was at the wheel, and she seemed to believe that she had gotten away from her pursuers. She started down the other side of the mountain and into the San Fernando Valley.

Tom followed her for another twenty minutes, until she turned into a residential neighborhood and then into a driveway. He stopped down the block and watched her get out of the car, take a couple of suitcases from the trunk, ring the doorbell, then go inside. Tom made a note of the address.

He made a U-turn and, back on the main road, found a phone booth. He called the city desk of the newspaper that had run the Hopper piece about Harmon and, without giving his name, gave the man who answered the make, model and license plate number of Harmon's car and the address of the house she had run to, then he got back into his car and drove back to L.A. As he came over the mountain he passed the car of a photographer he knew, going the other way. His work was done, for now.

He had another date, though. He drove to the bar where he had first met with Hal Schmidt of Milwaukee, went inside, took a booth and ordered a drink. Schmidt was ten minutes late. He slid into the booth, and Tom signaled the waiter for one more drink.

"How you been, Hal? Settling into L.A.?"

"I've been well, thanks, Tom, and I'm enjoying the city. The quality of the women is a definite improvement over Milwaukee."

"I can believe that. You want some dinner?"

"Sure."

Tom picked up the menus along the wall and handed Schmidt one. They ordered dinner and another drink.

"I guess you're wondering why I called," Schmidt said, looking pleased with himself.

"Yeah, I am," Tom replied.

"I've got something for you on those party membership cards your boss received."

"I'm all ears."

"I guess you know my boss at the union is a party member."

"I figured. He's also chummy with the mob, you know."

"Yeah, I've met Mickey Cohen in the office."

"Seems like he's working both sides of the street," Tom said.

"The party is not above dealing with anybody it finds useful," Schmidt replied.

"You want to be careful with Cohen," Tom said. "He's easy to get chummy with but hard to shake, and he can play rough."

"That's good advice I already gave myself," Schmidt said. "As I was saying, the party will deal with anybody it can use. I made a call to Milwaukee, to a guy I used to know who ran the local office, until recently. A few weeks ago, he heard from a guy at the union named Murray Fox. Now Murray used to live in Milwaukee, too, back when Louise and I were seeing each other, and he knew about my signing her up for the party. He asked my buddy to photostat her party card and send it to him."

"Aha," Tom said. "Progress. Did he give it to somebody at Centurion?"

"Hang on; I'm not finished. About three months ago, the party sent Murray to New York for some special indoctrination. They do that from time to time. He was based in the local office there, and he would have had access to the membership files. Now, I don't know for a fact that he was the one who copied the other guy's card, but he's a very good bet."

"Okay. Let's assume he got hold of both Louise's and the other guy's cards. Who did he give them to?"

"Hang onto your hat, Tom."

"Come on, Hal; the suspense is killing me."

"He gave them to Leo Goldman."

Tom sat back and shook his head. "That doesn't make any sense at all, Hal. We both know that Goldman is playing for the other team. How would he even know this Murray Fox?"

"He doesn't know him; Murray just mailed the two photostats to Goldman."

"This still doesn't make any sense, Hal."

"It does if you know how the party works, and you obviously don't."

"God knows, that's true."

"I already told you the party would use anybody to further its ends, right?"

"Right."

"Well, for some reason not known to me or, probably, to Murray either, the party wanted it known that Louise and your other guy . . . what's his name?"

"Sidney Brooks."

"Yeah, Sidney Brooks, the writer. For some reason, the party wanted it known that these two people are party members."

"But why would they want that? You'd think they'd protect their members."

"This was around the time when the subpoenas went out, wasn't it?"

"Yeah. I guess it was."

"Well, try this for a scenario: the party knows HUAC is investigating Hollywood, and they don't necessarily view that as a bad thing. Maybe they want it known that prominent members of the Hollywood community are Communists or fellow travelers, because it makes the party look good for the public to know that well-known Americans in a glamorous field see things the party's way."

"Boy, if I was a Communist Party official, that's not how I would run things. Don't they have any interest in protecting their members?"

"Not necessarily. You remember how the hearings went, right?"

"Yeah. A whole bunch of people got cited for contempt of Congress and are going to go to prison, unless the Supreme Court saves them."

"Right. Now the reason that happened is because the two party lawyers advising the twenty or so people who got subpoenaed, told them to use the First Amendment as a defense. If they had told them to use the Fifth Amendment, instead, they wouldn't be facing prison, because taking the Fifth can't be construed as contempt."

"So, you're telling me that the party *wants* a bunch of its most prominent members to go to prison?"

"Yeah, and to get blacklisted, too. What's better publicity than a martyr? I'll tell you: ten martyrs. If they'd taken the Fifth at the hearings, it would all be over. Okay, maybe they would have been blacklisted anyway, but they wouldn't go to jail and become martyrs."

"So why did they pick Leo Goldman to send the party cards to?"

"My guess is they did the same thing at other studios, too; maybe all of them. Leo is just the noisiest anti-Communist at Centurion."

"Hal," Tom said, calling for the check, "I owe you one."

D riving home, Tom's excitement turned to anxiety. How was he going to tell Rick Barron that the guy he had just promoted to a big job was the guy who sent him his wife's Communist Party membership card? Certainly, if he did that and word got back to Leo, he'd make an enemy of Leo Goldman. And, Tom reflected, in this town, word always got back.

52

Rick Barron sat at a table with the two stars and the director of *Greenwich Village Girl* and listened to the first read-through of the script. As the picture's producer he was entitled to sit in, but Rick had another reason: he wanted to find out how a director made a script funny or, at least, revealed the humor already there.

Sam Sparrow, the director, had a very simple technique. When the first read-through was done, he said to his two actors, "All right. Let's do it again but faster, and as the script progresses and the two characters begin to argue and snipe at each other, I want you to play it *very* fast. In fact, I want you to step on each other's lines. Got it?"

The two actors nodded, and Rick sat back and tried to see it on the screen. Pretty soon he was laughing, and soon after that he nearly had to leave the room, because he was laughing so hard. By the time they had finished, the director was laughing, too.

Rick stood up. "Well, thanks for the entertainment, folks," he said. "I'm obviously not needed here, so I think I'll go and scare up some work for myself." Sparrow looked pleased. As Rick left the building and started to walk toward his office he remembered that, although Hattie Carson was reading from her script most of the time, Vance Calder had never once looked at his and not once had he blown a line. Where had he learned to do that?

Rick looked up as Tom Terry drove up to him in an electric cart. "Can I give you a lift, Rick?"

"Sure, Tom." Rick got into the cart.

"I've got some news for you."

"What about?"

"About the Communist Party cards you got in the mail. And it comes from our old friend, Hal Schmidt."

"Tell me."

Rick listened as Tom ran through the story of how Murray Fox had gotten hold of the two cards and mailed them.

"Who did he mail them to?"

"I don't know," Tom replied. "Fox wouldn't tell him, but Schmidt said he wouldn't be surprised if Fox had done the same with other cards mailed to other studios."

"You think we have any chance of finding out who got the cards at Centurion, then sent them to me?"

"Frankly, no. I mean, what we've got came from a source inside the party, and we were very lucky to have that source. If he can't find out, I don't think we can find out without him."

"Well, I guess this is one we should just put behind us," Rick said. "After all, Sid Brooks has already been publicly humiliated, and you've destroyed any record of Glenna at the Milwaukee party office, so it seems unlikely that any further harm can be done."

"That's the way I look at it, Rick. Just forget about it."

Tom stopped the cart at the door of the main building, and Rick got out. "By the way, Tom, did you see the story by Hedda Hopper in the paper yesterday?"

"Yeah, and there was another one this morning."

"What did that one say?"

"Apparently Hank Harmon fled her apartment ahead of the press and moved in with a friend out in the valley, but they caught up with her there, too."

"With what result?"

"No result; she refused to come to the door. They've got her pretty well staked out, though, I would imagine."

"Tom, did you give Hedda the first story about Harmon?"

"No, Rick. I didn't."

"What's your best guess as to where it came from?"

"My best guess? From the LAPD, although somebody at RKO would run a close second. It may be that the studio wanted people to know that they'd fired Hank, but they didn't want to make any kind of official statement."

"I guess that makes sense," Rick said. "Thanks for the lift, Tom."

Tom waved good-bye and started back toward his office. As he drove along, a big, black Packard pulled alongside him.

"Hey, Mr. Terry!" the driver yelled.

Tom looked over at the man. "Morning."

"Remember me?"

Tom stopped and looked closer. "Oh, yeah. You're the studio driver I met at Vance Calder's house; you're the one who was supposed to drive Susan Stafford to the airport, right?"

"That's right. I was just wondering if anything new had come up in the investigation. I mean, I saw the stuff in the papers about the script girl at RKO, but I wondered if there was anything else."

"It's Jerry, right?"

"That's right."

"No, Jerry. Nothing new at all, and believe me, I've been keeping tabs on the investigation. I think that, short of a confession from Hank Harmon, the police are not going to get any further."

"Oh, okay. Thanks a lot, and take care."

The Packard pulled away, and Tom started for his office again.

53

Sid Brooks sat on a stool at the counter of the diner in Santa Monica where he had lunch nearly every day. He needed a midday break from his work, since he was at the typewriter for eight hours a day, compared to the four hours he had been working before he had been blacklisted.

He was deep into a bowl of homemade clam chowder and paid little attention when someone took the stool next to him.

"You're a real piece of work, Brooks," a voice to his right said.

Sid turned and looked at the man. He recognized him as Fred Blair, another blacklisted writer. He knew the man only from the meetings of the nineteen subpoenaed writers when they were discussing their legal defense. "Hello, Fred," Sid said. "What are you talking about?"

"We've heard what you're planning to do," Blair said.

"Who is 'we,' and what am I planning to do?"

"You're going to purge yourself before the committee, aren't you." It wasn't a question. "You're going to rat us out."

"I'm not going to rat anybody out," Sid said and turned back to his chowder.

"So, you're a liar as well as a rat."

"Did you hear what Billy Wilder said about us, Fred?"

"Huh?"

"Wilder said, 'Of the unfriendly ten, only two had any talent; the others were just unfriendly.' There's not much doubt which group you belong to. You have nothing to lose, because you were doing shitty work all along. Somebody always had to be hired to clean up after you."

Blair stood up and squared off. "You lousy son of a bitch. Stand up, and I'll make you eat those words."

Sid ate the last spoonful of his chowder, laid a dollar and a half on the counter, stood up and faced Blair. "Why don't you grow up, Fred?" He brushed past Blair and walked out of the diner.

Blair caught up to him in the parking lot. "Just a minute, you coward," he yelled and grabbed at Sid's shoulder.

Sid took a step away from him and turned; he saw it coming. Blair started at him and drew back his right hand. As he swung, Sid stepped inside the punch, blocked it and drove his right fist into the man's solar plexus.

Blair sat down on the pavement, clutching his midriff, and vomited into his lap. Sid wanted to hit him again, but he was too pathetic. He turned and walked toward his car, mentally thanking the instructor at the Lower East Side settlement house who, when he was twelve, had taught him to box, a handy skill for a Jewish boy in a public school.

"We're gonna get you!" Blair yelled from behind him.

Sid turned and used his whole arm in a very satisfying obscene gesture. He got into his car and drove away, thinking that any remaining doubts he had about testifying had been resolved.

Hank Harmon left her upstairs bedroom in her friend Sylvia's house and went downstairs in search of a pen. She went into the den and began opening desk drawers, finding all sorts of things, including a snub-nosed revolver, before finally finding a pen. She borrowed some stationery, went back upstairs and peeked through the drawn venetian blinds. They were still out there with their cameras. She sat down and started writing.

She had written, sealed and stamped her letters when, a little after six, she heard a car door slam outside. She peeked outside again and saw Sylvia elbowing her way through the little mob of reporters, then she heard the front door slam. Hank went downstairs.

"Hi," she said to Sylvia. "Did you have a good day?"

Sylvia sank into the sofa, not looking at her. "Sit down, please, Hank."

Hank sat down.

Sylvia looked up. "To answer your question: no, I didn't have a good day. First of all, when I left for work this morning, I had to wade through that bunch outside. Then, when I got to work, my boss showed me a newspaper article by Hedda Hopper that mentioned my name and address and that said you were hiding out here. I was pretty much told that if he read anything like that again, I'd be out of the studio on my ass."

"Sylvia . . ."

"I'm not through. Then I came home from work, and I had to wade through the reporters again." She held up a batch of mail. "I never get this much mail." She riffled through the envelopes. "All of it is from my neighbors on this street." She chose one and ripped it open. "Dear Miss Pound," she read, "We would appreciate it if you would come to a neighborhood association meeting at the school at seven-thirty this evening to discuss with us the ruckus outside your house and your choice of houseguests. And I would advise you to read the bylaws of the neighborhood association before you come." Sylvia tossed the letter aside. "I'm sure the others say pretty much the same thing, and I don't need to read the bylaws to know that there is a clause stating that any resident who is a bad neighbor for any one of a number of reasons can be voted out. They can actually force me, legally, to sell my house."

"Sylvia . . ."

"I'm not finished. When you called and said you needed a place to stay, you didn't mention that you were the chief suspect in a murder investigation and that the press would follow you to my house."

"Sylvia, I'm so sorry."

"Hank, I'd like you to leave tonight. You can go late, when those people have finally decided to go home and go to sleep." She went to her desk, rummaged in a drawer, came back with a brochure and handed it to Hank. "That's a seaside hotel in Santa Barbara that is friendly to sisters; I'd recommend it as a good hiding place until all this dies down."

Hank nodded. "All right. I'll go tonight. There's something I want you to know, though."

"What's that?"

"I didn't kill Susie."

"I never thought you did, Hank, and I would have been happy for you to stay here if you hadn't brought the entourage with you. Now, if you'll excuse me, I need to have a shower and wash my hair before this meeting tonight, and I think I'm going to have to wear a skirt, too, and my wedding ring. The neighbors all think I'm a divorcee." She got up and went upstairs.

Hank slept until the alarm woke her at two A.M. She got up and peeked through the blinds. The front yard and the street in both directions seemed clear. She got dressed, carried her bags downstairs, went into the garage and put them into her car. She put the top up, then went back inside for her handbag, which she had left on the desk in the den. She picked it up, then stopped and thought for a moment. She turned, opened a desk drawer, took the snub-nosed revolver and put it into her handbag.

She went back to the garage and opened the door. She backed out her car, got out and closed the door, then backed into the street and drove away. On the main road she found a mailbox and mailed her letters.

At the top of the mountain, instead of continuing down the other side, she turned right on Mulholland Drive.

54

Rick and Eddie were going over budgets in Rick's office when his secretary buzzed him. He pressed the button. "Yes?"

"There's a Lieutenant Morrison of the Los Angeles Police Department on line one," she said.

Rick picked up the phone. "Ben?"

"Yes, Rick. I'm sorry to disturb you; I tried Tom Terry first, but he was out, and I thought you should know about this."

"Know about what?"

"This morning a sheriff's patrol car found a car parked way out on Mulholland where that dump was where Susan Stafford's body was found. Inside was a young woman, dead, apparently of a self-inflicted gunshot wound. She's been identified by the contents of her handbag as Hank Harmon."

"Oh," Rick said, unable to think of anything else to say.

Eddie spoke up. "What is it?"

"Hank Harmon has committed suicide." He turned back to the phone. "Ben, is there any doubt that it was suicide?"

"None; everything added up. The gun belonged to a friend of hers, a Sylvia Pound. Harmon had been staying with her, and it was reported in the papers. I talked to Miss Pound, and she claimed ownership of the gun, said Harmon must have taken it from a desk drawer in her home."

"Do you think she did this out of guilt over Susan's murder?"

"No. There was a note in her handbag. She claimed she was innocent and her life was being ruined: lost her job, hounded by the press, et cetera. She left a list of phone numbers: her parents, a funeral home where she had made arrangements and her lawyer. It was all very well thought out and orderly."

"Was she your only suspect, Ben?"

"Yes, she was. I remain pretty confident that she killed Susan Stafford."

"Then it's over?"

"It is, unless some sort of exculpatory evidence comes to light, and that seems unlikely. I'll put her in my final report as the sole suspect."

"Ben, thank you for letting me know, and if anything else comes up, I'd like to hear about it."

"Of course, Rick."

Rick hung up the phone. He told Eddie about the note.

"I don't get it," Eddie said. "If she murdered Susie, why would she leave a note saying she didn't? Why not confess and save everybody a lot of trouble?"

"In my experience, some murderers have difficulty admitting their guilt even to themselves. I suppose it's natural to want to be remembered as innocent."

"Yeah. I guess so," Eddie said. "Well, it's a relief to know that this saga is over."

"I guess it is," Rick said.

As soon as Tom Terry got Morrison's message, he called him back and got the news.

"Tommy," Ben said, "I've got to ask you this: where were you from midnight last night until ten this morning?"

"Jesus, Ben. You think I killed her?"

"If it's not a suicide, then only a cop—or an ex-cop—could make it look that good."

"Well, I. . . I didn't kill her."

"You didn't answer my question."

"I went to bed at eleven last night, overslept, got to the studio a little before nine. My secretary will confirm that I was already here when she arrived."

"Were you in bed alone?"

"Yes."

"Tommy, I have to tell you, if any evidence turns up that this wasn't a suicide, you're going to be my first suspect."

"Aw, come on, Ben."

"You knew where she was staying, didn't you?"

"Well, yeah."

"Her friend says she left in the middle of the night to avoid the press and that she was heading for Santa Barbara. She would have taken Mulholland to Malibu, then gone on up the coast. You could have had her staked, followed her up there and pulled her over. You got a red light in your car, Tom?"

"Yeah, I do."

"You're my boy, Tommy."

Tom was starting to sweat, now. "Look, Ben, I swear to you that I didn't . . ."

Morrison burst out laughing. "Had you going, didn't I?"

"You bastard!"

"She left a note, Tommy. It was suicide; you're off the hook."

Tom loosened his tie and wiped his brow. "Did she own up to the murder?"

"No. In fact, she said she was innocent."

"Shit!"

"Don't you hate it when they won't confess, even if they're gonna off themselves?"

"Well, she did it. I don't care what she says in the note. What else did she say?"

"Just a list of people to contact. It was all very neat."

"Well, we can close the books on that one, I guess."

"I guess. Take care, Tommy." Morrison hung up.

Tom hung up, too. He had thought of killing her himself, but somehow he found it more disturbing that he might have hounded her into taking her own life.

The following morning, Vance Calder left his house, taking his mail and the morning paper with him. He drove to the studio to his bungalow and greeted his secretary.

"Good morning, Vance," she said.

"Anything that needs my attention?"

"No."

He dropped his mail on her desk. "Here are some bills for you to pay." He walked back to his dressing room, where his costume for the first day's shooting of *Greenwich Village Girl* was hanging, waiting for him. He got into the shirt, trousers and shoes, then sat down in the living room with the newspaper, to await the arrival of his makeup artist. He had learned that, although he wore almost no makeup, it was better to let her do something to him, just to keep her happy. After all, she wanted to get paid, just like everybody else, and who was he to deny her the work?

She arrived a moment later, and, taking the paper with him, he walked into the makeup room and sat in the plushly upholstered barber's chair. He glanced at the front page while the makeup girl did her work.

His secretary walked into the room. "Shirley," she said to the makeup girl, "Will you excuse us for a moment?"

"Sure, Connie," the woman replied. "I'll be outside."

"What's up, Connie?" Vance asked. She had a funny look on her face.

She held out a letter. "This was with your mail," she said.

55

S id Brooks left his Washington hotel with an hour to spare before the hearing. He thought that, since he was early, he'd take a look around the Capitol. The only time he had been there before was for the first hearing.

It was rush hour in Washington, and cabs were scarce. There was a line of people waiting for the doorman to get taxis, so Sid walked up to Pennsylvania Avenue to look for his own cab. He did not notice that two men were following him.

He stopped at the corner and put a nickel into a newspaper vending machine for a *Washington Post*, and as he straightened up, something hit him on the side of his head, behind the ear. The blow staggered him, but he kept his feet and managed to square off against his attackers. They were both bigger than he and wearing business suits and hats, and both had clenched fists as they came at him again. He threw his newspaper in the face of one of them, and that gave him time to kick the other man in the knee, effectively taking him out of the fight. The other man recovered and came at him. He caught Sid high on the cheek, but Sid counterpunched with a straight left to the man's nose, hoping to draw blood. He had been taught at the settlement house as a boy that an attacker's sight of his own blood would discourage him, and it worked. The man ran, one hand over his face.

He turned back to the other man, who was struggling to his feet and hobbling away. He looked back at Sid and shouted, "Fink!" Sid did not pursue them. He gathered his paper together and got lucky finding a cab. By the time he arrived at the Capitol he had stopped trembling, and his breathing was normal. He walked slowly around the rotunda for a while, looking at the pictures and the sculptures, then he found the hearing room, and a guard checked his name off a list and admitted him.

The hearing room was smaller than the last one he had visited. There were few people in attendance and only one photographer, who took his picture as he seated himself in the front row.

Shortly, the committee members filed in, and, after discussing some procedural matters, the chairman instructed a guard to call the first witness.

"Sidney Brooks!" the man intoned.

Sid stood, walked to the table before the committee and sat down.

"Mr. Brooks," the chairman said, "are you represented by counsel?"

"No, Mr. Chairman."

"Do you wish to be represented by counsel?"

"No, Mr. Chairman."

"Then be sworn."

Sid took the oath, then addressed the committee. "Mr. Chairman, I would be grateful if I could make a short statement before questioning begins."

"All right, Mr. Brooks, proceed."

Sid took a deep breath. "Mr. Chairman, some time ago I appeared briefly before this committee as what was known as an unfriendly witness. Since that time I have had an opportunity to reflect at length on my situation, and a number of life-altering events have occurred that have helped me in my thinking: I became unemployable, my wife left me, many people I had looked upon as friends stopped speaking to me and I was twice physically attacked, most recently when I was on the way to this hearing this morning.

"Perhaps if I were a more stubborn person, these events would have only increased my resolve; instead, they have made me see that, if I am to choose sides in this matter, I initially chose the wrong one. I am here today to rectify that.

"In 1935, when, like millions of Americans, I was depressed over the state of the country, I joined the Communist Party, because I thought that, based on their written statements, they might do something to improve things. I was wrong about that, of course; they have improved nothing and have been the cause of the disruption of a great many American lives. I am happy to say that, during the ensuing years, I have been a very bad Communist. Now, starting today, I am going to try to be a better American.

"Finally, let me say that I have not changed my mind that this committee has no constitutional right to question any American on his political views or to punish him for not answering. However, I have decided to freely volunteer to answer all of your questions today. I do so in the knowledge that having alienated half the people in my life, I will now alienate the other half, but I can live with that. Please ask your questions."

The chairman designated a man to his left as the first questioner.

"Mr. Brooks, you've already told us that you are a Communist, is that right?"

"I'm sorry, Congressman. I neglected to mention that I recently resigned from the party, so I am no longer a Communist."

"I'm glad to hear that. Sir, do you regret having joined the Communist Party when you did so?"

"I certainly do, Congressman. The experience over the years has given me much pain and little joy."

"You said that you were impressed by the written statements of the party and that caused you to join. Which statements impressed you?"

"Congressman, I have discovered that the party is very good at co-opting those things about this country that are good, like free speech and free association. I have also discovered that none of the things they advocate in this country would ever be allowed in the Soviet Union or any other Communist country. All the party has achieved in those places is to make its ordinary citizens more miserable than ever, and I am sure that, given the opportunity, they would do exactly the same here."

Sid was then asked to name names, and he dutifully recited those that he had been given.

"Are you aware, sir, that all those names were previously known to this committee?"

"I am."

"Is that why you chose to name them?"

"The names were proposed to me by committee staff."

"All right. Let's talk a minute about a name that was not included in your recitation, that of Alan James, the movie actor."

"The late movie actor."

"Yes, the late movie actor. Was Mr. James, to your knowledge, a member of the Communist Party?"

"Yes, sir. He joined on the same day that I did."

"Do you have any knowledge that he, in any of the films he made, voiced Communist propaganda?"

"No, sir, I do not. And may I point out that actors do not make up the words they speak in films; they read the scripts that are written by people like me."

"And have you ever voiced Communist propaganda in writing your scripts?"

"No, sir, I have not."

"Have you ever been asked to by other Communists?"

"On two occasions, sir, I was asked to include rather innocuous statements about the good life in the Soviet Union, and I declined to do so on both occasions, because I knew these statements were lies."

"Who asked you to do this?"

Sid paused for a moment. "I'm afraid I don't recall; it was a very long time ago, when I first began writing for pictures. I don't even remember if it happened at the studio or at some party function."

"Mr. Brooks, by testifying here today, do you hope to regain your former position in Hollywood?"

"Sir, I have no real hope of ever regaining my former position; too many people will hate me for what I say here today, no matter what I say. But I hope to be able, once again, to earn a living by writing for pictures, the theater and television under my own name. That is all I know how to do."

Sid was questioned for another half hour along the lines of the agreed script, then he was dismissed.

The chairman spoke the magic words. "Mr. Brooks, you are excused, with the sincere thanks of this committee."

B ack outside, on the steps of the Capitol, Sid discovered that his shirt, under his jacket, was soaked through with sweat. He found a cab and began the long trip back to Los Angeles, not knowing what awaited him there.

56

T om Terry was at his desk when Ben Morrison called.

"Good morning, Ben."

"Morning, Tom. I have some news, of a sort. I don't know if it means anything."

"I'm all ears."

"You remember that when we took prints from Susan Stafford's car, we came up with hers and one other set?"

"Right."

"And when we finally got to fingerprint Hank Harmon, the other prints didn't match hers?"

"Yes."

"Well, I sent the unknown prints to the FBI, and I finally heard from them in this morning's mail. They were a match to a P. J. O'Toole, no photograph available. He's six-one, two hundred pounds, brown hair. He has a record of two arrests for rape in Arizona, no convictions. We came up dry on his last known address, in Phoenix."

"What hope do we have of finding this guy, Ben?"

"On the assumption that, since his fingerprints were found here, he now resides in the L.A. area, we've checked the phone books and we've found eight P. J. O'Tooles within a twenty-five-mile radius of Los Angeles. I'm short-handed, but I'm going to check them out as fast as I can."

"Do you want me and my people to help?"

"No. I don't want your people to be seen to be doing our job. I hope we can whittle down the number with telephone calls before we start interviewing them in person."

"That makes sense."

"We've already started, but we've only found one Mr. O'Toole at home, and he's a man in his eighties who's in a wheelchair. We'll give the others time to get home from work, then make the calls again."

"Don't tell them you're the cops. Tell them you're looking for somebody who's won the Irish Sweepstakes or something."

"Right," Ben said drily. "We thought of that."

"You've got my home number?"

"Yes."

"Call me if you get anything good, no matter what time."

"Will do."

"And thanks, Ben. This is good news."

"That remains to be seen. He could be some guy in a gas station who worked on her car. Who knows? I wouldn't get my hopes up just yet."

"Okay. I'll stay depressed until I hear from you."

Tom hung up and noticed that his heart was beating very fast.

E ddie Harris answered the telephone in his suite at the Plaza Hotel, in New York. "Yes?"

"Mr. Harris, there's a Mr. Harvey at the front desk, asking to see you."

"Thank you, please send him up." Eddie hung up the phone and pushed the room service tray out into the hall, then sat down to wait for the man from *Red Targets*, a publication that was a primary tool of the blacklist in New York. There was a knock on the door, and Eddie went to open it. "Mr. Harvey?"

"Mr. Harris?"

"Yes, please come in. Would you like some coffee?"

"Don't mind if I do. Black, please." Harvey sat down and placed his briefcase next to him.

Eddie poured two cups from the pot on the coffee table and sat down.

"Well, Mr. Harris, what can we do for you?"

"There's a writer from Los Angeles that I want to get cleared."

"And who would that be?"

"His name is Sidney Brooks."

Harvey set his briefcase on his lap, opened it and took out a thick document in a ring binder. "Let's see," he said, leafing through the pages. "Ah, here we are: Sidney Brooks, born New York 1901, a Jew, joined the Communist Party 1935 in New York, was an unfriendly witness before the House Un-American Activities Committee earlier this year, cited for contempt of Congress, sentenced to a year in a federal prison, sentence stayed pending appeal. That the one?"

"That's the one. What your book doesn't say is that Mr. Brooks recently resigned from the party and that yesterday he appeared again before the committee as a friendly witness and purged himself."

"We read the papers, too, Mr. Harris."

"What hasn't been in the papers yet is that Congress will lift his citation for contempt in session today, or so I am reliably informed."

"Well, good for Mr. Brooks. Sounds like he's taken the first step toward cleansing himself."

"First step? What else could he possibly do?"

"Well, before we clear somebody, we like to have some time to watch his behavior and recheck his associations. Besides, we're just getting together our resources and working out our procedures; we haven't cleared a lot of people yet. Have you spoken to any other organizations?"

"I've had conversations with people at the Motion Picture Alliance," Eddie said, "and I've been assured that they have no problem with Mr. Brooks's clearance. I've had informal discussions with the American Legion as well, and they seem inclined to agree, although. . . ."

"Although they want to see what we think?"

"Your publication was mentioned."

"Yes, well, we're in the midst of a fund-raising campaign that should help us move things along with a bit more dispatch."

"I see," Eddie said. He picked up his own briefcase, which was sitting next to the coffee table, opened it, took a stack of hundred-dollar bills secured with a paper binder and placed it on the table.

"That's one hundred, hundred-dollar bills, Mr. Harvey; comes to ten thousand dollars. Do you think that might augment your fund-raising campaign to the extent that you could accelerate the clearance process?"

Harvey stared at the money and said nothing for a moment, then he licked his lips.

When Eddie saw that, he knew he had the man.

"Well, Mr. Harris, that's certainly a very generous donation . . ."

"It's not a donation yet, Mr. Harvey; it's just ten thousand dollars sitting on a coffee table. I'd like Mr. Brooks cleared today, and I'd like a news release to that effect hand-delivered to the United Press and Associated Press before five o'clock this afternoon."

"Well, I'd have to speak to my superiors . . ."

"There's the phone, Mr. Harvey. You might point out to your superiors that the money is in cash and that I don't care who gets it or what is done with it; I'm not going to deduct it from my taxes. I'm going to go brush my teeth and put on a necktie, and if you're not here when I get back, I will assume that we are of one mind."

Eddie got up and walked out of the room, leaving Harvey staring at the stack of bills. He brushed his teeth and put on a jacket and tie, taking his time about it. When he returned to the sitting room of his suite, Mr. Harvey and his briefcase were gone, and so was the ten thousand dollars.

57

Rick was sitting on his bed, tying his shoes, when the phone rang. "Hello?"

"It's Eddie. Glad I caught you before you left for the studio."

"How's New York?"

"Just great, kiddo. I bear good tidings of great joy."

"Let me have it."

"I spent yesterday afternoon with the network, and they loved your idea. We've got nine to eleven on Saturday nights, starting in September."

"That's wonderful, Eddie!"

"There's more: have you read the papers yet?"

"No."

"Well it's in the *New York Times*; I assume the L.A. papers will pick up the wire reports, too."

"Reports of what?"

"Congress voted yesterday to void the contempt citation of Sid Brooks."

"Great news!"

"Amazing what a campaign contribution or two will accomplish, huh? But there's more."

"What else?"

"I met with a guy from *Red Targets* yesterday and, after another contribution, maybe to their fund-raising drive but more likely to a pocket or two, they've cleared Sid. That should be in the L.A. papers, too."

"That's wonderful, Eddie. The best news I've had since we got Radio City for *Bitter Creek*."

"Call Hy Greenbaum and make him an offer. Sid may not be back from Washington, yet, but try and have a deal waiting for him."

"That would be my pleasure."

"I also looked at apartments yesterday, and I found one I like."

"Why? You're not thinking of moving to New York, are you?"

"Nah, I just think we spend too much money on hotels here. I'm going to buy us an apartment in the Carlyle Hotel, so we'll have a pied-à-terre. Tell Sid he can stay there until he finds a place in New York."

"I'm sure he'll be glad to hear that."

"The network has a big production space on the West Side where we can film our show, and they'll provide office space for Sid and his staff. You might ask him how much help he thinks he'll need."

"Did you say film? I thought we were going to do it live."

"We are, but we're going to film it simultaneously. If we don't, any reruns would have to be Kinescopes, which is basically a film of a TV set, and the quality is terrible. If we spend the money up front to film it, we'll stretch the reruns out for years. Also, we can shoot film in color; in a few years, we'll have color TV."

"That's a great idea, if we can manage it technically."

"I want you to go to work on that today. Find a way to shoot some tests, and make sure the scripts allow us to reload the film cameras while we're shooting live."

"I think that may be a tall order, but I'll get on it."

"That's all the news I have right now. I'll see you in a couple of days."

"Congratulations on a successful trip, Eddie. I'll look forward to seeing you back here." Rick hung up and went to tell Glenna the news.

Glenna listened to all of it before she spoke. "Well, I'm happy for Centurion and I'm happy for Sid, but the simultaneous shooting of TV and film is not going to work."

"Well, I know there'll be some kinks to work out, but . . ."

"It's not going to work. The reason is TV cameras have to work with very high lighting; it's very, very bright in a TV studio, and that's not going to work for film, especially in color. The only way you could do it is either before or after the live performance, light the sets for film and shoot the whole thing. You could still shoot it almost exactly like the live performance. Hardly anybody would notice the difference."

"I see your point, and I think you're right. I'm not sure that the economics would allow us to shoot the whole show on film on a different day. We'd have to pay the actors for that performance, and we wouldn't have any income from it until the reruns started at least a year later."

"You might be able to work out something with the Screen Actors Guild for deferred payment, but I doubt it. I think it's just one of those glorious ideas that isn't feasible."

"Well, I'm going to have to prove that to Eddie; he's very excited about it."

"Yes, I know what Eddie is like when he's excited."

"Maybe we could fix the simultaneous shooting problem with special film stock that's graded for high light."

"Now that's a thought, but Kodak would probably have to invent it."

"Yeah, most of their efforts are directed at getting the stock to work in low light, not high."

Rick wrestled with the problem all the way to work and decided that, barring some technical breakthrough, they would have to shoot the show three times: twice for live performances in different time zones, followed by once on film.

W hen he got to his office Tom Terry was waiting for him.
        "Hi. Rick. I have some news."

"Come on in, Tom, and tell me about it."

Tom followed Rick into his office and took a seat. "Ben Morrison called me yesterday about the fingerprints he lifted from Susan Stafford's car that turned out not to belong to Hank Harmon."

"Yeah?"

Tom explained about P. J. O'Toole and the eight P. J. O'Tooles living in the L.A. area. "Problem is none of the eight is our guy; they're too old or have alibis. Two of the P.J.'s turned out to be women. Apparently, some women list their numbers with initials to avoid getting heavy-breather phone calls."

"Maybe our O'Toole doesn't have a phone."

"Ben's people are working on the city directories now, but there are at least a dozen of them to go through, and every person they turn up who doesn't have a phone is going to have to be visited, so it's going to take time. Ben is short-handed, and he won't accept our help, says it doesn't look good."

"Well, we'll just have to wait for them to grind it out, I guess. At least the guy won't know the cops are looking for him, so he won't run."

"My fear is that he's already run," Tom said. "Some guy living in a boarding house who, when he thought about what he'd done, got out of town."

"Well, they've got a name and a description. He'll get arrested somewhere for some petty crime, and then Ben will nail him."

Tom stood up. "I wish I had better news to report."

"Not your fault, Tom. Just let the police do their work."

T om left, and Rick tried calling Sid Brooks but got his answering service. He sketched out a rough deal on a pad, then called Hy Greenbaum.

58

Rick was about to go home for the day when his secretary announced that Vance Calder wanted to see him.

"Send him in," Rick said and stood up to greet the actor.

Vance came in, looking a little somber, shook Rick's hand and sat down.

"How are rehearsals going?" Rick asked.

"Very well. In fact, I think we're ready to start shooting the day after tomorrow."

"Has Hattie caught up with you on the script?"

"She has it down cold. By the way, Sam Sparrow thinks we should shorten the title to *Village Girl*."

"What do you think?"

"I like it better."

"It's okay with me, then. Will you tell Sam for me?"

"Sure. Rick, I got a letter from Hank Harmon."

"Really? What did she have to say?"

"It's two letters, actually: one to me from Hank and one to Hank from Susie." He took two sheets of paper from his inside pocket. "I'll read them to you."

"All right."

To Vance Calder:

We've never met, and, I suppose, we never will, but there's something I'd like you to hear directly from me. I did not murder Susan Stafford. I returned to my apartment after she had taken her things and left. She had left me a note, which I enclose. I think when you read it, you will realize that I had no motive to kill Susie. I had nothing but love for her. I am ending my life, but I wanted you to know about our relationship.

Since I didn't kill Susie, that means that her killer is still on the loose, and I hope you will use any influence that you and your studio might have to see that her killer is brought to justice.

Sincerely, Hank Harmon

Rick nodded. "I believe she left a note to that effect for the police to find, and apparently they are no longer certain that Hank was the killer. They found some fingerprints in Susie's car belonging to someone named P. J. O'Toole, who had a record of arrests for rape in Arizona but no convictions. They're looking for him now."

"I'm glad to hear that," Vance said. "Do you want to hear Susie's letter to Hank?"

"If you want me to."

"Yes, I'd like you to, and then I'll destroy it." Vance unfolded the letter and began to read.

My dearest Hank,

I've packed up all my things and I'm removing them to Vance's house. I think you knew this was coming, and I don't want you to feel bad about it.

You know that I have always liked men almost as well as women, and Vance is a beautiful and delightful man in every way. Right now, it's good protection for my career for me to be with him. It will help to stop any gossip, which, if it became public, could destroy my career. I must tell you that, the way our relationship is going, Vance and I may even be married, maybe even have children. You know I have always wanted children.

But you also know, Hank, that you are the love of my life, my one true love, and I will never leave you. I'll see you at every opportunity and love you the way we have always loved. I think I'm going to make a lot of money as an actress, and if the relationship with Vance doesn't work out, then I'll be able to buy a really nice house for us.

I probably won't see you or talk to you for several weeks, as I settle in with Vance, and I don't want you to call me. He knows about my relationship with you or, at least, part of it, and I don't want him to hear your voice on the phone.

Be patient, my dearest, and we will be together again soon.

With love, Susie

"Do you want to see it?" Vance asked, holding out the letter.

"No, that's not necessary, but I'm glad you read it to me. I think you're right to destroy it."

Vance took a box of matches and an ashtray from Rick's desk and burned the two sheets. "There," he said. "Now life can begin again."

The two men shook hands, and Vance left.

Rick went home and told Glenna about the two letters.

"The poor girl," Glenna said. "I hope they get the bastard who killed her."

"They'll get him," Rick said. "It will just take time."

Sid Brooks got off the airplane and looked for an L.A. paper. He had already read the *Washington Post*, but he wanted to know that all L.A. would know that he had been cleared. He found only a two-paragraph story on an inside page, but at least it was there.

When he got home he found messages from both Hy Greenbaum and Rick Barron on his service. He called Hy first.

"Hey, Sid. Welcome back and congratulations," Hy said.

"Thank you, Hy, and thank you for talking me into testifying again. You were right; it was the right thing for me. What else do I have to do?"

"Not a thing, Sid. You're back in business. Eddie Harris has worked out a deal with a network for a two-hour show on Saturday nights, starting in September. I know Rick told you about this. Do you want to do it?"

"Yes, if you like the deal."

"I've been back and forth several times with Rick on the phone, and we've worked out what I think is a very fine deal. It's being typed now, and I'll messenger it over to you first thing in the morning. Talk to me after you've read it, before you talk to Rick. You have an appointment with him for lunch tomorrow at twelve-thirty at the studio commissary to talk over details."

"All right."

"I can tell you that, if the show runs, this will be a rich deal for you. You'll be paid both as a producer and a writer, and you'll have a percentage of the profits. If it runs for three years, you'll be a millionaire, and I think it could run a lot longer than that."

"Wow, Hy, I hardly know what to say."

"No need to say anything, Sid. My agency has a publicist on call who is going to see that your clearance gets noticed everywhere."

"I'm glad to hear it."

"Call me after you read the contract. If it's okay, you can sign it when you see Rick."

"I will, Hy. Good night." Sid hung up the phone, and, almost immediately, it rang.

"Hello?"

"Sid, it's Alice."

He was speechless for a moment. "Hello, Al."

"I saw the news in the *Times;* I wanted to congratulate you."

"Thank you, I appreciate that."

"I'm sorry not to have been able to talk to you before, but my lawyers wouldn't let me; they were adamant."

"I understand."

"I have some news of my own."

"Oh?"

"I'm getting married again."

"Well, congratulations. Who's the lucky guy?"

"Alex Bronsky."

"How about that," Sid said, since he couldn't think of anything else to say. Alexander Bronsky had produced all his plays on the Broadway stage. "Alex is a good man. I hope you'll both be very happy."

"Thank you, Sid. The wedding's this weekend at Alex's place in Connecticut. Nothing big, just a few friends."

Sid knew the Connecticut house well; he and Alice had visited there a dozen times. "That will be a lovely setting."

"I know this won't have occurred to you yet, Sid, but my getting married again means you won't have to pay any more alimony."

"You're right; that didn't occur to me."

"My lawyers will send your lawyer a letter confirming that."

"Thank you. Oh, I have more news, too."

"Tell me."

He told her about the television show. "So I'll be spending a lot of time in New York. I'm sure I'll bump into you and Alex."

"That's wonderful, Sid. I'm so happy for you."

"Give Alex my best and congratulate him for me."

"I will. Bye-bye."

Sid fell asleep that night, feeling somehow whole.

59

Rick and Sid Brooks met in the studio commissary, where they took a table in the area reserved for executives.

"It's nice that we can meet in public now," Sid said.

Rick was embarrassed. "It feels better to me, too." They had hardly sat down, when people began dropping by the table to say hello to both of them.

"I think people are glad to see you back," Rick said.

"I'm glad to be back."

"Did you have a chance to go over the deal with Hy this morning?"

"Yes, we talked a couple of times. I know he spoke to you about revisions."

"Yes, the contract is being typed now, and they'll deliver it to us before our lunch is over. Sid, have you thought about what sort of staff you're going to need in New York?"

"A little. I'll need a secretary, maybe two; I won't know until we're under way. I'll need a couple of assistants to read scripts and reports and a couple of typists to produce final scripts. We'll need some equipment, too: mimeograph, furniture, et cetera."

"I think the office suite the network is providing is furnished, but if you need anything more or better, let us know."

"I'm going to need a personal assistant on the set, too, especially when I'm directing, but I may be able to use one of the script readers for that."

"Our New York office is small, but please lean on them for anything you need. They'll know the good personnel agencies and that sort of thing."

"Good."

"Eddie wants us to film simultaneously with the live performances. We'll get a lot more mileage out of the reruns over the years if we don't have to settle for Kinescope quality."

"Do you think that's technically feasible?"

"There are a lot of problems to solve, but I've got some of our people here working on it now. As it stands, it looks like the best way is to do two live performances, one for each coast, followed by a filmed performance. Still, there are SAG and craft union problems to deal with, and the economics of the situation may be harder to solve than the purely technical."

"I can see how that might be."

"We'll have an office for you here this afternoon. I think it's a good idea to have an office on each coast, and you're going to need an apartment in New York, of course. If you want to buy, instead of rent, we'll help with that. Also, Eddie has bought an apartment at the Carlyle for the studio, and you can stay there until you've found a permanent place."

"I don't think I want to buy until we're sure this thing is going to work," Sid said. "I don't want to dig in, only to find out after a few months that we're being cancelled."

"As you wish."

Someone had approached their table, and Rick looked up to see Tom Terry. "Hi, Tom. Have you met Sid Brooks?"

"No, I haven't."

"Sid, this is Tom Terry, our head of studio security. Tom, Sid is going to be running a new two-hour live drama TV show for us in New York, but he'll be out here some of the time, too."

"Welcome aboard," Tom said, handing Sid a card. "Let me know if there's anything I can do for you."

"Any news on the search for P. J. O'Toole?" Rick asked.

"Nothing new this morning, but ..." Suddenly, Tom stopped talking and was staring across the room, looking stunned.

"Is something wrong, Tom?" Rick asked.

"My God," Tom said.

"Tom, what is it?"

"Everything just fell into place. Rick, please follow me; I may need you."

"What for?"

"To make an arrest." Tom strode off across the large room.

Rick excused himself and followed, wondering what the hell was going on. Tom seemed to be headed for a table where a lone man was just sitting down.

"Jerry!" Tom said. "How are you?"

Jerry, the driver, looked up. "Hi, Tom. I'm great, thanks."

"Jerry, have you met our head of production, Rick Barron?" Rick had just arrived at the table.

Jerry got to his feet and held out his hand.

"Rick this is Jerry ... I'm sorry, Jerry, I don't know your last name." Jerry shook Rick's hand.

"O'Toole," Jerry said, shaking Rick's hand.

"Peter Jerome O'Toole?"

"Patrick Jerome." Jerry turned and offered Tom his hand.

"I thought something like that," Tom said, taking hold of Jerry's outstretched hand and pinning his wrist to the table.

Jerry looked alarmed, and then he suddenly understood what was happening. "Let me go," he said, trying to free his hand.

"You killed her, didn't you?"

Jerry's expression turned to panic.

"What are you talking about?"

"You drove her all week long, got to know her, got to want her, didn't you? You waited for her at the house on that Sunday, and when she arrived, you came on to her. When she resisted, you dragged her around behind the garage, where you beat her and raped her in the bed of ferns. When she tried to scream you strangled her. Rick, frisk Jerry, will you?"

Rick started around the table, but Jerry reached under his jacket with his left hand and produced a revolver. Before Rick could reach him he had fired twice at Tom and had started running.

Tom fell backward onto the floor, clutching his belly. Panic ensued in the commissary, women screamed, people ran from the building.

Sid Brooks had run across the room and joined Rick, who was kneeling over Tom. "Sid," Rick said, "do what you can to help Tom." He grabbed a waitress who was running by. "You call the doctor at our infirmary, then call an ambulance and the police. Hurry! Sid, I'll be back as soon as I can."

Rick ran from the building and looked up and down the studio street. Two blocks down, he saw Jerry O'Toole sprinting down the street, then taking a right turn. Rick grabbed a passing man in cowboy gear. "I'm Rick Barron. Find a phone, call the front gate and tell them to seal it. Nobody gets out, got it?"

"Okay," the man said.

"And be quick about it." Rick ran after Jerry. A block down he passed the studio doctor and a nurse in an electric cart headed toward the commissary. Rick turned right, where Jerry had turned, and suddenly found himself on a New York City street, the studio's most-used standing set.

Jerry was nowhere in sight.

60

Rick rounded a corner and began to limp. He wasn't used to running without his knee brace, and his old war wound was starting to hurt. Halfway down the block a crew was setting up a street shot. Two police cars were blocking the street, and actors in cop uniforms were standing around, leaning against the cars and waiting for shooting to start.

Rick limped up to them. "Did you see a man run into this street?" he asked the group.

"Who are you?" an assistant director asked.

"I'm Rick Barron, and I run this studio. Answer my question."

"I didn't see anybody," the AD said.

One of the actor/cops spoke up. "I saw a guy down at the end of the block where you just came from, but I looked away, and when I looked back he was gone."

"Give me your gun," Rick said.

The actor pulled his .38 from his holster and handed it to Rick. Rick opened the cylinder and extracted a cartridge, a blank, as he had expected. "Where's the armorer?" he asked.

The actor turned and shouted at a man on the other side of his police car. "Hey, Frankie! The boss wants to talk to you."

A man trotted over to the car. "Yeah?"

"Have you got any live ammo?" Rick asked.

The man shook his head. "Not here. I'd have to go back to the armory."

"Go," Rick said. "I need a box of .38 specials and fast, and call the studio police and tell them to get some armed men over here."

The man hopped into an electric cart and raced away.

Rick could hear a siren from the direction of the main gate, then other sirens. That would be the ambulance and the cops. "You," he said to the AD, "grab a cart, get to the main gate and lead the cops back here, and be quick."

The AD drove away.

"What's going on?" one of the actors asked.

"There was just a shooting at the commissary," Rick said. "The shooter ran this way, and he's got to be found."

"Can we help?"

"The man is armed, and you've only got blanks."

"I'm an off-duty cop," one of the men said. "I work as an extra sometimes. What do you need?"

"Live ammo," Rick said.

"Here comes the armorer," somebody shouted.

The man screeched to a halt in his cart and handed Rick a box of ammunition. He gave some to the off-duty cop. "Okay, load up and let's start searching. Remember, this guy has already shot one man, so be careful."

"Okay. I'm with you."

"You take the shopfronts on the right; I'll take the brownstones on the left." Rick ran down the street as best he could and started checking doors on the brownstone mock-ups. The first three were locked.

"Everything over here is locked!" the off-duty cop yelled.

"Keep trying, and be careful."

There was only one brownstone left at the end of the row. Rick got up the stairs, turned the doorknob and pushed. The knob turned, but the door was stuck at the bottom. Rick leaned against it and pushed; it swung open. Rick simultaneously stepped over the threshold and found nothing but air on the other side.

He clung to the doorknob with his left hand and looked down into a large hole in the ground, perhaps twenty feet below. Rick had a loud taxi whistle, and he used it. "Help me!" he yelled. He stuck the .38 into his belt and tried to swing the door shut, but it was stuck, and there was no room on the doorknob for two hands. He swung his body toward the door opening and got one foot on it, then swung back. He was starting to lose his grip on the knob.

Then the off-duty cop appeared in the doorway, grabbed Rick's trouser leg and pulled him in until he could get a hand on Rick's belt, then on Rick's right hand. He braced himself against the doorway. "Let go!" he yelled. "I've got you."

Rick's hand slipped off the doorknob, and the man took all his weight, pulling him into the doorway. A second later he was safe but out of breath.

"Is that your guy?" the off-duty cop asked, pointing down.

Rick looked into the abyss and saw a man, lying face down, at the bottom, his revolver nearby. "That's the guy," he puffed.

Real police cars turned into the street, and cops began spilling out.

"Go around," Rick directed from the top of the brownstone's steps. "The guy is in a construction hole on the other side, and he seems to be unconscious, but his gun is there, too, so be careful."

A sergeant directed his men toward the rear of the set, then trotted up the stairs and looked down. "Jesus," he said, "did the guy run up here and through the door?"

"That seems to be it," Rick said. "He shot our head of security twice in the commissary, then ran here."

"Tom Terry?" the man asked.

"That's right." Rick heard the ambulance heading back toward the main gate, and he knew Tom was on his way to the hospital.

"You look a little winded," the cop said. "Are you all right?"

"Yeah, I'm all right."

The cop took the .38 from Rick's belt. "Can I have this, then?"

"Yeah. It belongs to the studio, but you can unload it."

The off-duty cop opened the cylinder of his gun and emptied the live ammunition into his hand. "I'm on the job," he said to the other cop, "just moonlighting here a little." He turned to Rick. "You used to be on the job, didn't you?"

"Yeah," Rick said. "I did, and I'm glad I'm not anymore. Will you call the front gate and tell them they can open up again?" The man left, and Rick looked down into the pit where the cops had reached Jerry O'Toole. "Is he alive?" Rick yelled.

"He's alive," somebody yelled back, "but we're gonna need a stretcher and some rope to get him out of here."

"I'll take care of that," the sergeant said, then left.

Rick walked down the steps of the brownstone and sat on the bottom one to get his breath back. An electric cart driven by Sid Brooks came around the corner and stopped.

"You okay?"

"I'm okay. How's Tom?"

"The doctor said he wasn't too bad; only one shot hit him and not in a fatal place, apparently. The ambulance took him away."

"Good."

"Rick, what was that all about?"

"The guy who shot Tom killed Susie Stafford. The police are taking him away now."

"Well, I'm glad nobody got killed."

"Just Susie," Rick said, "and a woman named Hank Harmon."

Rick got home on time, after visiting Tom Terry in the hospital, where he was recovering from surgery. His eldest daughter climbed into his lap. Glenna was holding the baby.

"Did you have a good day?" she asked.

"All in all, pretty good," Rick said. He started telling her about it.

EPILOGUE

1999

R ick Barron stood with a small group of people and an Episco-
pal priest in the marble hall of a mausoleum at Forest Lawn
Cemetery. Glenna stood next to him, dabbing at her eyes with a tis-
sue. The casket was slid expertly into the crypt, like a file drawer
into its cabinet, and a man used a battery-operated drill to screw in
a series of bolts, sealing the marble slab. Etched into the slab was:

VANCE CALDER

1928–1999[1]

Rows of similar crypts lined both sides of the hall, each with a
legend of its own.

Rick was eighty-seven years old, and Glenna was eighty-four;
they were great-grandparents. It was hard for Rick to believe that
Vance had been seventy-one; he had looked older than his age when
Glenna had spotted him at their construction site in 1947, and, re-
markably, as he aged into his forties, Vance began to look younger
than his age. That was a pretty good trick, Rick thought, especially
if you were a movie star, perhaps the biggest ever. Vance had won
his first Academy Award for *Bitter Creek*, the first of five Oscars and

---

1. For Vance Calder's death, see *L.A. Dead*.

twelve nominations. Rick had won, too, as had the cinematographer. Susie Stafford had been nominated.

Vance's young widow, Arrington, walked over to them, leading a man who appeared to be in his early forties. "Thank you for coming to the cemetery, Rick, Glenna."

There had already been a very large funeral on a soundstage at Centurion, but only a handful of invited guests had come to the cemetery.

"I'd like you to meet my friend, Stone Barrington, who is a lawyer, from New York. Stone has been very helpful over the last week, since Vance's death. Stone, this is Rick and Glenna Barron. Rick is the chairman of Centurion Studios, and Glenna is one of its greatest stars."

"How do you do," Barrington said, shaking hands with them both.

"I'm pleased to meet you, Stone," Rick said. "I've been hearing about you."

Arrington looked around. "There's a place here for me, too," she said, "next to Vance. He told me he bought these crypts fifty years ago. I suppose it's a peaceful place to rest." She turned to Rick and Glenna. "Do you need a lift home?" she asked.

"No, we have our car," Rick replied. "You go ahead. I know you must be tired. Good to meet you, Stone."

The two walked away, but Rick and Glenna remained for a moment. "Funny how everybody seemed to end up in this place," Rick said. "Eddie and Suzanne Harris are right down there," he said, pointing. Eddie had died of a stroke nearly ten years before, and Suzanne the year after. "Sol Weinman and his wife are a little farther down. It's like Centurion Hall. And Leo Goldman, too." Leo had blown his own brains out in what was thought to have been an accident, during the late eighties.[2] His wife had remarried soon afterward. Tom Terry had recovered from his gunshot wounds and was still alive in an old-age home out in the valley, having lost both legs

---

2. For Leo Goldman's death, see *L.A. Times*.

to diabetes. Jerry O'Toole had been sent to the gas chamber at San Quentin in 1952.

Vance had died the largest stockholder in Centurion as well as its biggest star, having bought Sol Weinman's widow's shares. Leo had been a big stockholder, too, and upon his death, Rick had bought his shares from his widow.

"Yes," Glenna said. "It's Centurion Hall, and we have slots down there somewhere," she said pointing.

"I forgot," Rick said. "You ready to go home?"

But Glenna wasn't listening to him. Instead, she was staring at another crypt. She moved closer. "Come here, Rick, and take a look at this," she said.

Rick walked to her side and looked at the marble slab covering the crypt next to Vance's. The legend read:

SUSAN ANNE STAFFORD
1924–1948

"And this one," Glenna said, pointing to the next one down.

HENRIETTA "HANK" HARMON
1922–1948

"My word," Rick said. "Do you suppose this is a coincidence?"

Glenna shook her head slowly. "I don't think so," she said.

"I remember that Susie's mother had said that funeral arrangements were being made for her in L.A. by a friend. I suppose that friend must have been Hank Harmon, who then joined her."

"Are you ready to go to Malibu?" They had moved into the beach house full time after the girls were grown.

"Yes," he said. "Let's go home."

They stood for a moment in silence, then the two old people turned and walked slowly toward their waiting car.

AUTHOR'S NOTE

I am happy to hear from readers, but you should know that if you write to me in care of my publisher, three to six months will pass before I receive your letter, and when it finally arrives it will be one among many, and I will not be able to reply.

However, if you have access to the Internet, you may visit my website at www.stuartwoods.com, where there is a button for sending me e-mail. So far, I have been able to reply to all of my e-mail, and I will continue to try to do so.

If you send me an e-mail and do not receive a reply, it is because you are among an alarming number of people who have entered their e-mail address incorrectly in their mail software. I have many of my replies returned as undeliverable.

Remember: e-mail, reply; snail mail, no reply.

When you e-mail, please do not send attachments, as I *never* open these. They can take twenty minutes to download, and they often contain viruses.

Please do not place me on your mailing lists for funny stories, prayers, political causes, charitable fund-raising, petitions or sentimental claptrap. I get enough of that from people I already know. Generally speaking, when I get e-mail addressed to a large number of people, I immediately delete it without reading it.

Please do not send me your ideas for a book, as I have a policy of writing only what I myself invent. If you send me story ideas, I will immediately delete them without reading them. If you have a good idea for a book, write it yourself, but I will not be able to advise you on how to get it published. Buy a copy of *Writer's Market* at any bookstore; that will tell you how.

Anyone with a request concerning events or appearances may e-mail it to me or send it to: Publicity Department, Penguin Group (USA) Inc., 375 Hudson Street, New York, NY 10014.

Those ambitious folk who wish to buy film, dramatic or television rights to my books should contact Matthew Snyder, Creative Artists Agency, 9830 Wilshire Boulevard, Beverly Hills, CA 90212–1825.

Those who wish to make offers for rights of a literary nature should contact Anne Sibbald, Janklow & Nesbit, 445 Park Avenue, New York, NY 10022. (Note: This is not an invitation for you to send her your manuscript or to solicit her to be your agent.)

If you want to know if I will be signing books in your city, please visit my website, www.stuartwoods.com, where the tour schedule will be published a month or so in advance. If you wish me to do a book signing in your locality, ask your favorite bookseller to contact his Penguin representative or the Penguin publicity department with the request.

If you find typographical or editorial errors in my book and feel an irresistible urge to tell someone, please write to Rachel Kahan at Penguin's address above. Do not e-mail your discoveries to me, as I will already have learned about them from others.

A list of my published works appears in the front of this book and on my website. All the novels are still in print in paperback and can be found at or ordered from any bookstore. If you wish to obtain hardcover copies of earlier novels or of the two nonfiction books, a good used-book store or one of the online bookstores can help you find them. Otherwise, you will have to go to a great many garage sales.